BRIDES OF WATE

Love forged on the batt

Meet Mary Endacott, a radical schoolmistress,
Sarah Latymor, a darling of the *ton*, and
Catherine 'Rose' Tatton, a society lady
with no memories of her past.

Three very different women united
in a fight for their lives, their reputations
and the men they love.

With war raging around them, the biggest
battle these women face is protecting their
hearts from three notorious soldiers…

Will Mary be able to resist
Colonel Lord Randall? Find out in

A Lady for Lord Randall
by
Sarah Mallory

Discover how pampered Lady Sarah
handles rakish Major Bartlett in

A Mistress for Major Bartlett
by
Annie Burrows

What will happen when Major Flint
helps Lady Catherine 'Rose' Tatton
discover her past? Find out in

A Rose for Major Flint
by
Louise Allen

Author Note

The opening scene of this book has been with me for some time—as has a mental picture of Adam Flint. But I was not sure exactly who he was or why the girl he rescued was on the battlefield. When I began to explore the world of Brides of Waterloo with authors Sarah Mallory and Annie Burrows I knew immediately that Flint would fit perfectly with the other two Randall's Rogues to make a perfect trio of hellraisers, and so I set out with him to find out who 'Rose' was.

Working with fellow authors is always a wonderful opportunity to create an even deeper and richer world than is possible with just one book. Each of the Brides of Waterloo novels stands alone, but if you read them together you'll catch glimpses of all our heroes and heroines in each book.

The realisation of who Rose is presents a challenge to Flint's honour, but also to the heart he does not believe he possesses. I hope you enjoy discovering how one hard, scarred, self-sufficient man finds happiness with a woman who is prepared to risk everything she is, everything she has, for love.

A ROSE
FOR MAJOR FLINT

Louise Allen

First published in Great Britain 2015
by Mills & Boon, an imprint of Harlequin (UK) Limited,
Large Print edition 2015
Harlequin (UK) Limited, Eton House, 18-24 Paradise Road,
Richmond, Surrey TW9 1SR

© 2015 Melanie Hilton

ISBN: 978-0-263-25572-0

Harlequin (UK) Limited's policy is to use papers that are natural, renewable and recyclable products and made from wood grown in sustainable forests. The logging and manufacturing processes conform to the legal environmental regulations of the country of origin.

Louise Allen loves immersing herself in history. She finds landscapes and places evoke the past powerfully. Venice, Burgundy and the Greek islands are favourite destinations. Louise lives on the Norfolk coast and spends her spare time gardening, researching family history or travelling in search of inspiration. Visit her at louiseallenregency.co.uk, @LouiseRegency and janeaustenslondon.com.

To Sarah Mallory and Annie Burrows.
It was such a pleasure exploring the Rogues
and their world with you both.

Chapter One

19th June 1815—the battlefield of Waterloo

The briar rose caught at her with grasping, thorny tentacles as she backed away. The pain was real, so this must all be real. The screaming inside her head made it difficult to think, but it hadn't stopped, not since she had found Gerald. *What was left of Gerald.* He had seemed untouched until she had grasped his shoulder and turned him over.

The noise in her head hurt so much. She lifted her hands to try and clutch at it, squeeze it out, make it stop. Then she could think, then she would know what to do about…*them.* Her arms wouldn't move. She looked down to the imprisoning briars, then up at what was coming towards her across the muddy, shell-ripped ruin of the spinney. This was real and this was hell and so those were demons. They laughed as they came, four of them, blood-soaked and mud-smeared, wild-eyed and ragged, baying like hounds on the hunt. She knew what they wanted, what they would do to her, even if she knew nothing else. Not her name, not how she had lived before this nightmare had begun, not how she had come to be here.

She opened her mouth to scream, but nothing happened. *Go away. Help me, someone. Help me!* Nothing. Only the sound of her heartbeat racing. Only the sound of their laughter and the words that made no sense as they hit her like fistfuls of slime.

And then *he* came. He pushed aside the shattered, wilting branches, strode through the mud and the nameless, stinking filth. *The Devil himself.* He was big and dirty, bare-headed, stubble-jawed, blood-soaked. He had a sword in one hand and a pistol in the other and a smile like death on his blackened face. He roared at the demons and they turned, snarling, towards him. He shot the first and came on, stepped over the body and waited, waited until they were on him and then...

She closed her eyes, stayed in the darkness with the screaming in her head, the screaming from the demons, the Devil's roars. She would be next. She had sinned and this was hell.

* * *

'Open your eyes. Look at me. You are safe, they have gone.' *Gone to a much worse place, the scum.* Flint looked down at the pistol in his left hand and the blood-streaked sword in his right, thrust one into his belt and pushed the blade of the other into a tussock until most of the gore was gone. He sheathed the sword and tried again. 'Open your eyes.'

The woman was tall and slim and her hair, where it was not wet and matted, was a dark brown. Rose petals had fallen from the briar that held her. They were fragile, pale pink, incongruously beautiful on the ripped, soaking fabric of her gown, the tangle of her hair. Long lashes fanned over white cheeks and her mouth was slightly open. He could hear her breath coming in short, desperate pants like a trapped animal in a snare. She had bitten her lips and the sight, amidst so much carnage, touched him despite his defences. Angered him.

'Let's get you untangled.' Flint kept his voice calm, used the firm tone that would steady an injured man. The briars tore at his hands, added to the bruises and cuts, the little rips of pain reminding him he was alive. After three days of hell, who would have thought it?

When he got her free she just stood there, swaying. Flint touched the back of his hand to her cheek, leaving a smear of blood on the cold skin. She flinched but her eyes opened, wide and dark, the pupils so distended he could not see the true colour.

'What is your name?' She stared blankly. Shock, certainly, and perhaps she did not speak English. He tried French, Dutch, German. No response, not a flicker. 'My name is Flint. Major Adam Flint. Are you hurt?'

They hadn't raped her, he had been in time to stop that, at least. The sound of their laughter had brought him here at a run. He had heard that unmistakeable excitement too often when men had poured into a besieged, defeated city and found the women and the girls. Children. Sometimes you could be in time. Often, not. *Badajoz...*

Still she stood there, a breathing statue. She must be a camp follower, but he couldn't leave her, not here. Her man, if he was still alive, would never find her, but others would. Flint put his arm around her, ignored the way her body shuddered at the touch, bent and swept the other arm under her knees to lift her against his chest. Pain stabbed from the sabre cut in his right side. The blood must have dried into his shirt and lifting her had ripped the wound open. He ignored it.

After a moment her arms slipped around his neck and she clung as he crossed the glade, stepped over the bodies. She was a reasonable armful, Flint thought as he found the track again and made for where he had left the men. Slim but not skinny, curved but not buxom. Feminine. Any other day he'd enjoy the feel of her against his body, but not now. Not here.

The men had sorted themselves out while he'd been away searching for that last missing private. Sergeant Hawkins looked up from the back of the ammunition wagon they had managed to patch back together that morning. 'Any luck, Major?' His right eyebrow—the left had been burned off in some half-forgotten skirmish when a gun had exploded—lifted as he saw Flint's burden.

'Jakes is dead.' There was a chorus of muttered curses from the back of the cart. 'I buried him.' He'd rolled him into a shell hole and kicked earth on top of him, to be exact. Not a decent burial, even for an alley rat like Jakes, but it would keep the looters from his body.

'We can all go then.' Hawkins knew Flint would never leave a man alive on the field, even if it meant staying back himself until he'd exhausted all hope. 'Get a shift on there, Hewitt! Get everyone stowed.' He jerked his head towards the woman. 'Not one of ours.'

'No.' Their camp followers were all safe back at Roosbos where they'd been stationed before the call to Quatre Bras, three days ago. Flint counted heads. 'Thirteen.' He'd lost the tally of the injured they'd sent back already, the dead they'd scratched graves for, but Hawkins had been jotting numbers down as they went. This was the lot.

'Aye, thirteen including us, Major. She hurt?'

'Don't think so, I can't see any wounds, but she's not talking.' In his arms she was as limp as a stunned hare. 'Found her cornered by a pack of deserters back there.'

The one tattered eyebrow lifted in question. Hawkins knew what happened to lone women in the aftermath of battle. Flint shook his head. 'No, I got there first.'

'They won't be troubling anyone else, then.' Hawkins didn't bother to ask how many constituted a *pack*, he'd seen Flint deal with scum like that before. 'Wonder if she'll scrub up any better than the last thing you picked up, Major.'

That had been Dog. Flint hoped the great shaggy beast had got out of this in one piece. Lord, but he must be tired if he was becoming sentimental.

'I'd got 'em all packed in tight,' Hawkins said. He shoved his shako back to scratch his thinning scalp. 'Llewellyn and Hodge can walk. Where'll we put her though?'

Flint went over and studied the cart. Two men leaned against it, one, with a rough bandage round his leg, sat on the shaft. Three men were laid out on the boards and the rest perched on the edge, fitting their feet and weapons in around the prostrate men as best they could. 'Potts, you can ride well enough to manage one-handed. Get up on my horse, I'll walk and we'll squeeze this lass in your place.'

The man shuffled out awkwardly and jumped down, swearing under his breath as he jarred his wounded shoulder. The others moved up to make room and Flint swung the girl up on to the edge.

She turned her head, stared wide-eyed into the cart and then fastened her arms around his neck in a stranglehold. Where did anything so fragile and helpless get the strength?

'I know they aren't the prettiest sight you'll ever see, but they're good lads and they won't hurt you.' He tried again, but she clung like a burr, her breath panting in his ear. He could use force, but there was enough pain to wade through here without adding to it.

'She looks terrified out of her wits, Major,' one of the men said. 'I don't think it's us, more like the blood an' guts an' all. We've done our best with Jimmy, but he's no sight for a slip of a girl.' He nodded towards one of the men on the floor, unconscious and, if there was any more mercy to spare for a scoundrel artilleryman, likely to die without waking up.

Flint reached into reserves of patience and kept his voice level. 'Back you go, Potts, I'll take her up in front of me.' The sooner they got going, the more chance they had of getting everyone back alive. Except Jimmy. But at least he'd die with his mates round him. Randall's Rogues didn't leave their comrades behind—not if they were breathing, at any rate.

Potts was hauled back in. Hawkins mustered his two walking wounded, went to the head of the nag between the shafts and urged it forward while Flint studied the logistics of getting on to Old Nick with a woman attached to his torso. The big black Spanish stallion rolled an eye and curled back its upper lip to reveal yellow teeth.

'Don't even think of it, or I swear I'll have your bollocks off,' Flint said. How the damned animal had the energy to even contemplate biting anyone after the past few days he had no idea. 'Come on, over here.' There was a shattered wagon and he used it like a set of steps to get high enough to fling a leg over the saddle and settle down with his burden uncomfortably in front of him. 'Stand!' Old Nick shuffled his feet, but obeyed while Flint arranged her as best he could across his thighs. 'Walk on.'

The rickety caravan set off on the twelve miles to Brussels. No distance at all when they rode with the guns. No distance at all to march on a reasonable road—but this was going to take a long time. He'd sent their guns with the fit officers and men of the unit back to muster behind the ridge for the return march to Brussels while he brought in the wounded and they'd be back well before his ragtag bunch.

Randall would be with them. Strange that he hadn't seen the colonel since mid-afternoon the day before, but he'd have heard if he was seriously injured and certainly if he was dead. Same went for Bartlett, the unit's wild man and resident rake. He was probably drinking claret and nursing his superficial cuts with his boots propped up on a gun carriage by now. Bartlett could find a decent claret anywhere and Dog would be there, too, waiting for his dinner.

That accounted for the officers and gentlemen. Which left him, an officer and definitely not a gentleman, the bastard in every sense of the word, to pick up the messy pieces.

Young Gideon Latymor was dead, cut down at Quatre Bras. He'd avoided thinking about Gideon and he wasn't going to start now. He had more immediate matters than one dead half-brother on his hands. Literally.

He tried again. 'What's your name?' The woman in his arms made no response. *'Votre nom? Wat is je naam? Wie ist dein Name?'* Nothing. 'My name is Flint. Adam Flint.' Silence. A rose petal fluttered down from her hair, brushed his knuckles in the ghost of a kiss and fell to the mud. 'Very well, then, I'll call you…Rose.'

They rode on at walking pace, limited not so much by the two soldiers on foot but the decrepit horse pulling the cart. Lord only knew where

Hawkins had stolen it from, some peasant's stew-pot probably, but horses were as rare as hens' teeth after that carnage and they knew from bitter experience that trying to get Old Nick between the shafts would result in more casualties than they had already. The stallion was trained to fight and to kill and it regarded being a carthorse as grounds for murder.

It was like a traffic jam in Piccadilly, Flint thought with unaccustomed whimsy. If, that is, one imagined Piccadilly knee-deep in mud and water-filled ruts, and the other traffic consisting of groups of exhausted troops, rough carts jolting along full of men biting back cries of pain and staff officers, their elegant uniforms filthy and torn, directing carts here, men there. And all along the margins of the road soldiers were lying where they'd dropped, dead or dying amongst the fallen horses, their bodies swelling, already turning black in the wet heat. The stench was an almost solid thing, clogging nostrils and throats.

They got to a particularly boggy patch and Flint kicked his feet out of the stirrups so the two artillerymen on foot could grip the leathers and swing themselves through the mud. Old Nick was used to this, the standard way of getting unhorsed men off the field in a hurry, and ignored the extra weight.

Waterloo village, when they finally got that far, was jammed. Hawkins forced the cart on through the road between high banks and Flint saw the parish priest on the steps of the church, his head in his hands, as more and more bodies were piled up at his feet. On the other side of the street men were chalking names on doorposts where senior officers had been carried in. *Ponsonby*, he read. Damn, another good officer wounded. He hoped he was going to make it.

'Rose?' They cleared the village and struggled on. Her back, beneath his arm, was still rigid, her face still buried in the frogging of his uniform. He wouldn't want to get that close to himself, he thought with a sour smile. He couldn't recall the last time he'd washed, he must stink of sweat, black powder, wet wool and blood. A cautious sniff confirmed it and brought a hint of her own scent. Hot, terrified, wet woman. Mud. The faintest hint of herbs and lemon.

Puzzled, he lowered his head until he was almost nuzzling the tangled brown hair. She had rinsed it in rosemary and lemon juice. It seemed such a harmless, feminine thing to have done just before plunging into hell. He imagined her humming to herself as she brewed the rinse, washing her hair over a bucket somewhere in the lines of tents, pouring the decoction over her hair and combing it through. Her man would have been cleaning his weapon, polishing his harness perhaps, his preparations all directed at killing while hers took no account of battles at all.

'What you going to do with her, sir?' Flint jerked out of the daydream. Peters, hanging on to his stirrup leather, looked up at him, bright blue eyes bloodshot in his dirt-smeared face.

'God knows. She needs women to look after her, but these peasants have too much on their hands to leave her with them.' Flint tried to think. His side ached like the devil, the bangs and bruises and minor wounds were coming to life, his guts were empty, his thighs were getting pins and needles, and the men depended on him to get them back to Brussels more or less alive. He could do that, or fight another battle if he had to, but safely disposing of unwanted women, now that was another kettle of fish.

He shifted the girl into a more comfortable position, for him at least. 'There's a nunnery a couple of miles ahead. That'll be the place.' *Problem solved.* Cheered by the prospect of getting the stray off his hands, he said, 'We're almost at the nunnery, Rose. You'll be better there, the sisters will look after you.' She made no movement. Was she deaf as well?

'Jimmy's gone, Major,' Potts called from the back of the cart.

Hell. Scurvy little sneak thief. And damned good artilleryman. This had been a very expensive battle. They would leave him at the convent, the nuns would bury him and he'd end up as close to heaven as any of the Rogues were likely to get.

'Rest stop at the nunnery,' he called and grinned, despite everything, at the chorus of coarse jokes that provoked.

'Here…Rose…nuns…get down…safe…' The Devil was talking to her, but the words jumbled in her head, half-drowned by the never-ending scream.

She tried to listen, to understand. Finally she managed to raise her head and focus. One of the tattered, bloody scarecrows was walking towards a high wall with a great gate in it. A bell clanged, jumbling the words in her head even more, and then a flock of great black crows flew out of the gate, flapping, waving hands, not wings. One of them came close, reached for her with long, pale claws.

'*Pauvre...monsieur...pauvre petit...*'

She huddled closer into the Devil's grip. He would stop them pecking her. They had one of the dead men now, bloody and limp as they carried him through the great gate. Like Gerald, only this one had all of his face. Perhaps they were going to eat him, peck at his eyes... Her fingers locked into the strap across the Devil's back. *No...no...* The words stayed closed in with the scream.

She felt the Devil shrug. The black crows chattered and flapped, then they rode on, her and the Devil on the great black hell horse. He said something, low, in his deep voice. It rumbled in his chest, against her ear, and this time she understood the words. 'What am I going to do with you, Rose?'

Who is Rose? It wasn't her, she knew that. Her name was...was... It had gone. He had told her his name. *Adam.* That could not be right, the Devil was not called Adam. *Beelzebub, Lucifer, Satan.* Those were the Devil's names.

Why wasn't he hot? He should be burning hot,

instead he was warm. And hard. He'd said he was made of stone… Flint, that was it. That was why he was hard, his thighs under her were rock that moved with the hell horse. His chest was solid, like holding on to an oak tree. His eyes were the blue of flames deep in the heart of a log fire, and he smelled of blood and smoke and sulphur.

Dare she sleep? It had been so long since she had slept. There had been a ball… Memory shifted, blurred, focused for a moment. The night before she had been too excited to sleep. Then the night of the ball she had lain awake with Gerald in her arms, stroking his hair, trying to give him some comfort for his fears. How long had it been since then? Two battles, a rainstorm… *Why was I at a ball? Who was Gerald?*

Could she sleep with all the noise in her head? She clung tighter to the Devil. He would keep her safe. It made no sense, but then nothing did any more. Nothing ever would again and all because she had sinned.

Chapter Two

'Oh, my Gawd, look at you!' Maggie Moss stood in the doorway, apron covered in flour, hair straggling out of its bun, elbows akimbo. 'That's a fine sight for a respectable Brussels boarding-house keeper to find on her doorstep of an evening.' The tears poured down her cheeks.

'We've been in a bit of a scrap, Maggie,' Flint said, knowing better than to notice the tears. Something in his chest loosened at the sight and sound of her. Maggie meant warm practicality, a sanctuary of normality after a voyage into chaos. 'Is there room? Twelve of us. Sergeant Hawkins, nine of the men and me. And Rose here.'

'Of course there's room, I made sure there would be, and never mind what those commissariat officers wanted when they came round. This house is for Randall's Rogues and no one else, I said. *Moss!*

Where is the man? Come on in. Tracking mud and worse all over my floors… And the noise! Those guns. Through here.' Her hands were gentle as she helped the men through into the kitchen, scolding all the time like a mother making a child believe his scraped knee was nothing to make a fuss about.

Her husband came stomping through from the back on his wooden leg. He'd been Flint's sergeant for three years until a spent ball had taken his leg off at Badajoz. Maggie had followed him through the hell of the Peninsular campaign and then, when peace had come and the English had flocked to Brussels, they'd come, too, to open a lodging house.

'I've got palliasses laid out in the outhouse,' Moss said. 'It's cool and dry out there and no need for stairs. Doesn't look as though it will be too crowded, either,' he added, low-voiced, to Flint. 'Fewer than I expected. Butcher's bill bad—or did you get off easy?'

'Could have been worse. Could have been a damn sight better. The ones I sent back earlier were with the rest of the non-commissioned officers under orders to go to the hospitals or nunneries. Hawkins, can you manage here for a bit? I can't do a thing with my arms full.'

'We'll manage, Major,' Moss said with a sharp glance at Flint's burden. 'The missus had best help you with that one. Hawkins, I've got hot water in the boiler, let's get them cleaned up and we'll see what's what.' He turned to one of the privates. 'Hey, lad, the pump's in the yard, you fetch everyone a drink, right?'

'Come on, Major, bring her through here. Hawkins and Moss will manage without us.' Maggie urged him towards the stairs. 'Up you go. How's your broth—Colonel Randall?'

'All right as far as I know. Gideon's dead,' Flint said. 'At Quatre Bras.' His younger half-brother had been a cavalry officer, full of courage and with, Flint thought bitterly, the brains of a partridge in shooting season. Gideon shouldn't have been with the guns, and he, Flint, was a fool to feel that somehow he should have stopped him, saved him.

'Oh, I'm sorry. Poor lad, he was only a boy.'

'Hardly knew him.' He'd stayed out of Gideon Latymor's way all his life—until those last minutes. What did an ambitious young cavalry officer want with one of his father's countless by-blows, even if their elder brother had, for some inscrutable reason of his own, promoted the by-blow's career? What did the bastard in question need with either of them, come to that? Randall was his commanding officer, that was as close a relationship as Flint wanted.

'Room on the left, the one you had before.' Maggie didn't make any further comment about Gideon, but he could feel her glare of disapproval at his words like a jab in the back from a bayonet. 'So who's this?' she demanded when he reached the middle of the bedchamber and she could look properly at the woman clinging to him like a burr to a blanket.

'No idea. Found her after the battle trapped by a gang of deserters.'

'Had they hurt her?'

'No. But something's wrong. She won't speak, doesn't seem to understand what I say to her in any language and she won't let go. Which is becoming uncomfortable,' he added, aware now he'd got where he was going that certain basic needs required attention.

'Come on, lovie, down you get now. You're safe here. I'm Maggie, I'll look after you.'

It took five minutes, and they had to unbuckle Flint's belt and peel off his jacket, before they had Rose huddled on the bed in the dressing room off

Flint's bedchamber. 'Quieter in here and snugger,' Maggie said. 'Poor little creature.'

'Not so little,' Flint said, stretching cramped shoulders. But she looked fragile. Not childlike, for even like this her womanly curves were obvious, but vulnerable. Something in Flint's chest twisted. Damn it, he was not going to get sentimental about one waif and stray. She'd probably been following the drum with some man or another since she was sixteen. 'I'll bring hot water up so you can get her clean.' This was women's work and Maggie, thank the saints, was the woman to do it. If anyone could bring some terrified camp follower to her senses, she could.

He lugged the tin bath along from the cupboard on the landing. The last time he'd used it was the afternoon before the Duchess of Richmond's accursed ball.

'I need you there,' his commanding officer had said. Justin, Lord Randall, who just happened to be his elder Latymor half-brother, had sighed as he'd looked at him, the sigh of a man whose butler has just spilled the best cognac on the Chinese silk rug. 'Get yourself cleaned up and try, just try, to look like a gentleman for a change.'

So Moss and Maggie had trimmed his hair,

nagged him into the closest shave he'd ever had in his life, dumped him in a bath with some fancy soap, dabbed at him with infernal cologne and eased him into his scarcely-worn dress uniform. He'd had to fight with ghosts from the past to make himself cross that threshold, but it had been worth it to see Justin's face when Flint stood there brooding in the corner, surrounded by the interested and predatory ladies who had deserted his handsome half-brother to simper at his scowls and stare unabashedly at his tight breeches.

'I forget that you scrub up quite well,' Randall had said, a smile on his sculpted lips, his blue eyes, so like Flint's, chill and unamused by what he had unleashed on the ballroom.

Flint had shown his teeth in response, knowing his smile and his eyes were identical to Randall's. 'I know,' he'd replied in the upper-class drawl he could produce when he could be bothered. 'Worried I'll cut you out with the ladies, *sir*?' And he could, they both knew that from their time in the Peninsula. Ladies who'd want him for one thing only. Randall, of course, was always too much on his dignity to allow his *amours* to be seen in public.

Focus. He could not let his mind drift, not stop

being a damned officer. Not yet. He stuffed the unpleasant memories away, dumped the tin bath in the bedchamber and went for hot water, leaving Maggie crooning reassurance in the dressing room. When he came down again Moss was tending to the worst of the injured while those who could stand were naked in the yard, sluicing themselves off under Hawkins's watchful eye.

'We've sent a lad with a note to HQ, sir,' Hawkins said. 'Let them know where we are. I've asked for the surgeon to call, but I think we'll be all right for now. They're checking each other over and washing the wounds out. Maggie's laid in plenty of bandages and salve. How's the girl?' he asked as Flint studied the battered bodies.

Yes, unless loss of blood or shock caught up with any of them, or a wound began to fester, they'd do. It had been, against all the odds and late in the day, a victory, and their tails were up as a result. 'The girl? I've called her Rose. We got her on to a bed and Maggie's doing what she can. Women's work, not our problem any more.' He began to strip. 'You, too, let's see what exciting holes you've acquired this time.'

'Nothing.' Hawkins stripped and grabbed for some soap. 'I'm filthy as a cesspit digger, but not a scratch on me.' He jerked his head at the slash over Flint's ribs. 'That needs cleaning.'

Flint grunted, splashed soapy water into the wound, swore and scrubbed the rest of himself mostly clean. The men were limping and hobbling back to the straw beds, wrapped in bits of sheet for decency.

'Lie down, the lot of you, and get some rest,' Moss ordered with the authority of the sergeant he had once been. 'I'll bring you more water and there'll be stew in bit.' He began to gather up the torn and filthy shirts, muttering over the state of the uniforms. 'The girl will get the linen into the copper and do her best with it.' He stomped into the house, shouting, 'Lucille!'

'You rest, too,' Flint said to Hawkins. He reached out to steady the other man as he balanced on one foot to scrub at the other. Hawkins grasped his hand, returned the momentary pressure without meeting his eyes. There was no need for more words. *We're alive. Hundreds aren't. We won.* 'Rest. That's an order.'

'And you, Major.'

'Aye.' Flint looked round at the yard and the outhouse. Nothing more to be done now for a bit except sleep. Immediately after a battle no one wanted to let their eyes close and risk it, the oblivion was too much like dying. Now they could all finally let go. He slung a towel round his waist, picked up his clothes. 'I'm upstairs if you need me.'

The dressing-room door was closed, but the tub was full of scummy grey water and a pile of damp towels were heaped on the floor. So Maggie had got Rose into a bath, at least, which meant she would have checked her for any injuries. He got rid of the dirty water and put the tub back in the cupboard, then stood in the middle of the room and eyed the bed. Yes, he could let go now for a while at last. He dropped the towel, climbed between the sheets and sank straight into a sleep as dark and still as death.

Light, softness and blissful quiet. The scream was still there, an echo in her head, but she could hear faint sounds from somewhere below and a rhythmic purring rasp like a big cat. Something had woken her. Footsteps? Voices? Whatever it was had stopped now.

She opened her eyes on to whiteness. Clouds...? *Heaven?* No, a big white puffy eiderdown, linen sheets, a lime-washed wall. She was in bed in a small, very simple, very clean room.

She sat up and looked down at her body. Someone had put her into a vast white nightgown. The plump woman with the big hands and the soft voice had bathed her and talked all the time with words that made no sense, but that soothed. Now she ached in every muscle as though she had walked a hundred miles, but that could not be right.

Where am I? Once there had been a house somewhere far away over the sea and then another one, smaller. Smiling faces. Love and arguments. What about? A man? A ball and a beautiful gown. Then kisses and a tent and tears and rain and mud and noise. The worst noise in the world. And then searching, searching and being afraid and then… The scream became louder and she fought back the memory, the images, until she huddled into the pillow, shivering with effort, and it was quiet enough for her to think again.

The demons had come and then the Devil who took her and all the other damned souls he was sending to hell. He had carried her off on his great black horse and she had felt safe, even though he was the Devil. And he had brought her here, to the soft woman and the warm water and peace.

None of it made any sense, because *this* was not hell, unless it was a cruel trick. Perhaps if she opened the door there would be flames and demons and mocking laughter. Perhaps that sound was a sleeping hellhound. But she had to get up. Surely if you were dead you did not need the chamber pot any more? That was encouraging. She made her way on shaky legs to the screen in the corner and emerged feeling a little better.

Now for the door and what lay beyond. It opened without a creak on to a bedchamber, another white room with muslin curtains drawn over early-morning light and the only flames those safely enclosed within a pair of lamps, burning low. There was a cold fireplace, a rag rug, a chair and a bed. A big bed with, in it, a big man. Her Devil. And he was snoring. That was the sound she had heard. Her face felt strange and she lifted a scratched hand to touch her mouth. She was smiling.

She stood beside the bed and studied him. His shoulders and one arm were above the sheets, muscled, brown, bruised, battered, marked with fresh cuts and old scars. His face was half-hidden under dark brown stubble, darker than the brown hair that partly covered the scar on his forehead. His nose was straight and imperious. He should have seemed vulnerable in sleep, instead he looked dangerous and formidable, a smouldering volcano.

Her Devil. He had saved her, so she was his now and she should be in bed with him. She eased back the covers and slid under, half-expecting the movement of the feather mattress to wake him, but he only muttered, shifted and threw one heavy arm across her, trapping her against him. He was naked, she could tell even through the sensible cotton nightgown. Naked and warm and big. Safe. She closed her eyes and slept, the rumble of his snores drowning the scream.

'Rose? Bloody hell, what are you doing here?'

Rose? Who was Rose? She snuggled closer against the solid bare body, into the warmth and the security, then had to clutch the edge of the bed as it shifted violently. She opened her eyes and found the Devil was sitting up, glaring at her.

She stared back, wondering why she was not afraid. There was no one else here, so she must be the Rose he was talking to. He was angry with her. What was she doing there? Foolish question, this was where she belonged. She laid her hand, palm down, on his chest and felt his heart beating hard and steady under it. He was very handsome, her battered, fallen angel. She had thought angels were sexless, perhaps feminine, all purity and light. He was dark and male and made her think of carnal, hidden, wicked things.

'Rose, you must go back to your own bed. You are perfectly safe there.' He muttered something that sounded like, 'But not here.'

No. She shook her head.

'You understand me? You are English?'

Yes. Two nods.

'Then talk to me, woman!'

Talk? But she couldn't do that. She had tried to scream when she had found Gerald, but nothing had come out of her mouth. All the words, all the screams, were trapped inside now. She spread her hands and shook her head.

'You can't?' He seemed to understand. 'That is a pity. Do you remember me? Adam Flint?' The intense blue gaze focused on her face.

I remember you. Yes, he read that easily enough.

His heart beat under her palm. His chest, his broad, solid chest, rose and fell with his breathing and the realisation came to her that he was alive and human. He wasn't the Devil, she wasn't dead. She had not, for all the sins she couldn't remember, gone to hell. But she had walked through it and he had shown her the way out.

Rose felt the smile coming back. It felt strange, as though she hadn't smiled in days…weeks?

Adam laid one hand over hers as his frown deepened. '*Rose*, you need to go to your room.' When she did not move he said, 'If you won't shift, then I must. And I'm stark naked.'

It was obviously a threat as well as a warning. She should be shocked, she seemed to recall from somewhere. Even his words were shocking. But she wasn't alarmed. She was curious. Curious about him or curious because he was a naked man? Both, she realised. *So I am not used to sleeping with a man.*

'Damn it,' Adam muttered. He gave her a look that could have curdled milk and, when she did not move, got out of bed on the far side. He turned away from her for the sake of his modesty, or perhaps hers, but Rose stared nonetheless.

Broad shoulders, muscled, scarred back tapering down to his waist, the strong lines marred by a stained cloth twisted around his ribs. Narrow hips and a backside that was tight and smooth. She wanted to touch him, curve her hand over those neat, firm buttocks. Long, strong horseman's legs furred with dark hair, big feet. He was male, beautiful, fearless. Hers.

Gerald. The image of a handsome face flickered into her memory. Blond, smooth, unmarked by life or trouble. So young and so unformed and, at the end, so very frightened. He had been hers, hadn't he? Had she loved him? She couldn't remember. All she could recall was holding him while he sobbed, and she tried not to tremble with fear and the realisation that everything was wrong. And then he had been… *No.* The scream began to build, shrill in her head and she pressed her hands to her temples to try and stop the pain. She focused on Adam and felt her breathing calm.

He had reached the chair and was pulling on the trousers of his uniform, filthy and ripped. Then he turned and she saw the cloth was a bandage and the skin around it was reddened and inflamed. He was hurt.

Something in her head cleared and came into focus. He was wounded and she knew what to do about that. Rose slid out of bed, tugging down the nightgown that had risen to her thighs. Adam glanced away and she saw the colour come up over his cheekbones. She had shocked him? She swept the clothing from the chair to the floor and pointed at the seat, then poked at his chest for good measure. He sat down, eyebrows raised. Apparently Adam Flint was not used to being pushed around.

The bandage was knotted tightly and she broke a nail undoing the ends. It had hardened over the wound and she went to the washbasin, poured out water and wetted a cloth to soak it off. Adam sat still while she worked, not flinching when she peeled off the bandage, even though it must have hurt. She shook her head at the sight of the long slash. It had lifted a flap of skin and that, she supposed, was full of cloth fragments and sweat and goodness knows what else that would irritate and fester. He made to get up and she shoved him hard in the chest. *Stay there!* It was like pushing a wall, and when he got to his feet despite her efforts she stumbled and fell against him.

'Bossy little creature, aren't you?' he said and put his arms around her. Instinctively Rose stepped closer, laid her forehead against the flat plane of his bare chest above his right nipple. He had washed after a fashion last night, she realised, inhaling the scent of just-woken man, plain soap and a lingering tang of black powder and sweat. She turned her head and rubbed her cheek against him and her lips brushed his nipple. It hardened and he became instantly still.

She did not know what to do, only that she had never felt like this before. Adam sat down abruptly, his hands on her forearms. Those blue-flame eyes narrowed as he studied her. Gradually her breathing steadied.

'Why won't you speak to me?'

Didn't he understand that she could not? Rose shrugged.

'You can trust me.'

She glanced down to where, even in her ignorance, his arousal was very plain. *Of course I can. I know that.* Although why she knew was another mystery. If he wanted to take her, then she would have no chance of resisting him.

With the knowledge came some confidence. She wagged a finger at him and pointed again, sternly. *Stay.* It worked with dogs. It worked, so it seemed, with big men. He narrowed his eyes at her, but did not move. She suspected he was amused.

The kind, soft woman would be somewhere below. Rose shot Adam one last look, then opened the door and went down the stairs. She followed her nose to the kitchen, her stomach grumbling. When had she last eaten?

The room was full of men. Men in trousers

and no shirts, men in shirts and no trousers, men draped in blankets.

'Gawd!' someone said and there was a mass scramble for the back door.

Rose was left with the kind woman, who was at the range stirring a pot of something that smelled delicious, and a thin man with a beak of a nose and a wooden leg. He glanced at her enveloping nightgown and looked away out of the window.

'You shouldn't be out of bed, lovie,' the woman said. 'I was going to bring up some tea in a minute.'

The place seemed as familiar and comforting as a childhood memory. Rose smiled. It was getting easier now she had remembered how to. There was a kettle steaming on the fire. She pointed to it and then looked round the kitchen until she saw a bowl of salt on the table next to a pile of neatly rolled bandages. She picked it up and took two of the bandage rolls.

'You want the hot water for the major, lovie? He's hurt?' the woman asked. 'Keep an eye on the stew, Moss, I'll see what's going on.' She wrapped a cloth around the handle and hefted the kettle off the hook as though it was a teacup. 'Come along, then.'

Adam was sitting where Rose had left him, his expression somewhere between amused and resigned. 'Caught her, did you, Maggie?'

'Caught her? Your lass here came down and made it quite clear what she needs.' She dumped the kettle on the nightstand and came to peer at the raw wound on Adam's side. 'And no wonder—although how she got a good look at it is best not to ask, I'd guess.'

'I woke up and there she was.' He did not smile, but there was a rueful twist to his lips.

'Seems as though you've got yourself a woman, then, Major.' Maggie winked at Rose. 'You know what to do about that?' From the jerk of her head towards Flint she might have meant either the injury or the man.

Yes. Rose nodded, sure about one and not at all certain about the other.

'I do not need a woman,' Flint growled, scowling at Maggie's retreating back.

Yes, you do, you need me. Rose poured hot water into the basin and ignored the way his brows drew together and his fingers drummed a rhythm on the arm of the chair. *You have to need me, because otherwise who am I and where do I belong if not with you?*

Chapter Three

'You seem to know what you are doing,' Adam remarked. Rose could feel his gaze on her as she swirled salt into the water. 'Did your man get wounded often?'

No. She shook her head and tried to work out why she was so sure of that. Of course, she had not been with Gerald long enough for him to be hurt...only killed. There were memories of bandages and salves, of pouring medicines, but that seemed to be in domestic settings. Humble rooms. Children, old people, a presence she sensed was her mother instructing her. *Our tenants, our duty.*

Wounds must be cleaned, salt water helped healing, she knew these things as she knew that her eyes were hazel without having to look in a glass.

Rose glanced at Adam, frowning with the effort to recall something more, something useful about who she was, and his gaze sharpened. 'I've seen you before. Where the blazes? Yes, after Quatre Bras, with the Seventy-Third's camp followers. Is that your man's regiment? I'll help you find him.'

No, he is dead. And he was never my man, not really. I was a fool who thought herself in love. How did she know that when everything else was a blur? How to make Adam understand? Rose gestured to the floor, then covered her face with her hands in a pantomime of grief.

'Dead? You are certain?'

She nodded and busied herself with the cloths and water, the memory coming back in frustrating flashes. His name had been Gerald and the belief that she loved him had lasted as long as it took to realise she did not know him at all. But after that there was no going back. She had made a commitment and she must stay with him, give him her loyalty even as his courage dissolved into the rain and mud and the dashing officer turned into a frightened boy in her arms. But how had they met, where had she come from? *Who am I?*

That could wait, she thought, surprising herself with the firmness of the intent. The traumatised, clinging creature of the day before was retreating, although she had no idea who would emerge in her place. Whoever she was, her true self was stubborn and determined, it seemed. Rose put the bowl on the floor beside Adam and set herself to clean the wound.

He sat like a statue as she explored the slash with ruthless thoroughness. Under her hands she felt the nerves jump and flinch in involuntary protest, but all he said was, 'There's some salve in my pack.'

Rose found it and smoothed the green paste on, wondering at Adam's stoicism. Was he simply inured to pain after so many wounds or was it sheer will power that kept him silent and unmoving? She rested one hand on his shoulder as she leaned over him to wind the bandage around his ribs and felt the rigid muscles beneath her palm. Will power, then. She knotted the bandage, touched her fingers to his cheek in a fleeting caress and sat back on her heels. *Finished.*

The soft touch on his bristled cheek was both a caress and a statement. *Finished.* Did she think he needed comfort? It was a novel sentiment if he had read it aright: no one ever thought Adam Flint in need of tenderness. He had believed he had acquired an inconvenient waif and stray, much as he had acquired Dog. Now he wondered if both animal and girl thought *they* had adopted *him*.

'Thank you.' Her eyes were asking a question. 'Yes, it feels much better.' In fact, it hurt like the very devil, but in a good way. It would not fester now. 'You go back to your chamber. I'll have hot water sent up for you and I'm sure Maggie can find something for you to wear. I need a bath and a shave.' He wasn't used to soft dealing, to people who needed gentle voices and kind words, but he would try for her.

Damn, but those wide hazel eyes were enough to make a man want to forget everything and just talk to her, find out what was going on behind that direct gaze. Pain and fear and stubborn courage, he would guess, and behind that there was doubt and uncertainty. But he had neither time nor inclination to explore her feelings. Rose needed a woman to look after her, not a man for whom a female in his life had only one purpose.

'Go on,' he said, his voice harsh with command, despite his resolve to be gentle. 'Back to your room.' If he spoke to Dog like that he got a reproachful look from melting brown eyes, accompanied by a drooping tail. Rose merely lowered her lashes and nodded. Yet somehow the gesture was anything but meek. She had assessed his mood and he suspected he was now being humoured with obedience while it suited her. Rose got to her feet in one fluid motion and walked to the door, the oversized nightgown swishing around her slim body, one moment cloaking it, the next caressing an almost-elegant curve of hip and thigh.

Flint cursed under his breath, low and fluent, as he dragged on his shirt, welcoming the distracting stab of pain as he tucked the tails into his trousers and looped the braces over his shoulders. His feet wanted to go straight to the dressing-room door, but instead he went downstairs.

The men had slept, it seemed, like the dead, but all of them had woken up in better shape than before. Maggie and Moss between them had sorted them into bed cases, the walking wounded who could care for their fellows and two who were in not much worse condition than Flint.

Maggie despatched those two upstairs with hot water for Rose—'And just knock and leave it at the door, mind!'—and for Flint's bath. 'Good thing you left a spare uniform here,' she grumbled at him when he handed her the wreckage of his shirt. 'Most of this is fit for the rag bag.'

'I know,' Flint said, straight-faced. 'Anyone

would think I'd fought two battles and been in a rainstorm in it.' He dodged the cuff she aimed at him. 'Can you do anything about fitting Rose out, Maggie?'

'Aye, that I can. My sister Susan leaves clothes here for when she visits, saves carting too much baggage back and forth. The size'll be about right, I dare say.'

'Anything else she needs, just give me the bills.' He stopped at the foot of the stairs and looked back. 'Her man's dead, Maggie. She's shocked, but I can't say she's grieving exactly. I don't know what it is, she doesn't seem the sort to just shrug that off.'

'Likely he knocked her around,' Maggie said with distaste. 'She's happy enough with you, by the looks of it.'

If he, a big, murderous bastard, made Rose feel happy, then her last man must have been a brute, Flint concluded as he stood in the bath and did his best to scrub off the dirt that had escaped last night's dowsing under the pump, without soaking the fresh bandage. The thought of unkindness to Rose made him angry, he discovered as he climbed out, feeling completely human again for the first time in days.

As he ran the razor through four days' accumulation of beard he heard the faint sounds of splashing from the little room. His memory, with inconvenient precision, presented the memory of Rose's body in his arms, in his bed against his naked chest, of her walking away with the wary grace of a young deer. Tension gathered low in his belly, heavy and demanding. With an inward snarl at his own lack of self-control he finished shaving, scrubbed a towel over his face.

She needed time and the last thing he needed at the moment was a woman. Sex, yes. He could certainly do with that, but a man could manage. His body protested that it *always* needed a woman and was firmly ignored while he rummaged in the clothes press for his spare uniform. Women were demanding, expected emotions he did not have to share. This one was tying him in knots and she wasn't even his, whatever Maggie said.

Maggie had brushed his dress uniform and he shoved it aside, smart, expensive, reeking of *officer* and *privilege*. It reminded him again of the confounded Duchess of Richmond's confounded ball where he had stood around, under orders to do the pretty, pretend to be a gentleman and generally give the impression that the nickname of Randall's Rogues that attached to their irregular unit of artillery was a light-hearted jest and not a mild description for a bunch of semi-lawless adventurers.

He'd even had to let Moss cut his hair, he thought with a snarl as he stood in front of the mirror and raked the severe new crop into order. *Fashionable*, Maggie had said with approval. Damned frippery, more like. Flint buckled on his sword belt, grabbed his shako and ran downstairs for his breakfast.

'Hawkins! With me.'

'Sir.' The sergeant came in, buttoning his tunic. He'd shaved and found a half-decent shirt from somewhere.

'We'll go and report in and see who is where.'

They walked out into the crowded cobbled streets where men lay on piles of straw under makeshift awnings with townswomen, medical orderlies and nuns tending to them. They kept their eyes skinned for familiar faces or the blue of an artillery uniform jacket.

The news on the street was that Wellington had left his house on Rue Montagne du Parc for Nivelles, where the army was bivouacked. 'We'd best start at HQ, see what staff he's left behind and get our orders, then locate the colonel,' Flint decided as they began the steep climb up from the lower town. It was slow progress.

'How's Miss Rose, sir?'

'Miss?'

Hawkins shrugged. 'She behaves like a lady, Major. So Maggie says.'

'She was living with a man from the Seventy-Third, now no longer with us, poor devil. I doubt that makes her a lady.'

'I think she's got a nice way with her, what I've seen,' the sergeant said stubbornly as they stopped to help a nun move a man on to a stretcher without jarring the bloody stump of his leg. 'Pretty little thing.'

'Most you've seen of her is a filthy waif glued to me like a kitten stuck up a tree. Her nice ways got her into my bed this morning,' Flint snapped. 'Not what I'd call ladylike.'

'Needs a cuddle, most likely,' Hawkins said, impervious to Flint's sudden bad temper. 'Women do when they're upset. Useful that, I always think. You know, you give her a cuddle, bit of a squeeze, buss on the cheek, the next thing you know she's stopped crying and you're—'

'You can discuss your techniques of courtship with the duke when we catch up with him,' Flint suggested as they returned the salute of the sentry at the gate of what had been Wellington's house. 'They say he's got about as much finesse as you have between the sheets.'

The scene was somewhat different from the weeks before the battle when the house had been mobbed by every person of fashion—or pretentions of gentility—hoping to gain access to the great man. Now it was all business, with red-eyed adjutants, scurrying orderlies and groups of weary men consulting notes and maps as they dealt with the aftermath of the Field Marshall's departure.

'Major!' Flint turned to see Lieutenant Foster, their brigade surgeon. He looked bone-weary, but he'd managed to change and shave. 'I was coming to find you. I've a list of which of our men are where, I just need the names and locations of any you brought back yesterday.'

'What's the butcher's bill?' Flint demanded.

'Eighty, unless any more go in the next few days, and that's always possible.' Foster shrugged philosophically. 'I've got as many of the badly wounded ones as I can with the nuns, they're better at offering comfort and the wards are cleaner and quieter.'

'Hawkins, take the lieutenant down to see the men at Maggie's, then get a list from him of where everyone is. We can add a few more to the dead list, Foster. Let me know what needs doing when we both get back to the house. And you, Lieutenant, when you've seen those last few men, you get back to your lodgings and sleep until this afternoon at least. That's an order.'

'But, Major, the colonel—'

'Go!' To hell with Randall, he could wait until Flint had reported in here at HQ before he started throwing out his orders.

The adjutant at the desk consulted a sheaf of papers. 'Your guns and the fit men have joined the line of march towards the border, sir. Any who recover in the next ten days are to be sent to muster at your base at Roosbos to await onward deployment. You, Major, and your sergeant, have orders here.' He rifled through the mass of documents on his desk and produced a sealed letter. 'They are not secret. His lordship has directed that for every hundred men who must remain in the city through wounds, sickness and for assigned duties, one officer, one non-commissioned officer and three men will also stay to keep order and look to their welfare and deployment. There is a list of the other officers included.'

Flint stared at the packet in his hands. This was

the end of his war. No more marching, deploying, fighting—the work he was trained for. Now it would be administration, paperwork, policing—the stuff he hated.

'…news of Lord Randall's condition when you've seen the colonel.' The adjutant was still talking.

'His *condition*? Randall is wounded?'

'Why, yes, Major. He has a chest wound and the blow to his head, of course. I assumed you were aware?' Something in the quality of Flint's glare must have penetrated. 'Ah, obviously not. There's no danger, sir, at least, not as far as the surgeon can see at the moment. I don't think he wants to operate to remove the bullet if it can be avoided.'

Lord, no, Flint thought with an inner shudder. Bullets in the chest were nasty enough, digging the damn things out was usually fatal.

The other man was still talking and Flint closed off the memory of having a ball cut out of his own shoulder. That had been bad, but at least it hadn't been rattling around his lungs.

'Concussion is always difficult of course, so they are keeping him in bed and flat on his back for a few days.'

'Where is he?'

'His usual lodgings, the house he took in Rue Ducale, sir.'

'Right.' Flint turned on his heel and strode out of the house. Damn it, his commanding officer wounded and he had not known. When had that happened? There were two rules: look after your men and watch your commander's back for him. He swore silently all the way across the Parc to the smart street where Randall had established a base for his frequent visits into the city.

He banged the knocker, strode in past the faintly protesting servant and up the stairs, guided by the sound of voices. *Conscious at least.* 'Laying down the law again, sir?' he asked as he pushed open the door.

'Where the hell have you been?' The question came on the merest thread of a breath. Flint made his face poker straight and his voice wooden to keep the shock from both as he advanced to the foot of the bed. 'Picking up the bodies, sir. Where was yours?' *God, but he looks bad.*

There was a movement behind him and a hand closed around his arm. 'Outside, if you please.'

Flint turned. A diminutive brunette in a gown that could best be described as *sensible*, with a hairstyle that was fighting a losing battle against escaping wisps of hair, regarded him with severity. A lady from her accent, a spinster of either Quakerish habits or a restricted budget to judge by her modest attire. Apparently a female fallen on hard times and taking employment where she might and a pocket battleaxe to boot, under that demure appearance. She turned towards the open door and, short of wrenching out of her grip, he had no choice but to follow her.

'Lord Randall was found in an old barn to the west of La Haye Sainte,' she whispered as soon as they were out on the landing with the door closed. 'Just at the moment, as he has a concussion in addition to a bullet wound in his chest, we are unable to establish exactly why he was there. I must ask you to leave immediately, sir. Lord Randall must rest.'

'Ma'am, I must report to my commanding officer. I follow his orders, not those of a hired nurse. With respect.'

'I am not a hired nurse.' Her lips thinned. She obviously knew just how genuine his remarks about *respect* were. 'I am Miss Endacott, a friend of the family.'

'The governess Randall escorted over from England?' *And the lady he danced every single dance with at the Duchess's ball,* Flint realised. *Only she hadn't been dressed like a schoolmarm then. What the blazes is going on? Surely not an* affaire*?*

Her expression became, if anything, stiffer. 'I own and run a school here, Major. I assume from your uniform and your likeness to Lord Randall that you are his half-brother Adam Flint? I believe I saw you at Roosbos.'

'Yes, I'm Flint. And I must report to him.'

She hesitated. 'I could use your help to give him the saline draught the doctor left. He is not a good patient. It is critically important that he lies still and does not get excited.'

Randall become excited? That would be the day they were ice skating in hell. But he would say whatever was necessary to get past this schoolteacher. 'Of course.'

'In that case you may have five minutes, no more.' Miss Endacott appeared to place little value on his word, even less when he showed his teeth in an approximation to a smile.

She shot him a glare that would obviously paralyse recalcitrant schoolboys—fortunately he had never been to school—reopened the door, moved to the bedside table and poured a clear liquid into a glass with brisk competence. 'I will administer the draught. You will please support his head, but do not allow him to sit up. Kindly do not jar his head when you lower it back to the pillow.'

Adam slid his right hand under the other man's neck and felt him stiffen in rejection. It was probably the first time they had ever touched this intimately. *Put up with it, Brother*, Flint thought as Miss Endacott lifted the glass to Justin's lips. She tipped the draught efficiently down his throat, then nodded to Flint to lower Randall back to the pillow.

His half-brother lay, eyes closed, white around the lips. His hands were clenched into fists as they lay on top of the covers.

He is in a great deal of pain and doesn't want her to see it, Flint thought, recognising the reaction. Expressions of sympathy wouldn't help.

'HQ are asking after you. I'll tell them to leave you in peace for a day or so. Everything's under control. I'll find Bartlett and we'll carry on. Any orders?'

There was no response from the man on the bed, then, 'Adam…look after the Rogues.' It was the first time his half-brother had ever used his first name.

'Of course, sir.' That was the closest Flint had seen Randall come to a display of emotion. Perhaps the effort of keeping every trace of his natural reactions under control when Gideon had died in his arms was having its effect on Justin now. Flint had thought he had no feelings for his legitimate family, but standing there watching his brothers in those final moments had been harder than he could have imagined. 'I'll fetch the body.' There was no need to say whose.

'Thank you.' Randall did not open his eyes.

Miss Endacott almost pushed him out of the door and closed it in his face without another word. She was worrying unduly, he told himself as he ran downstairs. Randall looked bad, and was suffering a lot of pain, but he was tough. He would pull through. But her protective attitude was interesting. Surely she and Randall were not…? No, of course not. Lord Poker-Up-the-Backside Randall fall for a schoolteacher? Never.

Chapter Four

Rose opened the kitchen door, uncertain of her welcome. Was she supposed to stay out of the way of the soldiers after their reaction when she had sent them scattering into the courtyard? On this, the second morning in the warm, cheerful house, she was beginning to feel stronger and the scream in her head had grown quiet, almost as soft as the buzzing of a field of drowsy bees on a summer's day. She had slept in the little dressing room and waited until Adam had left the bedchamber before venturing out.

Maggie was at the hearth, stirring something in a big pot, and Adam and Hawkins were slumped in chairs either side of the table, their backs to her, relaxed like two great hounds after an exhausting chase.

As Rose hesitated on the threshold, Maggie

jerked her head towards a battered armchair beside the fire and poured a mug of tea. Rose took it with a smile of thanks and snuggled quietly into the patchwork cushions as Hawkins picked up what was obviously a thread of conversation.

'If Boney's beat, then the war's over, surely? They've got the French king all ready to come back, the nobs in Vienna will carry on negotiating and drawing lines on the maps, and what'll happen to us?'

'West Indies?' Adam said.

'They say it's a death trap. Getting killed in battle's one thing, don't fancy going all that way to die of yellow fever.'

'Might get ordered home.' Adam drained his mug and set it down with a thump on the table. 'We could be Hyde Park soldiers, firing off guns for Prinny's parties. That *would* be fun.'

'Or we'd be harassing rioting industrial workers up north. Not what I call soldiering,' Hawkins muttered.

'Me neither, Jerry.' Adam slumped lower in his chair, his accent roughening. They were like two sergeants together, Rose realised. Mates, not officer and NCO. 'I've been a soldier half my life. This is family.'

There was a brooding silence. Maggie lowered herself into the chair opposite Rose and picked up a sock and darning wool from the basket beside her.

'East India Company looks the best bet to me,' Hawkins said. 'They're using more artillery, so I hear, and there's a chance of good money.'

'I'd been thinking about that.' Adam sat up straighter and reached across the table to rip a crust off the loaf. 'Or there's the Continental princelings. All those German states with standing armies, they need good artillerymen and they're prepared to pay.'

'You'd end up a general,' Hawkins said.

Adam snorted. 'You'd make major,' he countered, dragging the crust through the butter and biting into it. 'And think of the fancy uniforms.'

Hawkins snorted. 'Yeah, that's you all right, prancing about like a circus ringmaster, all gold braid and plumed hats.'

'East India Company, then. Sensible uniforms, a real army with real fighting, good money.' Adam sounded cheered. 'That sounds fine to me. Hate not having a plan.'

Rose's heart sank. *India? But why am I upset about that? He isn't mine... It is so far away.*

'You've always got a plan, thank goodness,'

Hawkins said. 'Puts the wind up me, not knowing what's happening next. What the hell would we do if we had to leave the army?'

'Damned if I know.' Adam dropped the remains of the crust on the table as though his appetite had suddenly deserted him. 'The army's who we are, not what we do.'

The door to the yard swung open as he spoke and Moss stumped in, bringing the smell of fresh air and stables with him. 'What are you two brooding about? Spouting philosophy by the sound of it.'

'East India Company,' Hawkins said as he got to his feet and caught the door before it closed, Adam at his heels. 'The major's got a plan.'

'Oh, aye?' Moss said to Maggie as the door banged closed behind the two men. 'Suppose that makes sense. It'd break the major, being a peace-time soldier.'

'He could sell out,' Maggie suggested, biting off a loose end of wool and rolling the socks up.

'Flint? You're joking. He made himself an officer and a gentleman from nothing. He belongs in the army, heart and soul. Not like me, I'd had enough by the time I got out. And I'd got you.' He winked at Maggie. 'Him, he wouldn't know what to do with himself.' He glanced across and saw who was in the other chair. 'Well, Miss Rose. You're blooming this morning. You want to give me a hand with the lads?'

Rose filled the mug with water again and looked across to the one remaining soldier she had not yet taken a drink to, the one with the head wound. He lay quietly on his straw mattress, some of his fitter mates playing cards at his feet. Occasionally one would look at him, murmur a few words of encouragement, touch his leg as if to reassure him they wouldn't leave him.

She had been avoiding him quite deliberately. Now, as she made herself look at the soldier's shrouded head, the scream in her head grew louder.

Coward, she told herself. It had helped to come downstairs, to make herself smile and work alongside Maggie and Moss, Lucille and the men. They had accepted her silence and treated her with more respect than she had expected from common soldiers. Their gratitude for anything she did for them seemed genuine.

Now she crouched down beside the still figure and forced herself to touch his arm. He started and turned his head with a jerk and the bandage slipped to reveal the mess of torn flesh beneath. From across the yard came a loud bang.

Gunfire. Then her head was full of the scream, her silent scream.

'Miss Rose!' someone shouted. Men jumped to their feet, people ran out from the kitchen. Hands seized her, shook her. She found she was on her feet, trembling violently, held by fingers so tight they hurt.

'Hysterical,' a man's voice said. 'I'll have to slap her. Fetch cold water.'

'Don't touch her.' It was a snarl, a familiar, fierce growl. Rose found herself in Adam's arms, held against his chest. *Safe.* 'Rose, what happened?'

'Dixon's bandage slipped,' someone volunteered. 'And then that shutter on the loose hinge dropped off and she jumped up, white as a sheet, and started shaking. Don't know why Miss Rose is so upset, sir. She was fine with some really nasty sights— Dan's leg, for one.'

'Facial wounds seem to distress her,' Adam said. 'It's all right, Rose. Lieutenant Foster is looking after Dixon, he's going to be fine.'

He made her walk and then pushed her down and she landed with a thump that jerked her out of the nightmare a little. She was in the kitchen, sitting on one of the hard wooden chairs. Not on the battlefield, not surrounded by mangled bodies and the screaming, twitching wounded.

Rose blinked and the now-familiar faces swam into focus. Adam, Maggie, Sergeant Hawkins, Moss. Little Lucille, the maid-of-all-work, her eyes wide and shocked.

'Best get her up to bed, Major,' Maggie said. 'Look how she's trembling.'

'No.' Adam hunkered down in front of her. 'Rose, this is not your nightmare, this is here and now. No more shooting, no more dying. The surgeon is here to look after the men. Take a deep breath and see.'

His voice was firm, without any sympathy or softness in it. Adam expected her to be calm and he would not ask anything of her that she could not do. Rose closed her eyes and took the deep breath, then another, and opened her eyes again. *That poor man, Private Dixon.* She got to her feet and saw Adam wave the others, who had tensed when she moved, back into their seats. The door to the yard seemed a long way away, but her feet took her there, and through and across to the outhouse where the surgeon was bandaging the private's head.

She knelt down beside Dixon, took his hand and held it until he was lying back down again. His one-eyed gaze stayed on her face. 'Sorry, Miss Rose.'

He was sorry? She lifted his hand to her cheek, then put it down and cupped her palm gently around his bandaged face, smiled and shook her head. *I'm sorry.*

The surgeon got to his feet and picked up his bag. 'Are you steadier now?'

Yes. She frowned at him. He was the one who had wanted to slap her, the one who had shaken her. She held out her hand and was pleased there was no tremor now. *Can't you see?*

'Are you dumb?' he asked, as he took her elbow and steered her towards the kitchen door.

Rose shook off his hand. *I can't speak. I* can *walk.*

Adam was standing by the window. *He was watching me.* The unsmiling nod he gave her was like a hug.

'Is this a congenital condition?' the surgeon demanded of the room in general. Rose found herself pressed down into the chair again. The man tipped up her chin. 'Open your mouth.'

No. She gritted her teeth and shook her head.

'There's a deformity of the palate perhaps. She can hear normally?' His fingers pressed against the hinge of her jaw.

'I suspect you are in a good way to having your fingers bitten, Lieutenant,' Adam said. 'Leave her be. Rose will speak when she is ready, not before.'

Thank you. She could tell that he could read her expression and the hard mouth just kicked up at the corner into a suspicion of a smile. She could understand the look on the men's faces when he spoke to them. They'd follow him into hell—they *had* followed him into hell—because they knew he had confidence in them and they knew he would never abandon them. He was not going to abandon her either, those blue eyes told her.

'If you say so, sir,' Lieutenant Foster said and, to Rose's relief, he left her side and went to take the mug of tea Maggie held out to him. He cleared his throat and flicked open his notebook. 'As I was explaining to the sergeant, everything is pretty much under control, Hawkins will fill you in with the details, sir, but I'm rather concerned about Major Bartlett.'

'What about him?' Adam demanded. 'He's not wounded, is he?'

'He is. It must have been a nasty blow to the

head. He seems to have significant memory loss, he's not exactly rational and the circumstances under which he is being nursed… To be frank, sir, I am not sure what to tell the colonel.'

'If he's in some hovel, then we must get him moved. Damn it, are there any more of our officers wounded that no one's bothered to tell me about?'

He looked furious, Rose thought, glad those hard blue eyes were not looking at her.

'Er…no, none, sir. And Bartlett's in very comfortable lodgings in the city. Perfectly clean, plenty of water, decent kitchens. A lady's um…residence.' The lieutenant appeared fascinated by something in his notebook.

'Stop stammering, man. So Major Bartlett has found himself yet another lady friend. This is hardly a novel scandal to rock Brussels' society, now, is it?'

'I couldn't…er…comment, sir.'

'Give me the address. I'll go now.' Flint extended a hand and the surgeon scribbled a few lines and passed the note across. 'Rue de Regence? Respectable area.'

'Quite. Very.' The surgeon was red around the ears.

Adam slapped his shako on his head. 'I won't be

long. Rose, you keep busy and don't tease Lieutenant Foster while I'm gone.'

'Well, and what are you blushing like a maiden for, Lieutenant?' Maggie demanded as the door banged behind Adam. 'He's not ended up in a brothel, has he?' She grinned at Rose. 'A bit of a lad is our Major Bartlett.'

'A brothel? No, far from it! I really do not consider it my place to say, Mrs Moss. I must be going. I will come back tomorrow and Moss knows my lodgings in case anyone needs me urgently.'

'If it wasn't that Randall's Rogues never ran from anything, I'd say the lieutenant was in full retreat,' Moss remarked. He stuck a taper in the fire and lit his pipe. 'Now what's Tom Cat Bartlett up to?'

Flint found the address easily enough. Foster had been correct, the house was in a respectable street, well kept and as quiet as any at the moment, given the state the city was in.

The door was answered by a woman as well kept and respectable as her house. 'Sir?'

'Major Flint. I am calling on Major Bartlett.'

Her lips thinned but she made no move to stand aside. 'Indeed, sir.'

'I assume, as he is wounded, he is in?' *Don't say he's died. We've lost too many.*

'Oh, he's in, sir, but her ladyship said I wasn't to admit anyone but the surgeon, sir.'

Ladyship? Bartlett had found himself very cosy lodgings indeed by the sound of it. Presumably he was languishing on the snow-white bosom of some high-ranking officer's wife while her husband was otherwise engaged chasing a fugitive emperor back to Paris. 'I am that surgeon's senior officer.'

'Oh, in that case, sir, please to come in.' She had decided he was another surgeon, it seemed. 'Top of the stairs on the right, sir. Can you find your own way? Only I've left the bread rising—'

'Thank you.' Flint was halfway up the stairs, too irritated with Bartlett to worry about interrupting a tender *tête-à-tête*. If he was well enough to be taking an interest in women, then he was well enough to get up and share some of the workload.

He gave a cursory rap on the door and strode in. 'Bartlett. They tell me you're—' Languishing certainly, and on a bosom which was probably snow-white, but which was, thankfully, covered by tumbling blond tresses. The owner of the tresses was curled up on the bed, her arms around the wounded major, her expensively simple muslin gown rucked up to her knees and her blue eyes glaring at Flint.

His own blue eyes, Randall's blue eyes, the eyes of his half-sister, Lady Sarah Latymor.

Of all the circumstances to meet his half-sister for the first time. 'What the *hell* are you doing here?'

Bartlett closed his eyes in a reasonable imitation of a manly swoon. Lady Sarah laid him tenderly on the pillows and bounced off the bed like a mother cat defending its sole kit. Flint averted his gaze while she wrestled her creased gown into some sort of order.

'*You!*' she uttered in tones that would have done credit to Sarah Siddons as Lady Macbeth. 'You're Adam Flint. Justin wouldn't introduce me to you at the review.'

'He wouldn't introduce you to any of the Rogues,' Flint snapped. 'And for very good reason.'

'I know the reason he wouldn't introduce me to *you*. You're my natural brother and I'm not supposed to know any of you exist, let alone associate with you.'

'None of the Rogues should be associating with you—let alone him.' He stabbed a finger at Bartlett. Damn it, now he had to worry about his sister's morals on top of everything else. Half-brothers were bad enough, but at least they were fellow soldiers, there was a connection there, an understanding. Sisters were another matter. He had never been responsible for a respectable lady in his life and he did not want to start now.

She swept her hair over one shoulder and began to braid it into a rough plait. 'And stop shouting. Poor Tom's head hurts.'

'Poor Tom's head is going to be ripped from his shoulders just as soon as he's on his feet,' Flint threatened. *And his balls are doomed as well, just as soon as Randall's halfway fit.* 'Now get your cloak and bonnet and I'll take you home this minute. You can't stay here.' He shouldn't feel anything other than irritated, he thought, but he did. Or was that just because he'd felt so unaccountably churned up over Gideon?

'I *am* home. This is my lodging.' She glared at him.

'Well, then, I'll take you to your brother.' He glared back. *I really do not like this chit.*

'You can't do that. Mary Endacott says Justin's too ill to be disturbed.'

'Then don't disturb him.'

'I will, if I could only get to him! They told me

that Gideon's dead, and I feel it, but I can't believe it somehow.' Her voice trailed off and she looked young and hurt and vulnerable.

'Believe it.' He couldn't cope with another female on his hands and he was damn sure he didn't want to revisit that tableau amidst the shrieking chaos of Quatre Bras as Randall held his dying brother. *Their* dying brother. 'What's wrong with Bartlett? If you won't leave, then I'll take him out of here.'

'You can't, he has a head wound. Lieutenant Foster said it would be dangerous to move him.' She shifted to stand between Flint and the bed. He took her by the waist and moved her bodily out of the way, then, before the first of her blows landed on his back, bent over the other man.

'Bartlett! Tom! Open your eyes.' He was very white, the bandaging was extensive and there was bruising everywhere Flint could see. There was, he realised, quite a lot of the major to be seen. The man was naked.

Slowly Bartlett's eyes opened. He stared up at Flint without any sign of recognition. 'Sir?'

'Don't *Sir* me, Bartlett, we're the same rank, damn it.'

'We are?' he asked dully. His eyelids closed before Flint could answer, as though this was of no interest to him at all.

'Have you shown him his uniform?' Flint demanded.

'He had been stripped by looters when I found him.' Sarah's angry colour faded. She compressed her lips for a moment as though fighting back nausea.

She had found him? This drawing-room darling had ventured into that hell and come back with Bartlett? No wonder she looked queasy—it was a wonder she could sleep at night. Perhaps his half-sister had her share of the Latymor backbone, after all.

'They had taken everything except his breeches and one boot,' she added. 'The vultures.'

'Vultures…?' Bartlett's voice trailed off.

'You see?' Lady Sarah tugged at Flint's arm. 'Leave him alone. He has no idea who he is, what happened. He doesn't know you. He seems to think he's a lieutenant. Perhaps in his mind he is back when he first joined the army.'

It looked genuine enough, and the man was no coward, nor a shirker, despite his overactive social life. On the other hand, it would be just like Tom Cat Bartlett to spot a good thing—and a lovely young woman—when he came across them. Something unexpected, something suspiciously like brotherly protectiveness, stirred. 'Have you seen the head wound?'

'Yes, of course.' She swallowed hard. 'It was dreadful, you could see the skull—and I had to stitch it. When Lieutenant Foster saw it later he said it must have been a cavalry sabre because nothing else could slice like that and give such a heavy blow at the same time.' She bit her lip. 'Tom *is* going to get better. He must.'

He probably would, unless there was internal bleeding within the skull. That could kill almost without warning, days after a blow, but there was no point in telling her that, she would only cling tighter to the man.

Something scratched at the door and Sarah hurried across the room. 'Oh, Ben, shush! You know Madame le Brun doesn't want you upstairs.' She opened it and staggered back as a great black hairy dog hurtled into the room and flung itself on Flint.

'*Sit.*' It subsided on to his feet, panting, its tail thrashing the carpet. 'How the devil did Dog get here?'

'His name's Ben. I found him tied to a baggage wagon, the poor thing. I recognised him from the review. And he led me to Justin. And Tom. And helped me fight off the deserter who tried to steal my horse. So I had to take care of him after he'd done so much for me.'

Flint snapped his fingers and the dog sat up, leaning against his leg. 'Good boy.' He scratched it behind the ear, obscurely comforted that the beast was safe. 'Dog is coming back with me, now. And so are you. Pack a bag. I'm taking you to Randall's house.'

'I won't go.' She sat down on the end of the bed, one hand possessively on Bartlett's leg. 'You'd have to carry me kicking and screaming.'

'It can be arranged,' Flint muttered.

'I don't have to do what you say. You're only my half-brother and if Justin won't introduce you to me, I'm sure you're not fit company for me.' She glared at him, full of fierce bravado and not far from tears, he thought. 'How are you so sure Gideon is dead?' she asked suddenly.

'Because I was there,' Flint said, caught off balance before he could think.

'Are you *certain*?'

'Certain I was there or certain that he's dead? Yes to both. You don't get up after wounds like that.'

'Was…was he shot? Was it quick? In the head…?' Her voice trailed off.

'Sabre wounds, several.' The angry colour ebbed out of Sarah's cheeks. She had been on the battle-field, she must have seen the slashed bodies. Her imagination was doing the rest. He though she was going to faint, or be sick, but it seemed he under-estimated his sister.

'Get out.' She sprang to her feet and pointed at the door. 'Get out and if you come back here again disturbing Tom then I'll use his pistols on you.'

Chapter Five

Adam crashed into the room like a sudden clap of thunder. The door slammed back against the wall as he strode in swearing and came to a fulminating halt in the middle of the room.

Rose dropped the shirt she was mending and stared. He appeared not to have seen her sitting in the corner. 'My own damned sister! The—' then something in French that Rose did not understand '—lascivious sod! I'll gut the swiving, good-for-nothing, fornicating—' Rose clapped her hands over her ears. 'And her, blast her, looking down her nose and announcing that as we've never been introduced she can't see why she has to obey me! I'll give her obey...' He unbuckled his sword belt and tossed the weapon on to the bed. '*And* she tries to steal my blasted dog. I'll...'

Something cold and wet nudged against Rose's

hand and she looked down to find a huge black dog watching her fixedly. It look a fold of her skirts in its jaws and tugged. Rose stood up. Adam was still swearing. The dog released her skirt and pushed her with its big head. When she stood her ground it growled softly.

'Dog?' Adam turned and saw them. 'For heaven's sake! *Friend*. This is Rose and she does not need herding.'

The creature gave her hand a swipe with a tongue like a rough red flannel and collapsed on her feet.

'I'm sorry. He's a Bouvier des Flandres and he's used to herding his flock. We rescued him and so he decided the Rogues were his.'

Rose raised her eyebrows and pointed a finger at Adam. *He believes* you *are a sheep?*

'Me? He seems to think I'm the shepherd. He rounds up strays which is what seems to have happened with the search party looking for the colonel. God, I am going to kill Bartlett, just as soon as he's fit enough. She's a wilful, irritating brat, but she's my sister. Randall can get in line behind me.' He began to pace again. Dog whined softly, lifted his head and followed Adam's movements with mournful brown eyes. His tail stopped wagging.

Rose took a step into Adam's path and shook his arm. *Tell me.*

'You want to know what I'm ranting about?' He shrugged. 'Sit down, it's a long story.' She went back to her chair and folded her hands in her lap. 'You look as though I should begin, *Once upon a time*, as though this was a fairy tale. Well, once upon a time there was Earl Randall, the father of our present colonel. He was a great man who thought that he could take anything he wanted, especially women.

'He had a large family—Justin, his heir; Gideon, who was killed at Quatre Bras; a pair of twins who're at school now; Augusta, now Marchioness of Blanchards, who was in Paris with her unmarried sister Sarah, Gideon's twin; and Harriet, who married some rural dean or another.

'And then there's the rest of us, the bastards.' He stopped pacing and drew a finger down the line of his nose. 'You'll see this nose and these eyes across every parish for miles around Chalfont Magna. My mother was a chambermaid. He forced her, used her and then when she fell pregnant, he tossed her out.'

The very calmness of his voice warned Rose just how angry he was, even after a lifetime of knowing the story of his own birth. She stayed quiet and still, out of his line of sight.

'The head groom took her in, gave her a room over the stables out of the old devil's way. She earned her keep cooking and looking after the lads and the grooms. I became one of them, learned to ride, learned to read and write, learned to mimic my betters.' His voice changed from the neutral accent with its faint country burr to an aristocratic drawl. '"Hitch up my chaise, lad. Saddle the bay. Clean up my hounds. Here's a penny for you."

'I stayed while my mother needed me, although I didn't take well to being a servant. Too bloody minded,' he added with a twist of his lips. 'Then when I was fourteen she married one of the grooms and the recruiting sergeant came to the village. I was a tall lad and they didn't ask about ages. I joined the army. Square peg, square hole.'

He fell silent and Rose stood up and went to stand in front of him, running her hands over the marks of rank on his uniform jacket. *As an officer?* Adam grasped her meaning as he always seemed to.

'Hardly, at that age and from that background. As a private at first, then a corporal. I learned my figures, found I was good at the mathematics you need for gunnery. Then I became a sergeant in charge of a gun crew, like Hawkins.'

He looked down at her as she stood there, her fingers still stroking the gold braid.

'And one day, after a particularly hot fight, I stood in the middle of what was left of the position, looked up and there was this officer on a big grey horse staring down his nose—this nose—at me. "Who are you?" he said. And I said, "Adam Flint, one of your father's gets, I'd wager," and he laughed and rode on. A week later I found myself with a field commission to lieutenant and a transfer to a unit they were beginning to call Randall's Rogues, under his command. One thing about artillery, officers are promoted on merit, not by purchase, which makes all of us not quite gentlemen in Wellington's eyes. So here I am now, a major.'

He shrugged as though that was an ordinary career path, not a climb from poverty and bastardy through skill and courage and sheer determination.

Just as Hawkins said, Adam had remade himself into the man he was now. The officer, the gentleman. The soldier. *And Sarah?* she mouthed.

'My esteemed fellow officer, Major Tom Bartlett, drinker, gambler and highly qualified rake, got himself hit on the head. Apparently Dog here found Sarah wandering about amongst the wounded—although how the devil she got there I do not know because she was supposed to be safe with our sister Gussie—and herded her over to him.'

But that is good, surely? Rose frowned up at him. *He's safe...*

'The idiot girl gets him back to Brussels and sticks him in her own bed—and that's where I find them. In bed. She says she's soothing his fevered brow and he doesn't remember who he is and I'm a brute to shout at an injured man. He lies there looking like the perfect wounded hero and calls me *sir*, as though he hasn't a clue who I am. Then when I order her out of there she announces it is her lodgings and that as Randall has never let her anywhere near my polluting and illegitimate presence I have no authority over her and she can do what she likes.'

Adam flung himself down in an armchair and Dog came and butted him anxiously on the knee. 'The only creature in that damned house who'd do what I told them was Dog.'

Rose repressed the smile tugging at her lips. The poor man was furious and frustrated, but it was somehow touching to see the confident officer brought to a stand by one concussed major and a defiant young woman. She perched on the arm of the chair and raised an eyebrow in question.

'What am I going to do now? I told Randall, managed to get past that dragon of a woman who is guarding him for a second. It seemed to bring him round, at least. He's sending a note to order her home. But if there's a hope in hell of getting the silly chit out of there before she's ruined, we've got to try. She won't listen to me, but perhaps she will to him.' He rested his head back and closed his eyes.

Rose slid to the floor and curled up against the chair and Dog's solid, furry bulk. *Ruined. I'm ruined, just like she will be, and that is my sin. I ran off with Gerald.* She looked at her hands, soft and white under the bruises and scratches. *I was a lady once, like this Lady Sarah, I must have been.* It explained the flashes of memory of big houses, it explained why she had been at a ball. It must have been the Duchess of Richmond's ball, the one that Maggie had been gossiping about.

She studied Adam's profile, aloof and severe, even with the piercing blue eyes hooded. *I saw you before, I was at the ball and so were you.* She'd looked in the closet while he was out and found a dress uniform, fine dark blue broadcloth and gold lace. *I was at the ball and then I ran away with Gerald and now I am ruined.*

Something brushed over her hair, Adam's hand, stroking it as though it was Dog's rough black coat. She shifted until she could feel his leg against her back. A shiver of desire ran through her. *I want this man.*

'And what the blazes am I going to do with you?' he enquired. 'I suppose I'd best find out where the Seventy-Third's camp followers are and get you an escort there.'

No! Rose swivelled round and came up on her knees so fast that she bumped her head against Dog's massive jaws. *Ouch.* He gave her a pained look and lay down, his muzzle on Adam's left foot. Rose shook her head emphatically at Adam.

'No? Then what do you want to do?' He was being patient, far more patient than she had any right to expect him to be when he had so much to think about, to do, to take responsibility for.

Rose got up, sat on the bed and looked Adam straight in the eye. She waved her hand to encompass the room, the house, then pointed a finger at him. *Stay with you.*

Rose had thought she was beginning to be able

to read Adam's expression, but now she might as well have been staring at a statue, so impenetrable were the strong, immobile planes of his face, the hard mouth, the steady blue eyes. Was there a flare of heat in the sapphire gaze? Something flickered and was gone.

'Stay with me?' He glanced at the sewing basket and the discarded shirt. 'I don't need a maid, Rose. I've got a batman at Roosbos.'

No. She stroked her hand over the coverlet, trying not to blush as she met his gaze.

'As my woman?' There was that flare of heat again. He was not indifferent to her.

Something very basic, very female, stirred inside her. Something she had never felt with Gerald. She had admired his looks, liked his sunny temper, enjoyed his kisses. Those memories were coming back and she had never fantasised about being naked with him, she was sure. She was reasonably certain she had never had fantasies like that about any man.

'You are too young for me, Rose.'

She gave a huff of exasperation. Men were supposed to want sex, weren't they? What was so wrong with her that Adam was fighting her off? She held up her hands, opening and closing them rapidly, confident about this at least. Ten, ten and three. *Twenty-three. And you?* She pointed at him.

'Twenty-eight. You don't look more than twenty-one, not that years have anything to do with it. I'm not a nice man, Rose and you deserve a nice man. No, don't look at me like that.' That half-smile put a crease in his left cheek that hardly qualified as anything so soft as a dimple. 'I might have rescued you back there on the battlefield, but I'm a bastard, a professional one. I fight dirty, I kill for a living and I'm not capable of being faithful to one woman for any length of time.'

You don't kill for a living, she wanted to protest. *You fight for your country.* She stretched out her hand, then let it drop back into her lap. No, of course she couldn't expect him to be faithful to her. What had she got that could hold a virile, experienced man like this?

'Rose, I'm not the marrying kind.' It was as blunt a warning as she could ever expect to receive. 'There are lots of good lads out there who'd take care of you, want to wed you, give you a family. Isn't that what you want?'

Was it? She'd thought Gerald *a good lad*. She'd thought she was in love with him and that they would marry and everything would be perfect. The daydream was as clear as if it were fresh minted. But life wasn't perfect, she'd mistaken infatuation for love and now she was ruined. Why not snatch what happiness she could?

Although why I think this big, hard, weary man would make me happy, even for a few weeks, I don't know. He obviously doesn't want me, not like that.

'Rose, don't cry.' It was the nearest to alarm she'd heard in Adam's voice.

I'm not crying. Then she realised that she was. She put up her hands to shield her face, ashamed of the weakness.

'You think I don't want you?' Adam stood up and pulled her to her feet. He tipped up her chin so she could not avoid his gaze. 'Of course I do. Who wouldn't?' One blunt thumb caught the tears under her eyes, rubbed them away. 'You're beautiful, brave, sweet. But we need to talk about this and you can't speak. I'm too old for you, Rose. Not in years, just in living. Don't mistake the need for comfort for something it isn't.'

She shook her head, helpless to explain her feelings when she hardly understood them herself.

'I've got to go and see Randall now, and then I

must get to the battlefield. I won't be back until tomorrow, late.'

She caught his hand and brought it down to her lips, kissed it, tasted the salt of her own tears.

'Hell, Rose.' She felt the control snap as Adam pulled her to him hard and his hands slid into her hair, held her fast as his mouth took hers. She had never been kissed like this, not with unconstrained masculine desire. Gerald had been respectful, aware she was a lady and a virgin. In the tent he had been clumsy, inept and afraid, too frightened for kisses.

She doubted Adam Flint had ever been clumsy or inept with a woman. She clung to the shreds of rational thought as he plundered her mouth with ruthless expertise. It was like riding a wild horse, she could only clutch at his shoulders and hope to survive the experience.

His tongue was in her mouth—when had she opened to him? She could not remember. His teeth nipped and pressed, his lips tormented and then soothed. His taste filled her senses: coffee, a hint of brandy, man. *Adam*. His hands stayed locked around her head and she found she was pressing against him, her breasts aching for his touch. Her thighs tingled and a compelling ache between them throbbed in counterpoint to the movement of Adam's mouth on hers. She snuggled closer and felt the evidence of his arousal hard against her stomach.

He released her suddenly and she sat down with a thump on the bed, one hand to her mouth, staring at him.

'You see?' His voice was harsh. 'I shock you. Maggie thinks your last man was a brute, but he wasn't, was he? He was a nice lad, I'd guess, just not around enough for you to get attached.' He grinned, without humour, when she nodded. 'I'm not a *nice lad*. I'll be back the day after tomorrow. While I'm away, think about where you want to go.' He opened the door and snapped his fingers at the dog. 'Come.'

It took time for her to recognise the trembling, the confusion of feeling, for what it was. Not fear, but simply desire stoked higher than she could have imagined. Rose got to her feet after a while and made her way on unsteady feet to the washbasin to splash cold water on her face, but even when she had done that, and stood with the linen towel in her hands, she could not do more than stare at the closed door, her mind a jumble of thoughts.

It took the sound of Maggie's voice to jerk her out of her trance. 'Rose! Tea!'

She made her way downstairs into the crowded kitchen, took her tea and perched in a corner while Maggie and Moss dispensed mugs and slabs of heavy cake for the men to carry out to their less-mobile comrades in the yard. There seemed to be fewer of the walking wounded than earlier.

The heat of the liquid penetrated the thick earthenware, a comforting, *real* sensation. Rose curled her fingers tight around it and listened to Maggie and Moss talking about Adam.

'What did the major want with those picks and shovels and the fitter men?' Maggie asked as she sank into her rocking chair.

'Gone to collect coffins. Lead-lined ones. Then they're off to the battlefield to bring back the officers,' Moss said and blew gustily on his tea. 'Bad job that, having to go back. I wouldn't have the stomach for it, not now, and I don't mind confessing it.'

Maggie shuddered, the ample flesh quivering. 'Poor man. And one of them his brother as well. That'll hurt, for all he pretends the boy was a stranger to him.'

Rose's imagination made a sickening lurch into

thoughts of mud and heat and… *No. Stop it. Think of Adam. He's strong and he wouldn't ever admit weakness, but he must be so tired and sick of this.* No wonder he didn't want some needy, helpless female tagging along, however convenient she might be for bed. And if he did want a woman, there must be plenty of tough, resourceful, experienced ones who understood a soldier's life and how to support their man.

And I'm useless and inexperienced and he knows it, she thought as she took a bite of solid fruit cake. *I'm less use to him than that great shaggy beast that comes to heel when he snaps his fingers. I've no voice and hardly any memory, so he thinks of me as a responsibility, another problem for him to deal with.*

'Aye, it's a nasty business, war,' Maggie said. 'Still, there's some good in it, too, even where you least expect it. Lieutenant Foster told me one of the infantry bandsmen found a French drummer boy, no more than a child, near where the colonel was lying. He says the regiment have adopted him and they're taking him back with them into France. Perhaps that's one boy who'll be going home to his mother.'

Rose found tears welling at the thought, blew her nose briskly and made herself focus on putting her few facts together. What did she know about herself? Unconnected memories flitted in and out, confusing, impossible to link up and make sense of. The sound of the scream was still there, almost unnoticed now until she tried to focus, then it swelled and clamoured. *This is impossible.*

'I'll just make a shopping list,' Maggie said. 'Pass me the pen and ink and some of that scrap paper, will you, Moss?' She began to scratch a list on the rough paper, muttering under her breath. 'Eggs, tea, butter, starch…'

Of course! I can write, I can put down all of the memories and then I can sort them out, like a puzzle. When Maggie had finished Rose gestured towards the pen and paper. Excitement and hope fizzed inside her. She'd been lost in a maze and now, finally she could glimpse how to get out.

'You can write?' Maggie pushed them over to her. 'You've found your memory?'

Yes and no. She waggled one hand. *So-so.*

The other woman seemed to understand. 'Look, there's more paper on that shelf. You take the things upstairs where you can be quiet, lovie. Your man won't be back today.'

My man? No, he's not. I doubt he is anyone's man but his own.

Chapter Six

Flint rode at the head of his sombre little cavalcade of carts, his mood as black as the cloths they'd covered the coffins with. Corporal Pitts, who'd been a clerk in some far-off life, had written the names in a large copperplate hand on each box and the carpenter had done a good job with sturdy elm and lead. These few dead, at least, would wait in decent order until their grieving families could decide where to lay them to rest. It took more of an effort than it should to shut out the thoughts of the many whose final grave was a mass burial pit or a pile of burning corpses.

I'm getting old, Flint thought. *Twenty-eight and bone-weary with this.*

It wasn't the fighting, it was the aftermath. They said that Wellington had wept over this victory and he could understand why. But this was the life he knew, the profession he had made his own. Peace was coming, surely—and then what? He'd been confident the other morning, talking to Hawkins about the East India Company. The armies of the Continental princelings sounded like toy soldiers from all accounts, but there was real fighting with the revolutionary armies in South America. If that was what he wanted… Hell, where had these doubts come from?

With an effort he dragged his mind from the future and thought about his errant half-sister. Randall had gone white with rage when he had reported where, and with whom, he had found Sarah and it had taken the concerted efforts of Flint and Randall's batman to keep him flat on his back in bed. Flint had left him dictating a furious letter.

'Report back the minute you have delivered the coffins to the Chapel Royal,' the colonel had called after him on a gasp as he'd left the room. 'If she's not here, then you'll go there and fetch her!'

And that was likely to get a positive response—one involving a slammed door in his face. Sieges were always tiresome and boring and he had an unpleasant premonition that he was going to have to remove Lady Sarah bodily, and probably end up answering a challenge from Bartlett into the

bargain. Always assuming his fellow officer regained his conveniently scattered wits and con-
sidered him enough of a gentleman to challenge
in the first place.

Whilst he was sunk in gloom he might as well
worry about Rose while he was at it. He wanted
her. Wanted her rather too much for comfort or for
decency. She couldn't speak, she couldn't remember who she was and he ought to leave her alone,
find somewhere, *someone*, to take responsibility
for her. As it was she was disturbing his sleep,
making him ache and ruining his concentration.

Perhaps one of the officers' ladies… He passed
the next few miles reviewing those he had some
knowledge of. The do-gooders who would take
Rose in and find her a *respectable* job were enough
to stifle any spirit the girl had. The frivolous and
the pleasure-loving wouldn't be bothered. Perhaps
Randall knew of someone, but whatever the out-
come, he was not keeping her, however much he
was coming to feel she somehow belonged to him.
A stray dog was one thing, a stray female, quite
another.

It was past midnight when Flint returned to the
lodging house. A grim day that had begun with

disinterring corpses had ended in something very close to a theatrical farce, with him hammering on the door of Sarah's lodgings and the infuriating chit hanging out of the window heaping insults and defiance on his aching head.

His temper had snapped. 'You are behaving like some Billingsgate doxy,' he'd roared. 'And I have just come from leaving your brother's coffin in the Chapel Royal.'

It was inexcusable, he knew it as soon as he said it. Gideon had been her twin and, from the little Randall had said, they'd been as close as twins so often were. He'd wondered at some point on that funereal journey whether her behaviour with Bartlett was not a reaction to that loss. Here was a wounded man she could tend to as she had been unable to tend to her brother.

'You...you *bastard*,' she'd screamed at him, hurled a potted geranium to crash on to the cobbles at his feet and slammed the window closed. The pretty blue-and-white-striped pot shattered along with any thoughts of empathy and the last shreds of his patience.

Now he walked through the deserted kitchen, dumped his sword belt on a chair, stripped off his clothes, grabbed soap from the stone sink and went out into the yard. Behind him he heard the click of claws as Dog made his way to his water bowl and then a gusty sigh as the animal sank down in his corner.

The cold water from the pump made him gasp, but it was clean, washing away the stink of death that had hung around him all day. Hawkins poked his head out of the stables, nodded, then closed the door again, his survival instincts sharp enough to recognise Flint's mood, even in the gloom.

He scrubbed himself roughly dry with his shirt as he climbed the stairs. Bed, sleep, oblivion. A woman would be even better, bringing the sort of oblivion that did not contain nightmares. Flint kept his back to Rose's door as he padded across the room in the almost-darkness of the midsummer night to the big white bed, dropping clothing behind him as he went. That way lay temptation. He knew he would not be able to resist her once he'd set foot in that room.

The bed was clean, soft bliss. Flint lay back, closed his eyes—and something moved beside him. He was on top of the warm body, fighting instinct taking over with his fingers tight around a throat, before the softness and curved shape beneath his own naked skin brought him fully awake.

'Rose, what the hell are you doing here?' He knew perfectly well. She was stubborn, she did not take *no* for an answer and that kiss had not deterred her. He was instantly hard, instantly aching. Flint dredged up the tattered remains of his will power and rolled away, on to his back, reaching for the edge of the bed to haul himself out. 'Rose—'

She moved, came up on her elbow, leaned across him and brought her lips to his chest, finding his left nipple even as her hand brushed up the length of his arousal with the merest hint of fingernails.

His head dropped back on to the pillow. A woman who knew what she was doing. The assured caress swept away the last of his will power. *Thank you, whichever god looks after tired, randy artillerymen.* With a growl of anticipation he turned to her, rolled her on to her back and pinned her between his elbows for his kiss.

Rose gasped and Adam took immediate advantage of her parted lips, his tongue sliding in, hot and wicked. She had reached for him almost blind, had meant only to curl her arms around him and rest her head on his chest. The sensation of his nipple hardening beneath her lips, the taste of his damp skin, the texture and length of the hard flesh her hand had found—they were shocking and exciting in equal measure. The sound he made as he'd reached for her sent tremors through her and a surge of something very like power.

She had done this to Adam, cracked his resolve, aroused him to passion simply because she'd reached out to hug him and then her lips and her hand had found parts that provoked this reaction…

His mouth did not leave hers as he lifted on one elbow and cupped her breast with his free hand. The weight and shape seemed to please him and he toyed with it, weighing it, kneading it gently. She moaned against his mouth and then gasped as he began to roll the nipple between thumb and forefinger, almost to the point of pain. An arrow of sensation shot down to her groin and she writhed, reached for him, found one of his nipples again and, purely on instinct, pinched it lightly, fascinated as it became hard at her touch.

Adam's growl resonated in his chest and he released her breast, slid his hand lower, over her belly, down to the triangle of curls. She was hot there, and wet. Was that normal? It was difficult to think, to feel embarrassed, as he slid one finger between the folds, raised his head and murmured something.

For a moment, as he shifted his weight over her, Rose felt a tremble of alarm. He was so very large, and experienced, and she knew nothing. The memory of what her groping hand had found made her quiver with something closer to excitement than the apprehension she knew she should feel and then she found she had shifted instinctively to cradle him between her thighs and the hard, hot length of him was pressing against her.

It will be all right, Rose assured herself as the blunt head nudged into her intimate flesh. *This is what all that dampness is for.* Then he was inside her.

'Rose—'

He was only just inside her, she realised as she managed to sort out one sensation from another. He rocked his hips, pushing a little, withdrawing, teasing himself as much as her, she suspected with sudden insight.

'You're so tight… Sorry, I was too fast. I want you too badly.' His head dropped until his forehead rested against hers, one hand slid between their bodies and touched her close to where he had entered her, stroking.

The sensation was intense and she arched up against his fingers, searching for more. The weight of his body held her down, but her movement pushed him deeper. He groaned and she felt the shift of his pelvis against hers.

The thrust of Adam's hips filled her impossibly, alarmingly, full. Perhaps the wetness was not enough, after all. Rose felt her body fighting him and struggled to relax, to stay calm, to control the instinct to reject this intrusion. She had known to expect this, only not how it would feel. Then he surged again, there was a sharp, sore pain and she realised Adam was hilted deep inside her.

Rose breathed deeply as her body begin to adjust. It would be all right in a moment. Her instincts knew what to do and he felt wonderful. This was a man, this was *Adam*, and they were joined in a way that seemed almost magically intimate and intense. There was more pleasure waiting just beyond the discomfort. She wasn't certain she wanted him to move though, not yet, not for a minute or two while she—

But shouldn't Adam be moving *something*? As her sensation-clouded mind cleared she realised he had gone quite still, rigid all over. Then he slowly raised himself up, pulled back and rolled free of her body, leaving her bereft. Surely this was not all there was to making love?

She could make out his silhouette as he sat on the edge of the bed, his head in his hands. After a heartbeat he raked his fingers through his hair and straightened up. 'You were a virgin.' His voice was flat, hard. 'A *virgin*, damn it.'

He shifted off the bed in one abrupt movement. Rose heard the rasp of a tinderbox and flung a forearm across her eyes to shield them from the sudden glare as he began to light candles, then the two oil lamps. Adam stood there in the wash of light naked, still half-erect, furious. 'You let me think you were a camp follower, that you had been with a man as his mistress. Why?'

How to mime that? Rose lifted her hands helplessly. How to explain?

'I may not be a gentleman, I may have been dragged up in the stable yard, but I have never, *never* despoiled an innocent.' He snatched a sheet from the bed and swathed it around his waist. 'Put something on. *Now.*' He began to pace, talking half to her, half to himself as she fumbled for her nightgown. 'A virgin this week…what will it be next week? Forcing an unwilling woman? I am obviously my father's son in every respect.'

No! She reached for him, the denial a silent

scream. No, how could he believe that of himself? What had she done?

The rant brought him up to the small table at the far end of the room. Rose saw Adam go still, watched his rigid back, felt her mouth go dry as he just stood there.

'What is this?' Adam turned and pointed to the ink bottle, the pen and the scraps of unused paper she had forgotten when she had tidied away her notes after hours of effort. 'You can write? Why in heaven's name didn't you tell me? This would never have happened if we had been able to have even half a conversation!'

Rose half fell out of bed and stumbled to the table. *Because I forgot*, she scrawled, blotting the lines in her haste. *I don't know my own name. Why should I remember about this?*

'You forgot.' Adam seemed to drag the breath down to his guts, then said, in the voice she had heard him use to give orders, 'What *do* you remember?' He pulled out the chair for her. 'Sit. Write.'

He looks like a Roman emperor in his toga, Rose thought, stupid with tiredness and frustration and unhappiness. *So I know about ancient Rome...*

She dipped the pen and began.

I ran away with a man called Gerald. We were going to get married. It was the night before Quatre Bras.

I realised almost at once I had been foolish, that I was not in love with him. He was very handsome—the uniform... Idiotic of me. But it was too late then. I had to stay with him. I'd promised.

I spent the night in his tent but we didn't... After the big battle I looked for him. He is dead. I forgot I could write until I saw Maggie this morning.

I am sorry. I don't remember much else, just little snatches.

Adam picked up the paper. She made herself watch the strong, long-fingered, scarred hand and not his face. The paper was quite steady in his grip. After a minute he laid it down again. 'Could you speak before the battle?'

Yes. Until I found him. His head...half his face...was gone. I wanted to scream, but nothing would come out. The scream is still there, somewhere, and words won't come.

He was reading as she wrote, one hand resting on her shoulder, his weight pressing a little as he leaned over, his body warm, close. It should have made her feel safe. When she put down the pen he pushed the cork into the ink bottle. 'It is shock. Probably another one will bring your voice and your memory back.' His hand brushed against her cheek as he straightened. She thought it was an accident, for his voice held no tenderness. 'Or time will. Go to bed now, Rose.'

When she looked towards the rumpled bed he shook his head. 'I need to sleep and to think. And I will not do either with you in my arms. Go to your own room.'

His voice was not unkind now, but she could sense the banked anger. *With me or with himself?*

She would have ignored his words, walked into his arms, tried everything she could to change his mind, then she saw the shadows under his eyes like the bruises left by the pressure of a thumb, saw the darkness in that blue gaze. He did not take what had just happened between them at all lightly and he was exhausted. *And he says he is no gentleman*, she thought with a wry smile as she turned and did as he asked.

Sleep refused to come in her narrow, lonely bed.

Her body was sore and restless. Rose felt cheated, as though she had been allowed the tiniest taste of something wonderful and then it had been snatched away. She moved, turned and heard the answering creak of bed ropes in the other room. Adam was not sleeping either.

Now the initial shock was past the realisation was creeping over her that she had hurt him very badly. He had not been born a gentleman and his sense of honour had been hard-won, something he held to himself like a shield. She had breached that, unwittingly led him to behave in a way he despised.

The temptation to go to him was like a physical force. To distract herself Rose got up, lit a candle and got out the slips of paper she had covered in notes. Each slip had one remembered fact or impression and she began to sort them out on the coverlet, searching for links and patterns.

I am a gentlewoman from a family that is comfortably off. I have a mother and father still living and I take after my mother in looks. Our home is somewhere in England but we have been in Brussels for...months? Weeks? Why?

I am well educated. I can ride and play the piano and sew. I play the harp very badly. I was at the Duchess of Richmond's ball. I was dazzled by a handsome face, a red coat and a dashing soldier who proved to be just a frightened boy, full of bravado.

And I am twenty-three years old.

Something about that stuck her as strange. Why was she not married, not betrothed? *Am I on the shelf?* Faint echoes of arguments came back. *'Why are you so stubborn? So fussy? So independent? You'll be left in the wallflowers' corner if you don't stop turning suitors down, my girl...'*

With a sigh she stacked the notes away, blew out the candle, burrowed down into the softness of the bed and willed sleep to come.

Hours later Flint lay and stared up into the darkness. His thoughts had circled all night, broken by snatches of restless sleep. *Rose.* A decent girl who had fallen for a pretty face and a scarlet coat and who'd had the sense to realise she had made a mistake, and the loyalty and courage to stick with her promise. By some miracle he had not been quite as tired, or as randy, as he'd thought himself, he'd withdrawn as soon as he had realised and at least there was little chance of a pregnancy. But the damage was done all the same.

He scrubbed his hands over his bristly jaw. Oh,

yes, a fine first experience that must have been, crushed under an unshaven, angry, aroused man using less finesse than a rutting bull. The courage of the woman struck him again like a slap in the face of his conscience. Never once in all of this had she wept, except those few tears when she thought he had rejected her. Not on the battlefield, not when she found herself dumb, lost and confused amongst strangers, not when he ordered her about, not when he took her innocence.

Rose had guts and grace and she deserved more of him. As an officer and a man he deserved more of himself than to treat her as a whore. He turned over yet again, seeking for a cool spot in the creased bedding, his nostrils full of the scent of her. Could he find Rose a decent man to marry? Something in him revolted at the thought although he did not understand why. Perhaps it was simply that he did not want to force her into anything until she had voice and memory back. He owed her that, at least, he thought as he dozed again.

The scream brought him out of bed before he could make sense of the sound. *Attack!* He stumbled towards his sword in the corner, dragged his eyes open on to the faint light of dawn.

Chapter Seven

'*Aah!*' It was wordless, desperate.

Flint flung open the door of Rose's room. She was thrashing amongst the sheets, her eyes closed, her face contorted in anguish as yet another scream was wrenched from her throat.

'Rose, wake up!' He fell to his knees, dragged her into his arms as the door to his room crashed open.

'Sir!'

He twisted round to see the figures jammed in the doorway. Moss, in trousers and braces, Maggie, her hair twisted into rag curlers, a rolling pin in her hand. Both of them stared aghast at him as he knelt there, stark naked, with a screaming woman in his arms. There was the sound of feet pounding up the stairs, Dog was howling. Moss turned and Flint saw the room behind was filled with the men, dressed anyhow, most of them with weapons in their hands.

'Adam Flint, what in heaven's name are you doing to that poor girl?'

'I had a nightmare,' Rose whispered against Adam's bare shoulder.

'Go on, downstairs the lot of you, and shut the dog up, for pity's sake!' someone said. 'The French haven't invaded, it's just a girl with bad dreams.'

It was Moss, she realised. The feet tramped off downstairs, Dog fell silent.

Adam's skin was slick with sweat, his breathing was short, as though he had been running. Over his shoulder she caught a glimpse of Maggie.

'Maggie, will you please leave?' he said harshly.

'The poor girl needs a cuddle. Take her to bed,' the older woman advised, ignoring the order.

He did not turn. 'She *is* in bed.'

'*Yours*, you dunderheaded man!' Maggie sounded torn between amusement and irritation.

'Then, with all due respect, Maggie—get the hell out of here.' The words seemed to escape between gritted teeth.

'Just admiring the view.' Maggie's chuckle faded as the outer door closed behind her.

'I cannot say I blame her,' Rose ventured when Adam stayed silent, holding her close. *How can*

I joke at a moment like this? What must they all have thought of me?

After a moment he released her, rocked back on his heels and stared. 'You can speak.'

'So I can.' She had a voice and she had not realised. *'I can speak.'* Rose sat up and tried to recall the nightmare before it vanished into incoherence. 'I had a dream, about the battlefield, about Gerald. It was just as it had happened, but this time, when I tugged at his shoulder and his body turned over...he spoke, even though he only had half a face. I screamed and this time the sound came out. I screamed and screamed.'

'I know.' He was holding himself rigid, but she saw the tremor in his hands, the sweat on his forehead.

'Adam? What is wrong? I can speak again, aren't you pleased?'

'I was asleep. It startled me.'

There was more to it than that. He was used to night alarms, she had heard the clang as he had tossed the sword aside. This was not a man who broke out in a sweat because of screams in the night or whose hands shook because of a sudden shock. 'Tell me,' she coaxed, encircling as much of the broad shoulders as she could, kissing the bristly cheek that was all her lips could reach. All he would let her reach.

'You don't want to know,' he muttered. 'You have seen enough of horrors.'

'Tell me.' She gave him a little shake.

Adam shrugged. His face was expressionless. 'When I woke just now I was back in Badajoz when the city had fallen after the siege. The men went wild and for almost three days we could not restore order. They were insane with anger over the length of the siege, the loss of so many comrades. For some the relief made them drunk.

'Those are the excuses, if there are any. There was shooting, pillaging. Women were raped, murdered. Many women. Girls, nuns. I can still hear the screaming. Officers were shot by our own men as they tried to control it.' His hand went to the scar she had noticed just below his right collarbone, he did not seem to realise he was touching it.

'You were hurt?'

Adam nodded. Shrugged.

'Not…not any of the Rogues?'

'No.'

Rose remembered his expression as he had charged across that clearing towards the men who threatened her, what he had done to them. Then she looked at him squarely in the face, put out her hand to tilt his head towards her.

This was not a man who had just been shocked out of deep sleep. His face was the face of a man who had hardly slept, a man whose thoughts were as painful as a wound. She remembered his reaction in the night when he realised she had been a virgin. *No. No, he cannot compare himself to those men, simply because he did not know.*

'Adam, you saved me.' Her voice felt rusty with disuse and screaming. 'It was not your fault…last night. It didn't occur to me that I should have told you I was a virgin.' Suddenly shy, she ducked her head. 'It was thoughtless of me. Selfish. I wanted you.' He was silent. After a heartbeat he shook his head, a tense jerk of his chin. From somewhere she found the strength to say, 'I still do.'

'No.' Adam got to his feet, walked out of the door, was halfway across his own room, then stopped as though he had forgotten where he was going.

It hurt how much she desired him, every battered, naked, weary inch of him.

'You are a respectable young woman,' he said without turning. 'Perhaps a sergeant's daughter, perhaps from a tradesman's family. You should not be with me.'

He hasn't realised. He thinks Gerald was a private. My voice...I don't sound like myself yet. If he knows I am gentry he'll send me away. She was deceiving him again and this time she knew full well what she was doing. But she was ruined now—not that it felt like ruin. How could this make it any worse?

'I was respectable till I ran off with Gerald,' she corrected him. A slight accent seemed to come naturally to her tongue. It wasn't much, just a broadening of the vowels. *My nurse?* Someone had spoken to her in that voice for years when she had been young. 'I'm not any more, not from then on, never mind what didn't happen that night in the tent.'

Adam stooped to search in the pile of discarded clothing on the floor, the muscles in his back shifting in the golden glow of the lamps. He pulled on his trousers before turning back to her, as though he was putting on armour. 'You deserve a decent man to marry you, give you children.'

'You're—'

'I'm a bit of rough from the stable yard, pretending to be a gentleman. I've seen too much, done too much and I am not the marrying kind. Faithful, yes, while it lasts. But it doesn't last long, never does. I get to feeling trapped.' He shrugged. 'I don't take up with women who want to cling and that way parting doesn't hurt anyone.'

I don't want to cling. *I want you to want me and to be with me. I want to understand what I feel for you. It isn't love, I've read about that, heard about it, thought I felt it for Gerald. I'm not faint or off my food. I don't want to sleep with your handkerchief under my pillow. I don't want you to read me poetry. I want to sleep with you in my arms, I need your weight over mine, your heart beating against my breast, your body sheathed within me. I want to live and explore and...*

'How do I get any less respectable than I am now?' Rose demanded. 'I ran off with one man and spent the night on a battlefield. I've been wandering round the place with a troop of soldiers, I've slept with you and I'm not a virgin any more. Doesn't get much less decent, does it?'

'Oh, yes, it does,' Adam said and sat down on the edge of the bed as though someone had kicked his legs from under him. 'You shack up with one of Randall's Rogues. You get pregnant. That'd do it.'

Rose marched over and sat down at the other end

of the bed. He was going beyond bone-weary, but she knew instinctively that she could show him no mercy now. 'Got many women pregnant, have you?'

'No!' He looked ready to fall asleep where he sat. That, or walk out.

'Then don't get me pregnant,' she said. 'I'm not asking you to marry me, just let me be with you till I know who I am.'

'Hell, Rose. It's a risk, you need luck, however careful the man is. I'm not—'

'Frankly,' she said as she got up, 'I don't think you are any risk at all, just now.' She gave him a sudden shove on the shoulder and then pinned him down on the bed with one palm on his flat stomach while she attacked the fastenings of his falls with the other hand.

Adam reared up on his elbows, then sank back with a groan of surrender. 'All right, you win. And you're safe for now, I suppose. At this moment I couldn't rise for the entire ballet at the Lyceum if they came and offered themselves. Let me get a couple of hours' sleep and we'll talk.' He lifted his hips as she dragged off the trousers, then rolled away on to his side.

Rose wriggled out of her nightgown and slid into

the space Adam had left. She pulled the covers over them both and laid her lips against his back, ran her hand lightly over the bandage around his ribs to make sure it was still secure. He was asleep already, she realised, hearing the soft purr of his breathing. *If they'll only let him rest...* She sank down into slumber beside him.

Rose woke to full daylight and the delicious drift of hands over her body. *'Mmm...'*

'Mmm?'

When she opened her eyes Adam was lying next to her, propped on one elbow. He had tossed back the covers and his gaze was on her naked body, sprawled in sleepy, immodest abandon.

'Is that, *Mmm, yes*? Or, *Mmm, what the devil's going on*?'

'Yes.' She lifted one hand to caress his cheek. The dark marks were still smudged under his eyes, but he looked a thousand times better than he had in the early-morning light. Somewhere a clock struck seven.

'I'm as bristly as an old badger.' He went on stroking his fingertips from collarbone to hip bone, just brushing the side of her breast, then back again. Down and up, up and down, savouring her skin as though she was made of silk and satin.

'I like your stubble.' She ran her nails through it and watched as he closed his eyes like a big cat being scratched. 'It is very masculine. I like it when you shave close as well, you look elegant then.'

Adam snorted and opened his eyes, deep, troubled blue. 'Rose, last night, there's no going back from that. But we don't need to go forward either. I'll think of something to make it right for you.'

'I am twenty-three years old. I may not have all my memory, but I know my own mind. Adam, I want to be your lover, for as long as…as long as we both want it. You don't need to worry, I'm not going to expect you to marry me, I swear it.'

'All women want to get married,' he said.

'Perhaps you aren't up to it, like last night,' she suggested innocently. 'You were so tired.'

Adam tweaked her nipple in retaliation. When she gasped, his eyes narrowed and he began to play with the hardening nub.

'That has a mind of its own,' Rose murmured, fascinated by the reaction, struggling to keep some control over her body and its riot of sensations.

'Not the only thing,' Adam said. When she

looked at him his mouth twitched into a reluctant grin. Against her hip she could feel the eager jut of his erection.

My heavens, I am glad it was fast last night or I would have been shaking with apprehension. Dare I ask how he really is this morning? No, he did not need reminding about those dreadful memories and the effect they had on him. He would see it as weakness. Masculine pride was a delicate flower, Mama had observed.

Mama. This was no time to be trying to recall her mother. Rose twisted round and began to explore the curls of hair on Adam's chest, scratched at his nipples and was immoderately pleased with herself when they tightened into knots.

'Baggage.' Adam's eyes were closed.

Daring, she looked down, then curled her hand around him. 'Is this right?'

His eyes flew open. 'Tighter.' It was a growl. 'Like this.' His hand closed over hers, moved as his eyes closed again.

Emboldened because he was not watching her, Rose came to her knees and bent over to study him better. So soft over so much hardness. So movable. With her free hand she cupped him below.

Adam groaned, pushed upwards into her fingers,

then opened his eyes and caught her hand with his. 'No…not unless you want this to be over very quickly.' He tugged at her hand, pushed and moved her until she was lying spooned against him. 'Lift your upper leg across mine, that's it.'

But this is backwards… Confused, Rose gasped when his fingers slid through the curls at her apex. She was spread open for him, pinned like a butterfly against his unyielding body, his free hand encircling her to toy with her breasts.

'Don't resist me, just relax,' he murmured in her ear and began to nuzzle the nape of her neck while one hand teased her nipples and the other explored the slick folds. One finger slid inside, then his thumb touched something that made her contract around the intrusive finger.

'Adam!'

'Shh. I have you.' He shifted his hips, pushed and then slid slowly, inexorably into her from behind. It felt deeper than the first time. There was no soreness now, only fullness and pressure in places that were new and startling. Her head fell back into the angle of his shoulder as he moved in and out with relentless care.

'I can't…I can't touch you.' She was panting, needing, not understanding what her body wanted, only that he was driving her completely out of her mind.

'You are all around me. Hold me.'

She tried to find some control of muscles she had never known she possessed and was rewarded by his gasp of pleasure. The pressure of his fingers on her nipple increased, the wicked, knowing pressure on that devilish little nub of flesh became more insistent, his thrusts slowed into deep, impossible, surging demands. She wanted to move, to thrash around, to scream. Rose jammed her palm against her mouth as everything reached fever pitch, erupted, threw her into lightning-spiked darkness.

She was barely conscious of her inner flesh convulsing around Adam, of his gasping breath, the urgency of his strokes. With a sudden jerk he came out of her body and she felt wet heat against her back as he pressed himself to her, groaned and went still, his arms lashing her to his torso.

'Rose?'

She blinked and opened her eyes. How long had they lain there, entangled? Her body hummed with an entirely new satisfaction and a tingling desire to experience it again. And again. 'I am here.'

'So am I. It seems improbable.'

'You…that was all right? I mean, I couldn't *do* anything.'

Adam's gasp of laughter tickled the back of her neck. 'All right? It was more than all right, Rose. We are going to be good together, I promise you.'

She wriggled round into a sticky, tangled embrace. 'I thought so,' she murmured against his chest and the delicious friction of hair.

'Wicked one,' Adam murmured. 'Are you tired or shall we try something else?' He hardly waited for her murmur of assent.

Flint drowsed, listening to the bells. Nine. He could not recall the last time he had lain in so late, simply out of laziness or to enjoy a woman. Beside him Rose slumbered. There was a certain smug masculine satisfaction to be had in reducing a woman to that degree of boneless content. He found he was smiling as he climbed cautiously out of bed, pulled on his trousers and moved, soft-footed, to the door.

Downstairs Maggie was folding sheets with the maid-of-all-work, their stately to-and-fro dance taking up most of the kitchen as they reduced each sheet to a neat package. Moss was cleaning a musket in a corner and through the open door he

could see the men lounging around the yard playing cards and yarning. One of the younger men sat
propped up against a pillar, throwing a stick for
Dog with his good hand.

All the heads came up as he entered the kitchen,
there was a murmur of greeting and then they all,
rather obviously, went back to what they had been
doing. Flint contemplated calling an impromptu
sick parade, just to shake them up, then settled for,
'Good day', before he dipped a pitcher full of hot
water out of the copper and went back upstairs.

Rose did not stir as he picked up his shaving
tackle and clean shirt and shut himself into her
room. Let her sleep. *Let me come to terms with this.*

Chapter Eight

Flint stripped and washed all over, uncoiled the bandage, slapped a dressing from his pack over the half-healed slash and then tilted the dressing mirror to the right angle for a shave.

Look at yourself, he addressed himself as he lathered his chin. *Great hairy brute. What the hell does she see in you?* Even the modish crop he'd suffered for the ball was growing out. The razor slid through the bristles and foam, leaving a stripe of smooth, tanned cheek behind it. Rose saw *something,* that was obvious, for she was not some little wanton hot for any man.

She was honest and loyal. She had said she didn't want or expect marriage, but might she possibly consider marrying him? Flint flicked soap off his razor into the basin. Where had that come from? He had told her he wasn't the marrying kind, or a man who stuck long with one woman. *But I might be.* If he had stayed a private, even a sergeant, he would have married by now, he supposed. But an officer, however murky his past, did not marry a camp follower.

But nor did an officer marry a lady, not if he was a bastard who'd clawed his way up from the ranks, even one with the support of an earl behind him. He had learned that lesson very early on. Flint missed a patch, swore and steadied the razor. The Honourable Miss Patricia Harte, blonde and pretty as a picture, had been very, very happy to flirt with the newly made Lieutenant Flint. And kiss him on the terrace and sneak away from her chaperone and sisters for clandestine meetings in the park.

He'd controlled himself with all the restraint of a young man in love who was determined to behave honourably, even if gentlemanly honour was a new concept he was still learning. He was not going to take advantage of the lady he loved, however much she ran her soft little hands over his shiny new dress uniform with its gold lace and tipped up her pansy face for his kisses.

So, like the fool he was, he took himself off to speak to her father and found himself out on the pavement five minutes later with threats of a horse-whipping ringing in his ears. And when he'd seen her in the park and had tried to speak to her she had laughed in his face.

'How could you think me serious? You aren't a gentleman.' She'd pouted. 'Now Papa is cross with me for encouraging your pretensions. I just thought you'd be fun later, when I'm married and it doesn't matter.'

He'd walked away, too hurt and angry to respond. The lesson was learned, not just about his place in society, but about the character of *ladies*. At least the cheerful tavern girls had no hypocrisy about them.

But Rose—even if she was ruined—was from a respectable family, he could tell. She'd had a decent education and upbringing, she had nice manners and an elegant way with her. She would be perfect for a mongrel officer.

He rinsed his face and stared into the mirror. She found him attractive apparently, she seemed to enjoy his lovemaking. They had communicated well even when she could not talk. Might she?

But what could he offer her? The war was over, that seemed certain. He was more than ever convinced he did not want to be a peacetime soldier in Britain. But could he drag her off to India and the heat and disease? Or into the unknown that was South America?

For the first time since he was fourteen he contemplated life outside the military. But if he sold out, what else could he do? Even farming was going to suffer with the end of the war, it always did as the demand for food dropped back to peacetime levels. Not that he had any idea how to be a farmer. Perhaps Rose had some thoughts about the life she'd like to live—but how could he give it to her?

Flint dressed with more care than usual, then stared again into the long mirror. The eyes that looked back at him were hard, cold as iced seawater, windows into what passed for his soul. What had come over him, thinking those thoughts? He was an artilleryman, an officer, a professional killer. That was what he was good at. That was his life. And as for women—he enjoyed them, he liked them and he seemed to be able to make them happy in bed. Not exactly qualifications for a respectable, genteel courtship, let alone marriage.

He retrieved his jacket and his sword belt from the main room and eased the door shut, leaving Rose still curled up under the covers. It was the aftermath of the worst battle he had ever been in, that was what had prompted this unexpected desire to settle down. Perhaps this urge was simply nature's way to repopulate the nation after all that killing, an animal reaction that a rational man should ignore.

Rose aroused feelings in him that ranged from fierce protectiveness to raging desire, but it didn't mean he had to marry her, or that he'd be anything but a dreadful husband. What did he know about marriage, anyway? He'd been brought up in a stable yard with a mob of other lads, more like a litter of puppies than a family. He'd no father to emulate, only one to reject and abhor. This unsettling feeling certainly didn't mean he had to throw away his career and the only life he understood.

Downstairs everyone was jammed into the kitchen, even Dixon with his bandages reduced to a pad over the cheek. By some miracle his eye had been spared.

'Where's Rose?' Maggie asked, handing round mugs of tea.

Flint picked up a mug in one hand and a roll stuffed with gammon in the other. 'Asleep.' He looked round for his saddlebags as he munched and made a mental list. *Randall, HQ, check the hospitals...* 'She's tired.'

There was complete silence. Not a word, not a snigger. When he glanced up sharply every face was expressionless. He recognised this. It was dumb insolence and he was very, very good at it himself, which was why he knew it when he saw it. He could hear the thoughts, the ribald comments, just as loudly as if they'd been shouted. *Worn her out, Major? Cor, you must be a demon in bed, sir! Well done, sir.*

Maggie cleared her throat. 'No more nightmares, then?'

'She can talk again,' he said curtly. 'The nightmare last night made her scream and that seems to have released the words.'

'Nightmare, eh? One word for it. Blimey, the major'll raise the dead next,' someone whispered, forgetting caution. *'Must be true what the girls say about him.'*

'I'll send Lieutenant Foster down to hold sick parade,' Flint said without looking round. 'The lot of you look fit enough to march back to Roosbos.' There was a general groan. 'And you can clean the place up for Maggie before you go. *Quietly.*'

He drained his tea and tossed the remains of the roll to Dog.

Hawkins followed him out to the stables. 'They could do with a flogging, all of them.' He sounded as though he could hardly suppress his own grin. When Flint spun round and glowered at him he raised his hands in a gesture of surrender. 'They'll not show Miss Rose any disrespect, sir. They're just feeling their oats and that's down to good food, rest and discovering they're alive and more or less in one piece. They need some work to straighten them out, that's all. Hard drill, camp food, some women to get a leg over.' It seemed to strike him that the last was not the most diplomatic comment. 'Er...want me with you, sir?'

'Found a horse yet?'

'Aye. Mouth like iron, but not bad. Paid a Hussar with a broken leg for it.' Hawkins opened the stable door and jerked a thumb at a bay gelding.

'In that case, yes, with me until we find Foster, then you go with him to the convents and hospitals, muster everyone who can manage the march and get them back to Roosbos. Take your own kit and stay there, knock them into shape. Moss can keep an eye on any of this lot who need to stay a bit longer.'

He hefted the saddle on to Old Nick's back, dodged a half-hearted attempt to bite his arm and tightened the girth. What was the matter with him? Flint puzzled over his own reaction to the knowledge that the men knew about his relationship with Rose as he argued the stallion into accepting the bit. 'Look, you want to go for a gallop. You know that means a bridle, so open your confounded mouth.'

He'd never had any shyness about life in camp. You just got on with it, despite the fact that everyone else was separated from you by the thicknesses of two pieces of canvas. You ignored their lovemaking, their rows, the sounds of bodily functions and their nightmares just as they ignored yours. The womenfolk were even less reticent than the men, or perhaps they were simply better at creating their own little world wherever they found themselves.

But Rose…Rose was different. He led Old Nick out into the yard and mounted, dealt with the stallion's predictable desire to trample on the stable cat and waited for Hawkins. He did not want speculation about Rose. He recoiled at the thought of anyone else hearing her soft cries, her murmurs of desire, her gasps of pleasure when she came to climax in his arms. She had been so beautiful, her lips swollen and parted, her face soft with passion, her eyes tender.

She'd be appalled if she realised the men had already accepted that she was his woman, with all that implied. They knew perfectly well that he kept no woman with him for more than a month or so and he knew, too, because he'd overheard the gossip, that they were well aware that married ladies sought him out and welcomed him into their beds.

He'd heard the ladies talk, too. 'My dear, the most deliciously wicked creature,' he'd overheard one colonel's wife say to another at one of Wellington's impromptu balls in the Peninsula. 'So rough and fierce and *big*.'

'All over. I can vouch for it,' the other lady had replied. She'd been an amusing and voluptuous bed companion for a few nights and very appreciative, given that her husband seemed more interested in his port and his hounds than her charms.

It had shaken him to discover that ladies gossiped as bawdily as men about bed sport. But Rose was different. He realised that if anyone else so much as looked at Rose with sensual speculation in his eye, then he'd gut the man. Slowly.

'Problem, Major?' Hawkins brought the bay out and mounted.

'No. Why?'

'Your…er…frown, sir.'

Flint stayed silent as they wove their way through the crowded streets. When they finally reached the Parc he reined in and watched a group of nurse-maids playing with their charges under the trees, the picture of innocence amidst the damage left by the mustering army in the elegant gardens. 'We were talking the other morning about what we'd do when peace is declared, Jerry.'

His use of the sergeant's first name was a signal that this was man-to-man talk. Hawkins shrugged. 'Thought we'd agreed. Find another war. There'll be one soon enough, that's for sure, and there's always the East India Company, like you said.'

'Yes, that was what I said. But…carry on fighting?' There was a small girl with auburn hair throwing a ball for a puppy. They both chased it, both tripped over their feet. The little girl burst into laughter. 'There's got to be something beyond that, I'm thinking,' he said slowly, his mind filled with the unsettling uncertainties again. 'What are we fighting *for*? All those men dying, all our wounds—we fight to win and for peace. But I just can't see peace in my head.'

Hawkins shifted to follow his gaze and watched the child's nursemaid scoop her up, laughing. 'Never had a yen to settle down. If I found a woman I liked well enough, then perhaps...' He let his voice trail off. Flint was very conscious that the other man kept his eyes forward.

'I'm changing my mind and I don't much like it. I'm thinking I should sell out, settle, if I knew what to settle to,' Flint admitted. There, he'd said it out loud. Something like panic lodged under his breastbone as the vague thoughts and uneasiness found solid words.

'Officers' pay isn't bad,' Hawkins said casually. 'I expect you've a bit put aside.' *Enough for a wife.* The words did not need to be spoken.

'I've been saving,' Flint agreed. A major's pay had been beyond his wildest imaginings when he'd enlisted. Now it arrived in his bank account regularly. *A bank account, for goodness' sake!* And what had he got to spend it on? His mother was dead, there was no one else relying on his support. He didn't patronise smart clubs—they wouldn't have him even if he wanted to—he wasn't fool enough to get fleeced in gambling dens, and he didn't keep high-flying mistresses. He certainly didn't bother Jermyn Street tailors. His two extravagances were his boots and his weapons.

Once he realised the money was mounting up he had swallowed his pride and asked Randall how to invest safely. That was years ago. His half-brother had put him in touch with his own man of business and now the quarterly reports showed an improbably large sum growing and growing. Enough to keep Rose in comfort, that was sure.

'I'd be bored out of my mind,' he said now, fighting the feeling of unease at the thought of life beyond the army.

'You could buy a tidy little property, manage that,' Hawkins suggested.

'Might breed horses, I suppose.' Flint slapped Old Nick's shoulder. 'This brute has the manners of a rabid leopard, but his bloodlines are incredible. Might run a stagecoach line...' Or look into investing in industry. Steam engines, now they sounded interesting. Didn't understand them, but that could be remedied. It was only machinery and mathematics, and so was artillery. Perhaps there *was* something beyond firing a cannon and killing people that he could be good at.

But whatever else he did, he wanted land, he

realised, the ideas galloping now he had let them loose. He might always be a half-bred *almost* gentleman, but if his sons had a decent education and land behind them, they'd rise. That would be the perfect revenge on the man who'd so carelessly fathered him—provided he could work out how to be a father himself first.

He was building castles in the air now. An estate, sons, good schools. He needed a wife for all that and Rose might very well change her mind about even liking him once she got her memory back and knew who she was. *He* might change his mind, the way he was feeling. It was the aftermath of battle, just a reaction, just a particularly solid-seeming daydream.

'Aye, well, enough of this.' He turned Old Nick's head towards headquarters. 'Let's run our surgeon down and set him on the men. We're still at war, so far as I know.'

Rose woke to find herself alone and Adam's side of the bed cold. Her stomach growled in protest at the lack of breakfast, but she lay there for a while, sorting her thoughts out, her spread fingers running over the place where he had slept. Everything had changed, totally. She could speak, she had some of her memory back, she was no longer a virgin and Adam had made love to her three times last night.

She still glowed with remembered pleasure and her body, despite its aches in unexpected and naughty places, was suggesting it would like it if he was back in bed now. Even the way she felt when she stretched, long and languid, sent little ripples of remembered pleasure through her body. Adam desired her and he had shown her just how much.

'Time to get up,' she murmured and went to investigate the wash stand. There was a pitcher of clean, cool water so she stood in the basin and had a standing sponge bath rather than go downstairs and draw attention to the fact that she had slept the morning away, worn out by passion.

Rose paused in the middle of a precarious one-legged balance while she washed her left foot. It was more than passion. She felt relief and happiness. She felt safe, as though she was somewhere she belonged. It was Adam, of course. He had saved her life, he had cared for her when she must have been nothing but an utter nuisance, and he had made love to her with a mixture of strength and sweetness, care and sensual abandon, that was beyond her wildest dreams of what the physical relationship between a man and a woman would be like.

She had never really trusted men, not emotionally, not to be honest, she felt that with a certainty. Why, she wasn't sure; there were memories, half-formed, of flattery and insincerity, of courtships based on wealth and status, not on emotion. Was that why she had talked herself into thinking she loved Gerald, because he had seemed guileless?

Adam was not guileless and she doubted he ever had been. He said he was no gentleman. He called himself *a bit of rough*, a bastard, a killer. 'Oh, Adam.' She put her foot down with a splash and reached for the towel. Was there any future for them at all? Why would Adam want her, other than for the rather obvious fact that he appeared to desire her sexually? She had no assets to bring him except her body. No family, no money. No past at all.

The hollow feeling inside that had been hunger turned to something else, something uneasy. There was a real world out there and sooner rather than later she was going to have to face it. And she did not know who she was as a person, not really. All she knew, with increasing certainty, was that she was not the helpless creature who had clung so tightly to the man who saved her that he had virtually to strip before he could shake her off.

She was usually a determined person, the memories of refusing to do the conventional thing and agree to marry for suitability, not love, told her that. She was unconventional enough to run off with one man and to persuade another into bed with her. Perhaps *wanton* was the word, although she hoped not. Adam had said *passionate, sensual*.

The unsettling suspicion grew that her infatuation with Gerald had been a kind of desperation. She had needed to prove to herself that she was perfectly normal, that she could fall in love and want to marry. But for some reason she had to fall in love with a man her parents did not approve of. They couldn't have done, or she wouldn't have needed to elope with him.

This was making her head ache again. *A convenient excuse for not facing facts*, she scolded herself as she dressed and made her way downstairs. *Do I really want to be with Adam?* That was the other worry that fretted at the back of her mind. Was the fact that every fibre of her being revolted at the thought of being parted from him simply a measure of how much she relied on him now? That and a sensual enchantment, she admitted ruefully.

I am not some waif to be rescued, I must do this myself. Perhaps Adam's strays would always turn out to be less waiflike than he thought. So far he had a dog with a strong protective instinct for his rescuers and a woman who would not do as she was told.

Chapter Nine

Maggie, Lucille the maid and two of the soldiers were in the kitchen. Rose greeted them absently, her mind still wrestling with her feelings for Adam. Then she noticed the very careful way they were keeping quiet and carrying on with their tasks. Not one of them looked at her.

They know. They know Adam and I are lovers. She sat down, uncertain what to say. *Is this disapproval? No, they don't want to embarrass me*, she realised as Lucille shot her a quick, half-smiling glance.

'I have my voice back,' she said. It was as though she had thrown a stone into a stage tableau. Everyone relaxed, heads turned.

'That's wonderful,' Maggie said, beaming. 'The major said you could talk again. And has all of your memory returned?'

'No. Not that.' And it was more than an inconvenience, she realised now. She needed to know who she was, *what* she was, if she had any hope of understanding her feelings for Adam. Any hope of holding him.

'Your poor friends, not knowing what has happened to you,' Maggie said as she peered into the flour bin. 'You run along, lads, let the women have a comfy chat. You find some breakfast for Miss Rose, Lucille.'

'My friends?' *Oh, my heavens. Not friends—my parents.* Somewhere, in the muddle of things half-remembered, was the comforting thought that she had left them a letter, explained she was safe with Gerald. Only she hadn't been safe with Gerald and they would have known that for days now.

'They must be frantic,' she whispered, sick with guilt. Eloping was bad enough, running off and getting lost in the middle of a vast and bloody battle was quite another thing. 'My parents. I eloped with Gerald, I left them a note.'

Did they know that Gerald was dead yet? She must ask Adam how casualty lists were distributed, how she could find out if anyone had been asking about Gerald. His own parents were in Wales, she knew that. News could not have reached them about the battle, let alone any enquiries from them come back about their son.

'Casualty lists,' she began as the door closed behind the soldiers. 'Gerald's name will be on them.'

'Not for rank and file,' Maggie said, apparently following her train of thought. 'Only officers.'

She couldn't tell them Gerald had been an officer, not before she talked to Adam. 'That won't help, then.'

'There's the knocker,' Maggie said.

Lucille was slicing bread. 'I'll get it,' Rose said.

A small, plainly-dressed lady in her mid-twenties stood on the doorstep. She held out a small leather-bound book.

'I am Miss Endacott. I have come from Lord Randall's lodgings. Major Flint left this when he called there.'

'Thank you.' Rose put out her hand to take the book. 'He told me that Lord Randall was injured in the battle. How is he now?'

'I, that is, he…'

The woman seemed extremely distressed. Rose wanted to offer her some comfort, to find out more details, but Miss Endacott was already backing away from the doorstep.

'We are hoping, praying—excuse me!' And with

that the woman turned abruptly and hurried away up the street.

'What was that about?' Maggie asked when Rose came back into the kitchen.

Rose recounted the short conversation. 'Miss Endacott seems very upset. Is she betrothed to the colonel?'

'I hadn't heard anything. But never mind them—Rose, are you going to marry the major?'

'He isn't the marrying kind,' Rose said with a casual shrug.

'None of them are,' Maggie said crisply as she slapped a lump of dough on to the kneading board. 'Not until they meet the right woman, that is. And then they usually need hitting over the head with it before they notice.'

Rose had a delicious image of Maggie taking her rolling pin to Moss until he admitted he loved her. 'Even if Adam did think…I don't know whether…' She ground to a halt and tried again. 'I don't know who I am, so how do I know what I feel for him?'

Maggie grunted and slapped the dough as if it was an uncooperative man. 'You had a nasty shock, he looked after you—good at looking after strays is the major—and now you don't know if you're just plain grateful, is that it?'

'It's more than that,' Rose admitted, hoping the heat in the kitchen accounted for the warmth in her cheeks.

'Aye, well, I've heard he doesn't disappoint in other ways.'

Now she was feeling jealous of all the other women in Adam's life. He said he wasn't the faithful kind, so why had the word marriage even entered her head? She had been looking for a man she could trust and love ever since she came out, that certainty was growing the more she thought about it. She was not swayed by wealth or power or titles, but she did care about honesty and faithfulness and love. Adam would give her the first of those in uncomfortable abundance, but he had also told her plainly that the other two were not in him to give.

'I can't think about any of that now,' she said aloud. 'I'll worry about it later.' *If he ever asks me.* 'I need to find out who I am and let my parents know I am safe.' And she had to do it without causing a scandal. They might well have been able to cover up an elopement, but a young woman enquiring of the British authorities whether any genteel family had misplaced a daughter would cause an uproar.

I need to take control, she thought. She could not simply lean on Adam until her memory came back, if it ever did. It muddled her thinking to be so dependent and it hurt her pride.

It was all very well to worry about her pride and her independence, first she had to know who she really was and what that woman felt about Major Adam Flint. She could simply go into the fashionable part of town—she could find her way around there, she was certain—and wait to be recognised, she supposed. But not dressed like a respectable but humble servant, which is how she looked now. She needed a gown and a bonnet. Gloves, a reticule...

'Maggie, Adam said something about letting me have money for anything I needed, didn't he?' She could pay it back as soon as she discovered who she was. She sensed she had never wanted for money, that her quarterly allowance had been more than generous.

'He left a wallet in the dresser.' Maggie nodded towards a chest of drawers. 'You help yourself, I'm all over dough.'

There seemed to be a considerable amount in the battered leather folder. How much would she need in order to present a ladylike appearance? She certainly could not go to a modiste and order a gown to be made, not with no name and no credit. But there were second-hand shops, places where ladies' maids took the cast-off garments that formed one of their most valuable perks. The simpler items they might adjust for their own use, but the money was more valuable to them, she knew from conversations with her own maid, Jane.

Jane. I can remember her. I can remember her careful diction and the efforts she made to put her East End background behind her. Rose put a number of banknotes in her pocket and shook her head in frustration with being able to recall so much and yet none of it the essentials. 'I need some things, so I will go out now. I might be a while. I want to see if anywhere looks familiar.'

'Do you want Lucille with you?' Maggie called as Rose ran upstairs for her borrowed bonnet.

'No, thank you.' She looked round the kitchen door with a smile, tying the bonnet ribbons, her spirits lifted by the thought of doing something positive. 'I will be all right when I reach the centre of town. Which way do I go?'

'Left out of the door,' Maggie said. 'Then straight on and you'll soon find the Grand Place.'

The plain straw bonnet had a large brim which

hid her face and gave her confidence. There were some respectable second-hand clothes shops in the network of streets behind the Grand Place, she knew, and the market stalls would provide cheap stockings and handkerchiefs, perhaps a shawl.

At first it was simply wonderful to be outside again. The sun was shining, the city, despite the remaining encampments of soldiers under awnings on the streets, was returning to its normal pristine, bustling self. Rose made her way rapidly along the pavement, wishing she could run, just for the chance to stretch her legs. As she went further into the centre of town her pace slowed. Buildings began to look familiar, she knew their names. She stopped on the corner of the Rue des Bouchers and stared around in frustration. Why could she not recall the name of the street where she had lived?

What would she do if she saw someone whose face she recognised? She had vague memories of social calls, of knowing people, of stopping to chat in the Parc. Whatever her family's station in life, their social circle was wide.

Rose began to walk again, more slowly now. If she saw a face she recognised, she would follow them home, she decided. Then, when she was re-spectably dressed, she could call on them. The thought of accosting someone in the street and asking what her own name was made her dizzy. Scandal, it seemed, was far from her normal experience.

But there was no one who looked at all familiar. Rose was not certain she was relieved or sorry. Relieved, she decided as she stood outside the second-hand dress shop Jane had mentioned. *Coward.* This strange bubble she lived in with Adam, with no past and no future, felt safe, even if that was only an illusion. She would have to prick the bubble and emerge sooner or later. But not just yet.

It was even easier than she had expected to outfit herself. This establishment only accepted garments in good condition and the gowns had been made by high-quality seamstresses. Rose found a walking dress that was an almost perfect fit at a much lower price than she had feared having to pay. A bonnet to match, gloves and a reticule and there was still money in her pocket. She could afford a day dress—or, rather, Adam could.

She smiled at the thought of his face if he had been dragged in here amongst the feminine frills and furbelows. Or perhaps he took his mistresses to dress shops and milliners, let them choose gowns and hats which he would pay for. But he did not have mistresses like some town buck, set up in a luxurious little love nest, she suspected. Adam's women lived with him for as long as the relationship lasted. Which was not very long, by the sound of it.

Rose blinked to clear the sudden blurring of her vision. She was here to shop, not to mope. That soft green fabric looked nice. In fact, it looked… familiar. She lifted the garment from the rack, held it against herself and studied her reflection in the long mirror.

'That is perfect, *mademoiselle*,' the shopkeeper remarked in accented English. 'It might have been made for you.'

It was *made for me.* Rose laid the gown on to the counter and examined the skirts. Yes, there was the place where a cinder from the fire had burned a hole. Jane had cut out a strip and resewn it, but Mama had turned up her nose at the result, convinced the reduction in the fullness of the skirt ruined the line, so Rose had given it to the maid.

Her hands shook as she looked inside for the dressmaker's label. It would have her name on it, or at the least, her initials. A few threads hung where it had been cut out.

Rose sank down on the chair beside the counter. She could have wept in earnest now. *So close...*

'Are you quite well, *mademoiselle*? A glass of water, perhaps?'

'I...I am just a little faint. I had no noon meal. I will take that gown, and the walking dress and other items. Tell me, *monsieur*, is there a respectable café nearby where a woman alone might eat?'

'But certainly, *mademoiselle*. The Pot au Feu at the end of the street is quite unexceptional.'

He began to wrap up her purchases in brown paper, looping and knotting string to create ingenious carrying handles. That was another clue, she realised. She was not used to carrying her own shopping, which meant the family kept at least one footman. Rose paid, took her parcel and made her way to the square in the direction the shopkeeper had indicated.

The café was more of a *bistrot* and was crowded with working people, including several young women. A couple got up to go as Rose entered and she slipped into a chair at the vacated table, right by the window.

The waiter was polite, the chalked-up menu short but appetising. Rose ordered an omelette and looked around. This was rather fun, she decided.

She had probably never eaten outside a private house before and certainly never alone. Now she relaxed and settled down to watch the passers-by.

She had just lifted the first forkful of egg and fried potato to her mouth when two blue-jacketed soldiers came into view, stopped and turned to look at the *bistrot*. Rose burned her mouth, choked and took a gulp of water. *Adam and Sergeant Hawkins.* Hawkins gestured towards the restaurant, Adam shrugged, then nodded, and they came up the steps and in through the door.

The room was crowded and there were few free places, except at her table. Hawkins glanced her way, apparently did not recognise the bonnet, said something to Adam. He turned as she sat there, fork halfway to her mouth, like a rabbit in front of a stoat.

Rose felt both exposed and curiously guilty, then common sense took over. What was she afraid of? She was doing nothing wrong, just learning to be herself again. 'Gentlemen, won't you join me?'

Hawkins's jaw dropped and Adam's expression darkened into one of his better scowls. The waiter began to move towards them and Rose realised what he, and everyone else in the place must think, that she was a woman of easy virtue soliciting the men's attention.

'Please lay places for my brother and his sergeant,' she said in French to the waiter. 'And bring some wine, I am sure he will need putting into a good mood when he sees all my shopping.'

The man glanced from the brown paper parcel to Adam's expression and winked. 'At once, *mademoiselle.*'

'What the devil are you doing here?' Adam hissed as they sat down.

'Shopping. And I missed the noon meal. A shopkeeper told me this was a respectable place to eat.'

'You did not tell me you were going out.'

'We were hardly discussing...' She noticed Hawkins staring out of the window with heavy-handed tact. 'I only made up my mind late this morning.'

'You should not be out by yourself.' Adam was still looking thunderous.

'Why not? This is a perfectly safe area and dressed like this no one will give me a second glance.'

Adam's expression suggested he would have more to say about it if it were not for the waiter putting the wine on the table. 'The special, for two.

And another glass for my sister.' He waited until the man was weaving his way back to the kitchen between the packed tables. 'It is perfectly safe until someone thinks you are a streetwalker.'

'Really, Adam, do you think you ought to be mentioning such women to me?' she enquired in mock-shocked tones.

Hawkins turned a snort into a cough and Adam's expression reminded her all too clearly that he was used to receiving unquestioning obedience to orders and no back talk. He was looking, she decided, exceptionally smart. His shave had been close, his uniform was brushed, his boots and his sword belt shone. *And I am not the only person here who thinks so*, she thought, noticing covert glances from the other women in the room.

Broad shoulders, straight back, an air of authority and danger. Really, he was a most impressive male specimen. My *impressive male*. It was a titillating thought.

'What is wrong, Rose?' Adam asked, his voice gentler now.

'Nothing at all. You just startled me, marching in here and scowling,' she said with a smile to soften the words. 'I feel as wary as any woman does when the man paying the bills spots a large parcel from a dress shop.'

And I do not like the knowledge that he is paying the bills, she realised. *I do not like feeling like a kept woman. Idiot, what did you expect when you got into bed with him? You made him your protector in every sense of the word. I really am ruined.* It had never occurred to her, she thought while the men were distracted by the mild confusion of plates of food arriving, that it was possible to be more than ruined. Eloping with an officer was one thing. Living as a mistress was a whole step more shocking.

But I want to be with him, part of her argued. *Yes*, her conscience retorted, *but who* am *I?*

They all fell silent, eating. Rose snatched glances at Adam under cover of sipping her wine, watched the muscles in his jaw and throat moving as he chewed. In profile it was a strong, determined jaw. The curve of his ear, the flare of his nostrils, had a masculine elegance that she suspected he would share with his half-brother, but she doubted anyone would ever mistake Adam Flint for a fashionable member of the *ton*. He looked half-tamed, feral, dangerous, even sitting quietly eating in a bourgeois *bistrot*.

She liked him, she was very attracted to him, she admired him and she was grateful to him. And that was the problem. Was she blinded by gratitude and sheer physical desire into thinking she felt more for this man than she really did? Rose watched the scarred, long-fingered hand close around the fragile stem of the wine glass and shivered. She was perilously close to believing herself in—

Chapter Ten

'Miss Rose, more wine?' Hawkins lifted the bottle, making her jump.

'Thank you, no.' She did not need anything else to cloud her thinking.

'I would walk you back,' Adam said. 'But we have the horses just down the street.'

'I told you, I am perfectly all right by myself. And besides, I still have shopping to do in the market.' *And I need to be alone, I need to be apart from you, just now.*

Adam's expression was as inscrutable as ever, but she sensed that her show of independence disconcerted him. Did he expect her to be fearful and clinging still? Surely his other women must have been strong and independent types if they had been camp followers? Perhaps he liked that in her, enjoyed the role of protector, but if that was the case he was going to be disappointed, Rose realised. She did not want to cling and be dependent, not with a man as strong as Adam Flint, or he would simply consume her.

Was that why I ran away with Gerald? she wondered. *Because I sensed he was not a strong character and I wanted to escape from home on my own terms?* That was not a comfortable thought, either about her relationship with her parents or her own motives in eloping. *Poor Gerald.*

'Rose?'

'Sorry, I was wool-gathering.'

Adam pushed money across the table to Hawkins. 'Go and settle up, will you?' He waited until the other man was halfway across the room. 'What's wrong, Rose?'

'Other than the fact that I still don't know who I am?' Her voice had risen, heads turned. She lowered it to reach only Adam's ears. 'Or that my parents must be frantic? Or that I am dependent on you for everything—the roof over my head, the clothes on my back, my food?' She gestured at the empty plate, then snatched her hand back. That had been theatrical, almost wild. She needed calm and rational thought, not to succumb to panic and drama.

'I'm sorry. I think the shock of everything is catching up with me. I will be fine, I'll just go and finish my shopping.'

Adam rose as she did, his chair scraping back on the tiled floor. 'Rose, it will be all right. I will make it all right.'

If sheer force of will could, then he probably spoke the truth. Rose found a smile and reached up to press a kiss on his cheek. 'I know.' She managed a gay little wave to Sergeant Hawkins and then she was off down the steps and heading for the market.

I have worried Adam now and he has too much else to worry about. But I am not going to lie to him, not once I discover who I am. Then I am not going to deceive him about anything. Anything except how I feel about him.

Adam came back to the house late that afternoon, along with Hawkins and the surgeon. Rose hung out of the bedroom window to watch Hawkins form the men up in the street outside and then start marching them up and down again.

'What on earth is going on?' she asked Maggie when she found her, as usual, in the kitchen.

'Sick parade. Everyone that the lieutenant thinks

is fit will march off to Roosbos, to join the others. It takes a while to sort them out. There's those who shouldn't go yet who'll pretend they are fit and those who are fit who fancy lying around some more and those who are fine.'

'I wouldn't want to try to deceive the major when he's looking like that,' Rose said and Maggie laughed. But that was just what she was doing. Deceiving him about the fact she was far better born than he believed, deceiving him about her confused feelings for him.

Dog sat whining by the front door. 'No, you can't go out there and join in,' Rose scolded him. 'The major isn't going to go away and leave you.' Dog looked at her and scratched at the door. 'You need to go out? Well, come to the back with me then.'

She let the dog out of the kitchen door to the courtyard and followed him as he ran over to his favourite post, watered it liberally, then trotted off purposefully through the arch into the stable yard. 'Stay,' she called. 'I'm not chasing you across half of Brussels.' But it seemed he was only concerned with treeing the stable cat and once that was out of reach, spitting and muttering on the grain-store roof, he was content to trot around the yard, sniffing for rats and marking his territory against the neighbourhood dogs.

She had not been in the stable yard before and Rose poked around, enjoying the dusty smells in the grain store, the satisfying tang of saddle soap and oil in the tack room, the military precision of the stacked bales of straw and hay.

The top half-door to the stables themselves was hooked back and Rose opened the lower half and let herself in. There were three stalls. The first contained a pitiful wreck of a horse with its coat covered in sticky patches of salve and a bandage around one leg. It was pulling hay from a net with the air of an animal that was going to stuff itself while the opportunity was there. Clouded memories of it between the shafts of a cart came back to her. This was the horse that had brought the men back from the battlefield, poor creature. At least it had found a safe home here.

It twitched nervously when she spoke to it, so she moved on to the next stall and a large, sturdy bay that was unfamiliar. She clicked her tongue, interested to observe her own familiarity with horses. She was comfortable with them and it occurred to her, when the bay came to have its nose rubbed, that she would welcome riding out.

'You're not a lady's horse though, are you? More of a cavalry troop horse by the size of you. No, I haven't got a carrot.'

There was the stamp of a hoof and a great black head appeared over the final door in the row.

'My heavens.' Rose blinked at the apparition. If she had thought the bay was large, this creature was enormous, with the arched, muscular neck of a stallion and a flowing, wavy, mane. It snorted and rolled its eye at her. 'You must be the hell horse. You brought me back from the battlefield. That does deserve a reward. Let me see if there is something...'

She searched amongst the sacks and found some lumpy carrots. The thin horse eyed the offering nervously, so she tossed it into his manger and the bay accepted his with good manners, but the big black showed a fine set of yellow teeth and stamped impatiently.

'Behave,' she chided, taking care to flatten her palm completely before she put her fingers anywhere near those teeth. He lipped up the carrot with surprising delicacy and Rose laughed. 'You are a gentleman, after all.' He butted her shoulder so she began to scratch his nose, then under his chin until he leaned his head heavily against her, begging for more.

'You are like your master,' she murmured. 'You look fierce and underneath—'

The tug on her arm that jerked her back flattened her against a solid wall of man. 'Adam!'

'Dear God, that horse is a killer, what in blazes were you thinking of?' Adam shook her, none too gently, picked her up and dumped her on a bale of hay. He had shed his uniform jacket, pulled off his stock, rolled up his sleeves, although the curved sabre still hung by his side. He looked ready for a fight, for a battle and somehow she had got in his way.

The fact that there was real anxiety in his eyes did nothing to quench the flare of irritation at being taken for an idiot. 'I know horses and I knew he'd be safe. I hadn't gone into the stall, I have sense enough for that.' She stood up. Adam's hands on her shoulders promptly pushed her back down again.

'You know about horses? Since when have you known that?'

'Since I came in here just now and felt confident with them,' she retorted. 'The big black is the horse you brought me back on, isn't he?'

Some of the tension went out of Adam's stance. 'Old Nick. That's what I called him after ten minutes' acquaintance. He's Spanish and trained in all the classical manoeuvres of a fighting horse and he works on the general principle of kill first, ask questions afterward. I bought him from a Spanish grandee who had eaten his way through his entire stable just to keep his household alive. The stallion had been left until last. I lived on credit for the rest of the year—' he shrugged '—but he was worth it.'

Rose ducked under his arm and went back to the stallion. 'He likes me.' The animal's eyes were half-closed as she rubbed the soft spot under his chin. 'If he was a cat he'd be purring.'

'Interesting.' Adam came over. 'He must like women, or he was trained early not to hurt them. He tolerates me—under threat of being gelded—until I'm mounted and then he's totally obedient.' He stoked the proud arch of the stallion's neck and Old Nick bared his teeth. 'See? One day, when we've access to a field, I'll show you what he can do, although I suspect I don't know the half of it. I must find a dressage master to put him through his paces.'

'Will you breed from him?'

'Yes, if I can find mares big enough.'

'English or Irish hunters,' Rose suggested. 'Something meant for heavy country. It would be interesting, breeding horses.'

'Hmm.'

That was hardly forthcoming. Rose peered round the stallion's nose. 'What are you thinking about, Adam?'

'The future.'

'Peace will be declared soon, I suppose. Napoleon can't recover from this, surely?' Silence. 'But I suppose you'll have your orders soon.' It was more of a question than a statement.

'I'm stuck in Brussels for now. The Rogues could be split up between other artillery units while I'm pushing paper around. Even if Randall recovers I doubt he'll stay in the army now the war is all but won, he's too many responsibilities back in England.'

Rose noticed he did not say *back home*. 'How is Lord Randall?'

'They had to operate on him, remove the bullet. Foster says he became agitated and it shifted.' She could not see his face, but he sounded shaken. 'And that was my fault for telling him about Sarah. Chest surgery is hideously dangerous. For them to decide to operate then it must have moved close to his heart or his lungs or a major blood vessel.'

She thought she heard him mutter, 'If Randall dies, that really is all I have of family gone. And that's a damn selfish way to look at it.'

There was a silence she did not know how to break, then Adam said, 'Foster thinks he'll recover. We've fought the war we were formed for. Time for change.'

'Adam, you are talking to *me*, not telling the men what you think they ought to hear. I can tell you aren't happy.' Her hand slid under Old Nick's nose to catch his wrist. 'What are *your* orders? Could you take over the Rogues?'

'Perhaps. Or Bartlett. I can't see him leaving the army. As for me, nothing has changed. For now I am still a cross between a hospital superintendent and a constable.' The sudden burst of anger made Old Nick toss his head and her hand slipped from Adam's wrist.

'I don't imagine you enjoy being separated from the army. No action, no excitement.'

'Are you attempting to be soothing and understanding, Rose?' His voice was a dark growl. The stallion shifted uneasily.

'Probably,' she admitted. 'What do you *want* to

do, Adam?' She was still sounding reasonable and soothing, she realised. Probably patronising.

'Want?' Adam ducked under the horse's head and came up right in front of her. 'I want the war back. I want the certainty of one enemy and my duty. I want to carry on doing something I know I am good at. I want to keep the only family I've had since I was fourteen. And I am damn sure that none of that is going to happen, not if I don't shift for myself.'

He smiled at her, a curve of his lips that left his eyes bleak. 'You did ask. So now I have to work out what I *can* do, so you will have to forgive me if I am rather less positive than my fellow officers, all gentlemen who have something to go home to.' He closed his eyes and took a deep breath while she struggled for the right words. 'And I apologise for inflicting my temper over my lack of purpose on you.'

He had become a soldier, like many a lad before him making the best of a difficult home life, a limited upbringing. And then he had made himself, *remade* himself, as an officer, as a gentleman. And now he was going to have to remake himself all over again.

'And now...' The sentence petered out. She had

no words of comfort, only platitudes. Adam had to work this out for himself.

Old Nick tossed his head, a solid blow between Adam's shoulder blades that pushed him the final few inches against her body. 'And now, what I do know is that I am your lover, Rose.' He lifted her, his hands at her waist, and carried her, his mouth hard on hers, the few long strides that brought her against the wall.

'Hold on,' he rasped before his kiss sucked the air from her lungs.

Rose clung to his shoulders, curled an arm around his neck and by instinct hooked her leg up, over his hip. 'Adam.' She managed a gasp when he came up for air. 'Here?'

'Here. Now. Like this.' Somehow he wedged her firmly enough to be able to free a hand and pull up her skirts, bundling them into the small space between their bodies. She felt him fumbling with the falls of his trousers and then he was against her, insistent flesh against her own damp, yearning softness.

A voice said, 'Yes, Adam. Yes, *now.*' She recognised it as hers, recognised a desperate need that matched his.

He shifted, pressed into her, held her against the

rough boards as he impaled her. 'Rose, forgive me, but I can't be gentle.'

'Good. Stop talking,' she gasped and heard the huff of laughter shaken out of him as he buried his face in the angle of her neck and thrust. It was completely without finesse, relentless, yet she came apart in his arms on the first stoke, shuddering around him as he drove into her.

'Again.'

'Adam, I can't.'

'Yes. Come with me. *Again.*'

Through the ebbing shock waves of pleasure she felt another surge growing, realised that she had both legs wrapped around his hips and that her mouth was fastened on his neck, the taste of desire and man and heat on her tongue.

'Now,' he demanded and she obeyed, cresting another impossible wave of pleasure, her body arching into his, her cries muffled against his neck as he groaned and shuddered and went rigid against her. Inside her.

Afterwards Rose had no idea how long they stayed like that, locked together against the stable wall. The sound of a hoof stamping on the stone floor finally shook Adam out of the trance.

'Old Nick approves,' he said, a grim smile tugging at the corner of his mouth. 'Two things he understands, sex and violence.' He helped her on to unsteady feet. 'Did I hurt you, Rose? I'm sorry.'

'No, I don't think so. I didn't notice, it was too good. I hurt you, though.' She reached up to touch the red mark at the angle of throat and shoulder. 'I bit you.'

'I didn't notice—it was too good,' Adam echoed. He pulled a handkerchief from his pocket, dipped in a bucket of water, wrung it out and offered it to her. 'There, just until you can get to your room.' He turned aside to give her privacy for a moment, then spun back, his face stark with realisation. 'Hell, Rose, I didn't withdraw. I could have got you with child.'

Surely a heart cannot stop from alarm, can it? Rose gasped, breathless with sudden panic until the sheer horror on Adam's face acted like a slap on the cheek.

'Unlikely, surely, after just the once?' she said as calmly as she knew how. *When are my courses due? About two weeks? Not long to have to wait.*

'It only takes once.' Adam still looked grim. 'We'll marry.'

It was hardly a resounding declaration of devoted love, Rose thought miserably, more a statement along the lines of, *Impossible odds, but we attack at dawn.* Or, *All the ammunition has gone, fix bayonets.*

'No we will not. Not unless it is absolutely necessary,' she said with a brisk confidence she was far from feeling. 'I promised you I did not expect marriage. Stop looking like that, Adam. We were both carried away.'

The expression on his face said as clearly as words that he did not consider she had any responsibility in the matter whatsoever.

Chapter Eleven

'I'll go in. Give me a moment.' By some miracle her hair was not the bird's nest she feared. Rose pushed in some pins, brushed dust from her skirts and walked out of the stable as briskly as her trembling legs would allow her. Once she was round the corner she sat down with a thump on the mounting block. There was the sound of tramping feet and the little yard was full of the men forming up in ranks, shouldering packs and weapons.

'Where are you going?' Rose asked Hawkins.

'Roosbos, which is where we were based before Quatre Bras.' He looked at her, a very straight, fatherly look. 'You take care of yourself, Miss Rose.'

'I will. Good luck, Sergeant.' She managed a bright smile as she went down the row of men, wishing them goodbye. And then they were gone, marching out of the yard, out of her life, the motley crew of brave, foul-mouthed artillerymen, some of them rogues in more than name, all of them unlike anyone she had ever had contact with before.

Rose drifted into the strangely quiet kitchen, then jumped as Moss shouldered his way through the door and dumped a load of sheets into the boiler in the lean-to. 'Lord, but those lads made a lot of work. Still, I'm sorry to see them go. They're forming up at Roosbos while they wait to see what Wellington wants them to do. Could be Paris, could be home to England, could be the Lord knows where.'

She went upstairs, washed, changed, but still Adam did not come. When Maggie called she went downstairs and ate supper with the strangely reduced household, then dipped a can of hot water to take to her room. 'I think I'll have an early night,' she explained when Maggie sent a look of surprise at the kitchen clock.

It was not true. She had no intention of going to bed and she was not at all tired. She washed, a proper hot sponge bath this time, then shook out her new clothes and began to dress without looking in the mirror. Chemise, petticoat, light stays, stockings. She slipped the morning gown over her head, fastened it and put on her shoes.

Still without using the glass she assembled the

ribbons and hairpins she'd bought at the market and began to put up her hair into a simple style that her fingers seemed to know very well indeed. When it was done she shook out her skirts, stood in front of the long glass and looked up.

Staring back at her was a young lady in a simple but fashionable gown. She appeared groomed, even elegant. Her hair, a shining dark brown shot through with mahogany lights, needed no ornament other than the moss-green ribbon threaded through it.

She was completely familiar. Rose dropped into a formal curtsy to her own reflection. 'Catherine.'

Catherine. That was her name, but who was she? 'Catherine,' she whispered again. 'Miss Catherine...' No that was not quite right. She was an only child so she was *Miss*... No, the surname would not come. But the *Miss* was correct.

She touched her earlobes. They were pierced and there should be pearl earrings. She wore her pearl set a lot, and the citrines, too. There was the amber necklace her godmother had given her...

'Rose?' Adam came through the doorway from the landing into the main room. She heard the snap of his boot heels across the boards, the clank as he set his sword belt and weapon in the corner, the sigh as he sat on the edge of the bed and began to lever off his boots. Familiar sounds, the sounds a husband coming home after a long day might make. She stood frozen, staring into her own wide eyes in the glass.

'Rose?' The pad of bare feet now. 'Are you all right? Maggie said you are having an early night. I'm sorry, I had to go with the men as far as headquarters. This afternoon…' His words trailed off as he reached the doorway and she turned to face him.

The silence seemed to stretch on and on. His voice when he did speak was deadly quiet. 'Who in blazes are you?'

'Rose,' the apparition said.

Flint stared. Of course it was Rose, but a Rose transformed. She shifted, uneasy under his regard, like a woman hiding something. *Hell, of course she's hiding something. Look at her, you fool.*

'Still Rose,' she murmured.

'You look like a lady.' Yes, he had been a fool, or perhaps he'd seen exactly what he wanted to see all along. 'You *are* a lady, aren't you?' Flint did not trouble to keep the bitter edge from his voice. 'You keep forgetting to use that accent. I should have guessed, just from your handwriting alone.' He studied her in the candlelight, kept quite still while everything shifted under his feet. She was not just respectable, she was well bred, possibly an aristocrat, the precious daughter of some titled household. Not only had he taken her virginity, but that afternoon he had poured his seed into her like a careless rutting fool.

'I think I may be, yes.' She stood as still as he did, as if chilled by the suppressed anger in his voice. Rose was not afraid of him, not physically, but she kept her own voice level, as though she was reasoning with a dangerous dog. He fought the urge to growl.

'I found this gown in a second-hand clothes shop that ladies' maids use to sell their mistresses' cast-offs. It was made for me, I remember it, I gave it to my maid. But the name label has been cut out.'

He came fully into the room and fingered the fabric of her skirts, the finest wool, the smooth-est silk ribbons. *Silk like her skin.* 'You can afford gowns of this quality, you had your own lady's maid. Tell me, what rank was this Gerald of yours?' *An officer, of course.*

'A lieutenant. I...we eloped from the Duchess of Richmond's ball. I think I saw you there. Adam, I am worried about my parents—I remember I left them a letter, telling them about Gerald. They will know he is dead by now and therefore that I am missing.'

'What was his surname? I can find out who is asking about a lieutenant of the Seventy-Third of that name.' He made himself walk away from her, kept his voice level and reasonable. The world was falling away beneath him, but an officer had to keep calm, had to resolve the crisis, *damn it*. 'Your parents will have made enquiries. The sooner we find them, the sooner we can get the horsewhipping element of this farce out of the way.'

Trust him, the blundering soldier who tried to ape the gentleman. First he had innocently asked for one lady's hand in marriage, now he had managed to ruin another.

'I can't remember his last name...' Her voice trailed away as his words registered. '*Horsewhipping?* What are you talking about?'

Flint picked up the walking dress from the bed and shook it out. He had to move and that was better than shaking her, or slamming his fist into the wall or going out and getting dead drunk. Or what he really wanted to do, drag her into bed and forget all of this doubt and conflict in the simple, glorious certainty of making love to Rose. *My Rose, not this fine lady.*

'You have excellent taste in clothes, my dear.' He laid the gown down with exaggerated care and turned back to her now he had himself under control again. 'And you are not stupid. You know your father or your brother are not going to call me out for ruining you. Gentlemen do not duel with bastards, they have other ways of dealing with them.'

'I do not have a brother,' she said with certainty. 'And it wasn't your fault. You thought I was a camp follower, you thought I was experienced, not a virgin.'

'It is my responsibility.' He shrugged. 'I saw what I wanted to see, I expect. Not for the first time.'

'We won't tell them. I am certain I will not fall pregnant.'

'Sure about that?' He watched her face, the colour ebbing and flowing under her skin. 'Your courses started this afternoon?' God, he really had ruined an innocent if she thought they could brush through this with a few lies.

'No!' Rose's cheeks were flaming now. She had never discussed such a thing with a man, not even the family doctor, he was sure.

'Well, then, we cannot be certain. And I am not going to lie to your father, whether you are with child or not. I do try to at least counterfeit some pretence of honour.'

'I wish you would stop doing that,' she snapped. Flint raised an eyebrow at the sudden flare of temper from the woman changing before his eyes into a lady he did not know. 'Stop putting yourself down. You are an officer and you have made yourself a gentleman.'

'And you are exceedingly naive, Rose. Unless your father has a gullible candidate lined up, then we are going to be married once I have given him whatever satisfaction he requires, but I can assure you, he will know exactly what I am.'

'I do not know if I wish to marry you.' Rose turned on her heel and went into the main bedchamber. It was clearly a retreat.

'What has that got to do with it?' Of course she did not want to marry him. All she'd wanted, like all the well-bred ladies who made eyes at him, was his body in her bed. 'Just when did you realise you were a gentlewoman?' Flint demanded, staying close on her heels. There was no way she was going to wriggle out of this, or charm him out of doing the right thing. 'Before you got between my sheets?'

'I realised when you were talking about Lady Sarah being ruined. I was beginning to piece things together,' she admitted.

'You knew the consequences of what we did. How in heaven's name can you say you do not want to marry me after that? The scandal is going to be bad enough as it is, but if we don't marry it will be infinitely worse and you know it.'

'Because I do not *know* myself.' Rose threw up her hands in obvious frustration and began to pace. 'I know how I feel about you now. I admire you, I feel safe with you, I like you. I desire you. But I am not the real me, now. I am changing, you must have seen it. I am not the frightened, speechless, helpless creature you rescued. What will I be when I am my real self again? What will I think and feel when I know who I am, when my memory comes back?'

'You will think you were a damn fool.' Rose flinched at the roughness in his tone, the language, but he did not relent. 'You will bitterly regret that desire. You will certainly not *want* to find yourself married to me, my lady, but married you will be.'

'Not *Lady*. Miss, I am certain,' Rose said, coming to a stop right in front of him.

'Oh, that is excellent news, I *am* relieved,' he jibed, fighting with the only weapon he had, words. 'A viscount or below for a father. At least I have not ruined a duke's daughter.'

'I do not know myself,' she repeated, standing her ground, toe to toe with him as if that would somehow make him take her more seriously. His words, his sarcasm, his bitterness slid off her skin as though she recognised them for what they were, a desperate deceit.

'You don't know me, either, but that did not stop you coming to my bed,' Flint pointed out.

'Yes, I do,' Rose said slowly. He saw himself reflected in the wide, honest depths of her eyes, saw his own bitterness staring back. 'I knew who you were the moment I saw you, Adam Flint. Even when I thought you were the Devil himself come to take me down to hell for my sins, I trusted you.'

'You thought I was the *Devil*?'

'I thought the men who were coming for me were demons, but you vanquished them. You smelt of fire and brimstone and blood and you rode a great black horse. It was the only way to make sense of the world I found myself in.'

'Rose.' Flint took her shoulders. Within his grasp they felt as fragile as eggshells. He made himself keep the hold gentle, acutely aware of how big and calloused his hands were. He must not drag her towards him, kiss her until she yielded. 'We will find your parents and I will marry you.' *And somehow I will make it right for you.*

'You do not want to,' she said stubbornly, her eyes fixed on the topmost button of his jacket.

'Yes, I do. I was thinking about it today.' He banished all the doubt from his tone, pushed away the uncertainty, the vagueness of his plans. When you were leading men into a situation you knew was lethally dangerous, but your orders gave you no choice, you put just that certainty into your voice. It wasn't deceit, it was survival and he'd always come through alive before. He had dishonoured her, so he must marry her. It was that simple. That complicated.

'Liar. In the stable you were far from sure about anything.' Her voice shook, just a little.

He forgot to be gentle, simply pulled her hard against his chest and wrapped his arms around her and felt her tremble. His anger ebbed a little with the realisation of just how frightened and confused Rose was for all her composure and her brave words. 'I would fight any man who called me a liar.'

'There is no time for this. You'll be leaving for Paris soon,' Rose muttered, her voice muffled in broadcloth. She had been washing her hair in something herbal again. Rosemary, lemon and a herb he could not identify.

Flint closed his eyes. 'I told you, my orders are to stay here in Brussels. I have no expectation of being ordered to Paris.'

'But you will be sent somewhere eventually, won't you? Moss seems to think so. Or you'll be ordered back to England or off to somewhere else unless you sell out now and I don't believe you'll forget the army, just like that. Wellington isn't going to let you sit around in Brussels, finding my parents. Then you'll need to arrange what you are doing next, join the East India Company. I heard you talking about it.'

'I will resign.' He could not drag Rose to India or to follow the drum in whatever foreign land he ended up. Nor could he leave her alone in England while he was away for months, years. He avoided examining why it was that fellow officers routinely left their wives behind, but he could not contemplate it.

He held her, his cheek against the crown of her head and felt himself relax, just a little. There was a certain relief in having the decision taken away. This was what must happen and now all he had to do was to make it work, however unpleasant the process.

'No! Adam, you can't do that.' She strained back against his arm to look up into his face. 'You are a soldier, an officer. This is what you do, who you are. And you need time to decide what to do next, not be pushed into a marriage you don't want. I can't do that to you.'

'But I can. I don't want to be a peacetime soldier, putting down unrest in the industrial towns or marching about Hyde Park firing gun salutes as one of Prinny's toy soldiers.' He buried the other options, the other armies, the other wars.

'No.' Rose wriggled free and sat down on the edge of the bed. 'You can't make a rushed decision. What about India? What about the German states? Moss said you'd be a general. I'll find my parents, we'll soon see I am not pregnant, they don't need to know where I was. Oh...'

'Oh?' Flint spun round the upright chair so the back was towards her and straddled it, his arms along the top rail, its wooden frame a fence against the urge to touch her, pull her into bed and make love to her until they were both convinced this was the only thing to do, without any further argument.

'Miss Endacott. She came round today with your notebook. She might guess...'

Flint scrubbed one hand over his face and sighed. 'Rose, you have a very strange idea of male honour. I will not pretend I have had nothing to do with you and I do not care if anyone else knows or not. I have ruined you and I *will* marry you.'

Rose reached out and closed her fingers around his as they clenched on the chair rail. 'Shall we go to bed, Adam?'

'You have just refused to marry me. Have you changed your mind so quickly?' The words seemed to come from a long way down. Was she going to yield and agree without any further struggle?

'One might as well be hanged for a sheep as a lamb,' Rose said with a shrug. 'There is nothing we can do tonight except argue ourselves into knots. I want to be hugged. I want to hug you.' She looked at him and bit her lip, but not before he saw the betraying tremor. 'We don't have to make love, if you don't want to.'

'I'll always want to make love to you, Rose.' And he wanted to sit in the corner and howl like a dog, but that was not an option. He had a duty to Randall if the man was at death's door. He had a duty to Rose. He had a duty to his own hard-won sense of honour and to the army in which he was still an officer. He was sick of duty. 'But I am not going to make things any worse than they already are. A hug sounds tempting.'

He wondered, fleetingly, if he could simply seduce her into compliance, make love to her until she was too befuddled to protest any longer. No, she had to agree because her head told her this was right. But agree she would. From somewhere he dredged up a smile, a lightness in his voice, and was rewarded by her answering smile. A somewhat uncertain one, to be true.

'Can you manage the fastenings on that gown?' Heaven preserve him from having to unbutton it, wrestle with stay laces, feel her skin warm under his fingers as he unwrapped her like a delicious ripe fruit nestled in tissue paper.

'Yes, thank you.' Her eyes were cast down, there was colour on her cheekbones. Somehow not having sex was more embarrassing than the intimacies themselves, it seemed. She went to her own room and closed the door.

Flint shrugged, undressed, fell into his own bed

and wondered whether he wanted Rose to come to him or not. He had decided she was staying in her room and his hand was on the edge of the covers, ready to get out and snuff the candles, when her door opened and she came out clad in a nightgown that fitted her, made from a filmy lawn that fluttered around her ankles. He closed his eyes and waited, focused on his breathing and not the uncomfortable excitement that the sight provoked. Obviously he had sinned very badly if this temptation was to be his punishment. There was a soft huff of breath and she dealt with the lights, then she slid in beside him, turned trustingly into his arms and laid her cheek on his chest, her hand on his shoulder.

He had endured sleepless nights before, Flint told himself. This time it would be his conscience keeping him awake, not the fear of French snipers.

Chapter Twelve

'Adam, what are we to do first?' Rose sat up against the pillows and watched Adam shave, the long, steady strokes of the blade cutting through the foam-covered bristles to leave a track of shining skin behind it. His chin was tipped up, displaying the strong lines of his throat, and his hands were sure on the ebony handle as he wielded the razor.

He was naked except for a damp linen towel slung around his hips. It seemed, if anything, to enhance the sheer masculinity of his body. Rose told herself it was only natural to want to look at him like this. There was no surplus fat on him, nothing that was not necessary to make a strong, supple fighting machine out of a frame that was naturally tall, broad and perfectly proportioned.

Rose jerked her mind back to all the things they

had to be worried about. There were enough of those, surely, to counteract inconvenient physical attraction? She had slept all night, safe and peaceful in Adam's arms, but the dawn had brought no answers.

Adam flicked soap off the razor. 'I must call on Randall, find out about this operation. Then I will go to headquarters, talk to the surgeon, see how Bartlett is. After that I'll find out if anyone has been asking after your Lieutenant Gerald. While I'm away you can go back to your notes and do your level best to remember more. We've got days to resolve this, Rose, not weeks.'

Should I tell him I can recall my first name? But that wouldn't help, it would simply be confusing. She couldn't think of herself as Catherine.

'I know. I'll try, I promise. Adam—'

'Hush.' There was the sound of knocking at the front door. Adam took a last stroke with the razor and wiped his face, his head cocked to one side, listening.

'It is a woman's voice. Miss Endacott with news, perhaps?' Rose suggested as she reached towards the end of the bed for a wrapper. The caller sounded agitated.

There was silence, then the bedchamber door

was flung open so hard it slammed back against the wall. From the foot of the stairs came Maggie's voice raised in protest, ignored by the young woman who stood there, clenching a frivolous little parasol like a weapon. Her fashionable ensemble seemed to have been flung on in haste, her blond hair was already coming loose where she had jammed it under her bonnet.

She swept into the room, apparently uncaring about Adam's near nudity or Rose watching aghast, half in, half out of bed. She stalked up to Adam and poked him in the chest with one ungloved finger. 'Justin is going to die and it is all your fault, you horrible man!'

Rose gasped and the intruder spun round. Her jaw dropped and for a moment they stared at each other. Rose met furious blue eyes that were suddenly very familiar. This was Adam's sister, Lady Sarah Latymor.

'You!' Recognition and surprise quenched the fury for a moment.

She knows me? 'Lady Sarah, who am—?' Rose's foot tangled with the bedsheet and she landed on the floor in a sprawl of limbs.

Adam took a step towards her, but she waved him away. Perhaps he could calm his furious half-sister down and then she would tell Rose just what her real name was.

Sarah rounded on Adam again. 'You hypocrite! You storm and shout at me about immorality, you put Justin's life in danger by telling tales, you pretend to be so sanctimonious with your protestations about how young ladies should behave. You called poor Tom a rake and accused him of corrupting my innocence while all the time you have your own little love nest here. You say I am ruined—well, what about her?' She pointed a quivering finger at Rose.

'At least I am with a *gentleman*. You are going to be sorry you ever crawled out of your gutter, Adam Flint! If Justin survives he'll see you drummed out of the army—if Tom hasn't killed you first. To think I told him it was a stupid idea to shoot you. I should have loaded his pistols for him and sent him straight after you when I had the chance!'

Adam reached for his robe and pulled it on. 'Stop ranting, you foolish chit. Is Bartlett recovered?'

'You mean you don't know? He isn't here?' Momentary alarm flitted across her face. 'Well, I still hold you to blame. And I'm going to make you both sorry you ever set foot in Brussels!'

She was gone before Rose could speak. They

heard her run down the stairs, then the front door slammed behind her.

'Are you all right, Rose?' Adam asked in the echoing silence. When she nodded and got up from her tangle of sheets, he remarked, 'You guessed that was my half-sister, Lady Sarah? Sounds as though Bartlett is up and about if she's misplaced him. That's good news by the sound of it. He's not with her and he can take over from me if it comes to it.'

'Over your dead body, from what she said about his pistols. Adam, I am so sorry. You won't fight him, will you?'

Lady Sarah knew who she was. But if she told Adam that now he would chase after his sister, demand to be told Rose's real name. And she wanted to discover her identity and come to terms with it before she told Adam. *Leave it today*, instinct told her. *Go tomorrow.* She could recall the address Lieutenant Foster had blushingly revealed. Surely if she spoke to Sarah calmly, without Adam there to inflame her, she would help.

'I'm not dead yet and Tom Bartlett has more sense than to issue a challenge, let alone commit murder, on the say-so of my little sister.' Adam seemed unaware that her silence was anything more than shock over the scene. 'The man was the worst rakehell in the regiment, Rose. Even if he's fallen head over heels in love and reformed, he's not going to forget that. He knows as well as I do that he shouldn't have been with Sarah.

'If they are lovers, he is going to have to marry her.' He raked his hands through his hair. 'I'd have said he'd make a worse husband than I would, but the girl's got guts and determination, I'll say that for her. Perhaps she can cope with him.'

Adam was dressing with the economy and speed of a man used to dawn emergencies. 'Have a decent breakfast, then sit down quietly and see what you can recall and I'll be back by noon.'

He took her in a swift one-armed embrace, his kiss rapid, hard and possessive. 'Find out who you really are, Rose. And then be prepared to choose a wedding gown.' He clattered down the stairs, called 'Good morning' to Maggie and was out of the front door, before she could react.

Rose took her slips of paper to the kitchen and sorted them on the table as she ate sweet rolls and sipped Maggie's strong coffee in an effort to calm her stomach. If she could remember who she was without having to rely on Lady Sarah, so much the better. She had an uncomfortable feeling they had never been friends.

Maggie had frowned when she heard who the visitor had been. 'Spoiled little madam by the look of her. She'll make trouble if she can.'

'Childhood... My likes and dislikes. England. People,' Rose muttered as she shifted the slips around into piles and tried to ignore Maggie's warnings.

'Why don't you want to marry the major?' Maggie demanded, demolishing Rose's attempts to duck the issue. She planted herself on the opposite seat and reached for the butter.

'I don't know who I am and neither does he. And all Adam said about marriage before he realised I wasn't a camp follower was that he wasn't the marrying kind. So he doesn't *want* to marry me. Or marry at all.'

'There are plenty of things in life we don't want to do—it doesn't mean that things aren't worse if we do what we like.'

'That's what Mama said to Papa when he didn't want to go to dinner with the Hutchinsons around the corner in Rue du Nord,' Rose said, half-listening to Maggie as she pushed the papers around. 'He said Mr Hutchinson's a bore and Mama said,

"James Tatton, for once in your life do...'" Her voice trailed off as she stared at Maggie. 'I remember. I know who I am! I'm Catherine Tatton and Papa is Lord Thetford and we've been living in Rue de Louvain for six months because it is so cheap over here in Brussels and Papa wants to economise.'

'A lord?' Maggie had turned pale. 'Oh, my goodness,' she added faintly. 'You're Lady Catherine.'

'No. Papa is a viscount. I'm just Miss Tatton.'

Maggie was fanning herself with a napkin. *Just? A viscount's daughter in my house and in Adam Flint's bed. Now what are we going to do? And what is the major going to say when he finds out?'

'I'm going home and I'll tell my parents something. Something so Adam won't have to marry me or ruin his career or change his life,' Rose said grimly. 'He saved me and I am not letting him do this to himself.'

It was not so very far to the smart rented house on Rue de Louvain, not if you ran, the breath sobbing in your throat until it was raw, and not if you went by the steep steps up the hill past the cathedral towards the Parc and the fashionable quarter.

It took her twenty minutes. Rose arrived gasping and clung to the railings of the house at the end of the street while she fought for composure. Her breakfast rolls lay like lead in her stomach, she felt dizzy with the implications of what she had remembered and what she must do.

She had to look perfect. Untouched, ladylike. Not a bedraggled victim, not a ruined woman. She smoothed down the skirts of the walking dress, tucked an errant lock of hair back under the brim of her bonnet and fanned her flushed face with her pocket handkerchief while she rehearsed her story.

There was no escaping the fact that she had eloped. She could tell the truth about that, about what happened on the battlefield, about how Major Flint had rescued her. How he had taken her to stay with the respectable wife of his old sergeant. There was no need to say anything about her relationship with the major, except to tell how gallant he had been. All Adam had to do when her father called on him with his grateful thanks was to look starched up and modest and mutter about doing his duty towards defenceless females.

Her breathing was back to normal and her face felt no more flushed than could be excused by emotion, although the churning in her stomach was pure nerves now. Just as long as her courses came when they were due, everything would be all right. Rose started to walk in a ladylike manner towards the house. It would be wonderful to see Mama and Papa again, but it would be harrowing, too. They must have been frantic with worry and that was all her fault.

She was halfway to the door when it opened and someone came out. A young lady in a forget-me-not-blue spencer and a darker blue bonnet paused on the top step, opened her pretty little ivory silk parasol and made her way down to the pavement and then along the street towards the Parc. She was too late. Lady Sarah Latymor had taken her revenge on Adam.

There was no going back now, her plans were in tatters and there were no lies or evasions that could serve. Rose forced her unwilling feet on, up the steps and knocked.

'Miss Tatton!' Heale, their butler, looked ready to burst into tears as he held the door wide. 'You are home, praise be!'

'Yes, thank you, Heale, here I am, safe and sound.' Years of training in deportment kept the smile on her face, the cheerful tone in her voice. You never showed weakness in front of the servants, you certainly did not lose your breakfast in front of them through sheer nerves. 'It is good to see you, too. My parents?'

'In the drawing room, Miss Tatton.' He bustled down the passage in front of her. 'I'll send for tea,' he added as he threw open the door. 'Miss Tatton, my lady.'

'Catherine!' Her mother was huddled on the sofa beside her husband. She looked up, her face blotchy with tears, and burst into fresh floods at the sight of Rose.

'You foolish, wicked girl.' Her father thrust a handkerchief into his wife's hand and got to his feet. 'And before you attempt to cozen us with some cock-and-bull story about where you have been, I should tell you that we know all about it. As if eloping with that moneyless whelp wasn't enough!'

'Lady Sarah Latymor has been here, I know. She has taken her brother, Major Flint, into dislike and as a consequence is determined to do him harm.' Somehow she kept her face calm, even as she recoiled from the anger and grief she had caused. 'Mama, Papa—I am truly sorry I ran away with Gerald Haslam. I thought I was in love with him and I wasn't. I never meant you to have so much worry and distress over me.'

'And now he's dead and you cannot even marry him.' Mama emerged from the white linen and gazed at her hopelessly.

'I would not want to marry him. It was all a horrible mistake and besides we didn't…I mean, we never…' *Oh, for goodness' sake, you are not some innocent girl, say it.* 'We were not lovers.'

'Then why did you not come home as soon as you realised you were mistaken?' her father demanded. He seemed to have calmed down a little. 'We would have done our best to salvage the situation. And sit down, for goodness' sake, Catherine.'

Catherine, that is me. But I do not feel like that woman any longer. I am Rose now. Adam Flint's Rose. But I must not be. She shook her head, dizzy with impossible choices.

She sat beside her mother and reached for her hand. The desperate clutch of fingers around hers was a knife to her conscience. 'I had promised to marry Gerald and I could not go back on my word. Then we were caught up in the preparations for battle. I was with the baggage train during the fighting.'

'With the camp followers,' her mother lamented.

'The women are brave and loyal to their men,' Rose protested. 'They helped me. After Quatre

Bras we retreated to Waterloo and then there was the battle and Gerald did not come back. I went to look for him.'

'On the battlefield?' Her father sat down with a thump on the nearest chair. 'What were you thinking of?'

'That I had a duty to Gerald,' she said. 'If he was still alive but wounded, I had to help him. But I do not think I was rational by then. I was very tired and wet. Hungry and terrified. Then when I reached the battlefield…' She could not go on, not with her mother gasping in distress beside her. She would never comprehend one tenth of the horror and Rose could not put those images into her head. 'I found his body. I think I must have been in shock after that. I tried to scream, but my voice would not work, I didn't know who I was.'

Her father was white around the lips. 'Then what happened?' he asked as though the question was being dragged from him by force.

'I was being threatened by four deserters and Major Flint rescued me. I couldn't tell him who I was because I did not know and, besides, I could not speak. He took me to the lodging house that one of his old sergeants and his wife keep. They are a respectable couple and very kind. My voice came back after a while and then little bits of my memory. I only remembered who I was today.'

'Lady Sarah said that she found you and this man *together*,' Lady Thetford whispered, as if by keeping her voice low she could pretend that this was not happening. 'In his bedchamber. You were in his *bed*. She said he was…unclothed.'

What could she say that would protect Adam? Rose struggled to find some form of words as the door opened.

'Are you receiving, my lady? A Major Flint is here asking for his lordship.'

'Is he indeed?' Lord Thetford rose to his feet. 'Show him in. My dear, take Catherine into your boudoir.'

How did he know I was here? Maggie must have told him. Rose stood up. She must go to Adam, stop this confrontation before he said something that would ruin his career.

Then she looked across the room at the erect, steadfast figure of her father braced to defend his family and realised with a sudden pang of affection that he was no longer a young man, not even a young middle-aged man. The skin of his neck was beginning to sag, his hair was more grey than brown, he had a little paunch and there were the beginning of bags under his eyes. She loved him and she had worried him desperately, had disappointed him dreadfully, and now he was squaring up to deal with this threat to her from a man half his age.

'I will stay here, Papa,' she said. She had two men to shield from the damage she had wrought. Somehow.

'Major Flint, my lord.'

Lady Thetford rose, quivering with outrage as Adam came into the room and stopped when he saw the tableau in front of him. She swept up to him. 'You libertine,' she hissed and slapped him hard across the face. 'Scum. How dare you presume to lay a finger on my daughter?' Without waiting for a reply she walked out of the room. The door closed quietly behind her.

Adam would stand like that, look like that, if he faced a court martial or a firing squad, Rose thought, aching to go to him, knowing that to do so would be another slap to his pride.

'What have you to say for yourself?' her father said at last.

'I am at your disposal, my lord.' The marks of Lady Thetford's fingers stood out like a brand on Adam's face.

'You think I would duel with a bastard? I should horsewhip you, rather.'

'If your lordship feels that would help.' Adam was as still and as controlled as he had been when she had cleaned and dressed his wound. To anyone who did not know him he would appear simply stoical, or perhaps unconcerned. Rose knew this was hard-learned self-discipline, just as she knew that if her father sent for a horsewhip and led the way to the stable yard, Adam would follow him, strip off jacket and shirt and submit to the older man's fury without flinching.

'Major Flint believed I was a camp follower,' she said.

'He thought *what*?' her father roared.

'Ro...Miss Tatton, I think you should leave.'

'And have you take the blame for this?' she demanded, coming to stand as her mother had, toe to toe with Adam.

'Of course. It is mine to take, after all.' His smile was like a touch on the cheek, gentle and reassuring, transforming his face.

'How dare you look at my daughter like that!' her father snapped.

'As if she is a lady I respect and admire? A lady for whom I feel great fondness?' Adam enquired.

'I understand your anger, my lord, and your desire to do me damage. But I do intend to marry Miss Tatton.'

'You, a bastard, marry a viscount's daughter? Oh, yes, I know who you are, your half-sister has been here before you to carry the tale.' Her father flung up his hands and turned away, but Rose could tell he was already beginning to realise that shooting Adam was not an option, that pretending nothing had happened was not possible either.

'My father, for whose numerous sins I do not feel I can be blamed, was an earl. My half-brother, who recognises me, is an earl. I am financially in a position to support a wife in comfort and respectability, if not luxury.' Adam was hanging on to his temper by his fingernails, Rose suspected, but he was hiding the fact well. 'I understand and accept your anger, my lord. If I were in your shoes I would be tempted to reach for a pistol, but that will not help your daughter now.'

'Catherine, come away from that man,' Lord Thetford ordered.

'I cannot quite get used to that name, Papa. I have been Rose for days, with no idea who I was.' She put her hand on Adam's arm and shook it gently until he looked down at her. 'I do not need to marry. You do not need to marry me.'

'No?' The ghost of that smile was still there.

'We will know in a few days,' she murmured.

It was not soft enough for her father's hearing. 'Scoundrel!'

Chapter Thirteen

'Miss Tatton, I think it best if you join Lady Thetford,' Flint said with a wary eye on the red-faced viscount. They'd have a heart seizure on their hands in a moment. 'I fear we are doing your father's health no good at all with this exchange.'

Rose sat down on the sofa, folded her hands in her lap and asked her father with commendable, and infuriating, calm, 'Is it known that I eloped with Gerald?'

'Fortunately not, which is the one bright spark in this whole sorry mess.' Her father flung himself down into the nearest chair. He did not ask Adam to sit. 'At the ball your mama developed a headache. We went to look for you so we could return home but could not find you. The footman in charge of cloaks said you had left an hour earlier and described Haslam. Your mama was…

overwrought. That attracted an audience.' He grimaced. 'However, she did not say anything indiscreet and I think I passed it off as a bad attack of migraine.

'I went to find Haslam's commanding officer, but they had left for Quatre Bras. I assumed he had hidden you in his lodgings, as your note that we found when we returned home said nothing of you leaving with him to the battlefield. When there was no word afterwards we could not understand it, for we were sure you would have tried to discover his fate. We saw his name on the lists, but we had no idea you were not in Brussels and we dared not make any enquiries about him by name. For what it is worth we have put it around that you are in bed with the influenza.'

'I am very sorry to have caused you so much anxiety, Papa.' Rose was within a breath of tears, Adam could tell, but she kept her voice steady. He wanted to go and sit beside her, put an arm around her in support, but that risked shattering her control. 'You see, I thought we could run away to Antwerp, get married, then come back within a day or so. But then Gerald received his orders to march as we left the ball. I was going to be an army wife, so I thought my place was with him.'

'I never liked that boy,' Lord Thetford said. 'He was immature, and too pretty by half. I had told him I would not accept his offer for your hand. What was he thinking of, to take you with him?'

'He was as green as grass, I would guess,' Adam said. This at least he could understand after years of dealing with callow youths. 'He'd been a Hyde Park soldier until this, no doubt. He had probably never seen a battle, had no idea what it would be like. He expected to leave Miss Tatton in a pretty little tent and gallop off to fight. There would be gallantry, glory, the thrill of a cavalry charge. Then he would return to her, bloodied but unbowed, perhaps with a captured eagle to lay at her feet. What he got was two battles, mud, blood and noise and a desperate encounter that almost overwhelmed even those of us who had been fighting for a decade or more.'

'You would defend him to me?'

'I would explain him to you, my lord. He was an inexperienced officer trying to do his duty, even though he found himself in hell.'

The older man looked him in the eye, without speaking. Flint felt as though he was being assessed, fairly, even if coldly, for the first time since he had entered the room. Rose's father gestured towards a chair. 'Sit, Major Flint.' It appeared a decision had been reached. *No horsewhip, then.*

The sigh that Rose gave showed that she, too, must have noticed that unspoken decision. She then rushed into speech before Flint could build on the moment of understanding. 'The point is, Papa, that I was technically ruined simply by eloping with Gerald. If no one knows of it, I am not *actually* ruined. Major Flint does not need to come into it.'

'I do if you are carrying my child,' Adam pointed out with, he thought, unarguable logic. He could not afford to regard her blushes, or her father's likely reaction to the blunt confirmation of his worst fears. 'And the unfortunate Lieutenant Haslam is dead or we wouldn't be in this position.' This *unfortunate* position. He did not need to spell it out to her, surely? 'Lady Sarah knows and feels angry enough with me to bring the story straight to your parents. Who can tell what she will do with the information? But even if no one else ever knows, I have been your lover. You need a husband, Miss Tatton, and you are my responsibility now. Child or no child,' he added.

'No,' Rose said flatly.

Flint caught the viscount's gaze. He, too, seemed baffled by whatever feminine logic Rose was employing. She was not a fool, she was an intelligent woman. Why could she not grasp the inevitability of this? Presumably because marriage to him was worse than ruin in her mind.

'I will try to persuade Sarah to keep quiet about it,' Rose said. 'We were never friends, but I cannot believe she wants to hurt me by tattling about this all over Brussels. She is too involved with Major Bartlett and with worries about Lord Randall to be attending social events, in any case, surely?

'I was wrong to elope with Gerald when I did not truly love him,' she added earnestly. 'And do not ask me why, Papa. It is one of the things that I still do not understand. But everything that happened afterwards was a consequence of that action. I am going to be punished enough for my deeds, please do not punish me further by forcing me into a marriage I do not want.'

Adam felt his body tense and forced himself to relax. That was clear enough, she did not want to marry him, which considering she had been so eager to join him in his bed, and was perfectly well aware of the fate of disgraced young ladies, argued a strong objection to something about either his personality, his birth or his character. Probably all three.

'What we want and what we need are not the same things, my girl,' her father said. He looked at Adam and Adam looked back. After a moment her father nodded and Adam inclined his head in assent to the unspoken question. Somehow, for her own good, they were going to have to unite to persuade Rose into this union and form an unwilling truce to do so.

'Take yourself off to your mother, Catherine. The major and I have business to discuss.'

'I am not going to go and leave you to trap Adam into marrying me.' Her hand tightened on the arm of the sofa, rucking the chintz cover under her fingers.

'It would be an unusual thing to find a man in Major Flint's position wishing to turn down the opportunity to marry the well-dowered daughter of a viscount,' Lord Thetford said drily. 'Especially when society will think him gallant indeed for rescuing you from disgrace if a whisper of your elopement ever comes out.'

The idea that he would have anything to gain from marrying her, other than the sense of having done the right thing, had obviously never occurred to Rose. Now she stared at him and Flint saw the colour rise and then ebb in her cheeks, saw the flicker of disquiet in her eyes.

It had not occurred to him either, which only proved he was not thinking very clearly. Whatever he wanted to do now, whether stay in the army or buy land, would be made easier by a marriage to Miss Tatton. She would bring a dowry, influential relatives, an established place in society—and she thought he had been thinking about that from the moment he discovered that she was a lady.

'I think it would be better if you do leave, Miss Tatton. Your father and I must have a practical discussion.'

'Horse trading,' Rose said with scorn in her voice. She stood, sweeping her skirts around her with ostentatious care. 'But I would remind you both that clichés usually have a kernel of truth in them. You may lead a horse to water, but you most certainly cannot make it drink.'

Flint stood to open the door for her, but she was already across the room. She paused in the open doorway and curtsied. 'Papa. Major Flint.'

'On her high horse, to carry a weary metaphor further.' Lord Thetford sighed as he dropped back into his chair. 'What have you got to say for yourself now the ladies are out of the room, Flint?'

'I genuinely believed that the woman I found on the battlefield was a camp follower, my lord. I had seen her at Quatre Bras, her clothing was that of a common woman, there was nothing out of place and she could not speak. I found myself drawn to her, fond of her. I wanted to keep her with me, treat her well. I did not see the clues that should have led me to a realisation of who she was, although I will be frank with you, even if I had, it was too late.'

Her father grimaced. 'Yes, that is frank indeed. Tell me about yourself then, Major. I know you are the old Earl Randall's by-blow.'

'One of them, yes.' An angry man, a worried man, but a fair one, he decided as he studied the viscount. Flint took a deep breath and cleared his mind as though he was about to give an intelligence report. 'My mother…'

Half an hour later Lord Thetford leaned back in his chair and grunted. 'Not as bad as I thought. You've more behind you financially than that boy Haslam had.'

'I can give you my bankers' direction for confirmation of my assets. I would refer you to Colonel Lord Randall if his health was not in such a precarious state. The duke might speak for me.'

'He may well. Wellington likes rogues, provided they get the business done,' the viscount said drily. 'You'll want to know about Catherine's dowry. No, don't wave it away, we're talking business here and I'll think you a noddy if you aren't concerned. I'm rich in land, poor in ready money like many a title-holder. I make no secret of the fact. That's why we're here in Brussels, a cheap place to live, as the Duke of Richmond would find if his duchess didn't keep throwing damn-fool entertainments. But Catherine inherited from her godfather and from her mother's mother.' He named a sum that had Flint feeling mildly queasy. 'And there is property, of course. All the unentailed land is settled on her and for now there's her godfather's nice little estate I'm looking after for her. That would suit you, I have no doubt.'

'I cannot…' Money? Land? A *nice little estate*? 'The settlements will have to be put in trust for the children. Whatever is the usual practice. I don't want any of it, I am not a fortune hunter.'

'Then you're a fool. Do you want your wife having to live in Brussels on the economical plan like the rest of us here?' Bushy grey eyebrows rose in scornful enquiry. 'Do you want your children growing up as a major of artillery can rear them or as a rich man can?'

'If you put it like that, the latter, I suppose.' It seemed there was no end to the blows his pride was expected to take. 'My lord, Miss Tatton is a beautiful, intelligent, elegant young lady. She is also past the age one would expect the daughter of a viscount to be unmarried. Is there something I should know?'

'Some broken heart in the past, you mean?' Lord Thetford gave a bark of laughter. 'Nothing that simple. The girl declares she will not marry except for love, mutual love. Romantic poppycock. I had met her mother half a dozen times before we married and we have rubbed along very well. Why Catherine lost her head over Haslam I cannot say, given that she regained her senses soon enough.'

Love? Rose wants a love match and she gets me.

'I will do everything in my power to make her happy, my lord,' he said, keeping hold of the fast-disappearing tail of his temper.

'You had better. I'll not have her marry you unless I am certain you will be kind to my girl, even if it means we have to go and live in Italy to avoid the scandal. Will you strike her if she displeases you? Keep a mistress? Come home drunk and gamble her fortune away?'

'No, damn it!' There went his temper.

The older man's expression hardened as he studied Flint's struggle to get his annoyance under control. 'If it turns out that you treat her badly despite what you say, then I'll make you sorry you were ever born, believe me. I will be quite frank with you—you are not what I had hoped for as a son-in-law, far from it, but a live major of dubious pedigree is better than a dead, feckless youth, under the circumstances. All you need to do is to convince Catherine, because I haven't been able to turn her will on anything important to her since she was eleven.'

Nature might be taking care of that without any further help from him, Flint mused, maintaining his composure in the face of Lord Thetford's stony gaze. He had been careless just the once, but once could be enough. He thought of the bone-deep pleasure of spending inside Rose, of feeling her body joining his in ecstasy. If ever a coupling deserved to produce a child, that one did. But if she was forced into marriage she would never forget it or forgive it. He needed her to agree because she wanted him as a husband, not because she was forced. He was becoming as romantic as she was, it seemed. Or perhaps it was simply that he could not bear the thought of her unhappiness.

He looked across into the face of the man who would be his father-in-law, the grandfather of his children. The man who looked down on him, barely trusting his word. 'I will do my best, my lord.'

'And treat her right, Flint, or I'll have you gelded.'

'Just what I told my Spanish stallion yesterday, my lord.'

The older man threw back his head and laughed, a sharp bark of reluctant humour, and Flint laughed with him. His was a diplomatic laugh, the acknowledgement of mutual amusement that he might offer a senior officer who had cracked a joke during a briefing. He was not fooled for one moment by the viscount's laughter. Beneath that moment of mirth was a proud man who was hating this accommodation he was having to make for his daughter's sake. *That makes two of us.*

Lady Thetford's boudoir was above the drawing room. With the windows open in the June heat the sound of male voices from below reached the two women sitting silent amidst the feminine comfort of pale blue upholstery, vases of roses and soft carpets. The deep voices had not risen in anger yet, no doors had slammed. Adam was presumably gritting his teeth and accepting the blame, just as he had said he would. He must be hating this, his pride would be shredded.

The disloyal, nagging suspicion about her dowry surfaced and was firmly pushed aside. He could not have known. She felt guilty about having those thoughts about Adam.

'If you twist that ribbon any harder it will be in shreds,' her mother said, her own sodden handkerchief a knot between her fingers. 'And look at the state of your hands. Your maid must find a pair of chicken-skin gloves for you to wear at night.'

Rose looked down at her tense fingers. The thin red marks where the briar had scratched her were fading, but she had broken several nails and the skin had caught the sun on that long ride back from the battlefield. 'Yes, Mama,' she said. She had been proud of her soft white hands. How foolish that seemed now, set against all the other things to worry about.

'What is taking so long?' her mother demanded. 'Oh, that it should come to this, to you having to marry a man like that.'

'You mean a courageous officer who has risen on merit? A man who saved my life? A gentleman who was a guest at the Duchess of Richmond's ball?'

'A baseborn man. A hardened soldier.'

'That hardened soldier saved me from rape and probably death, Mama. He killed four men for me.' Her mother went white and closed her eyes as though in pain.

Laughter floated up from the room below. Adam's rarely heard laugh sounded genuine. What was amusing him? What could possibly be amusing about this situation? Rose stood and went to lean over the windowsill.

'Catherine! Stop that this moment—what if someone sees you?'

After a second Rose recalled who Catherine was and moved away from the casement.

'The major seems pleased enough with the prospect of marrying you,' Lady Thetford said, her lips pursed. 'He must think his ship has come in and no mistake.'

Adam was no fool. No saint either. He was a practical, pragmatic man who could not be expected to ignore the benefits of marrying a well-dowered viscount's daughter. After all, none of the gentlemen who had courted her disregarded her dowry or her breeding. Why should he? But he would no more let that weigh in his decision to marry her than he would betray his country to the enemy and she was ashamed that she had doubted him for a second.

'I have to accept him first.' She tugged at the sash cord and watched the window slide down with a soft thud. She did not want to hear any more evidence of Adam's good humour.

A tap on the door broke into the awkward silence. 'Yes, Heale?' Her mother was the picture of composure, her back ramrod straight, the twisted handkerchief out of sight.

'Major Flint would be obliged if Miss Tatton would join him in the drawing room, my lady.'

'Very well.' Her mother waited until the butler had withdrawn before she let her shoulders slump again. 'I imagine any attempt at chaperonage is pointless, you had better go and see what he has to say for himself.'

'Yes, Mama.' Best to be obedient in everything that she could. But how was she ever to satisfy her conscience, her desires and her duty when they were all pulling in different directions?

* * *

Adam was alone in the drawing room when she went in. He stood in front of the empty hearth, hands clasped behind his back, head lowered as if in thought. It was exactly the position the other men who had offered for her hand had taken, she realised with an unsettling return of unwanted memories. Perhaps there was a rule book for a gentleman about to make an offer.

'Miss Tatton.' He lifted his head as she closed the door and there was no light in the blue eyes, no smile on the firm lips.

'Major Flint.' She dropped a nicely calculated curtsy. Two could play at this game of masks.

'I have your father's consent to ask if you will do me the honour of giving me your hand in marriage.' It appeared that all men used the same textbook for the words as well. Falling to one knee and kissing her hand appeared to be optional, however.

'Thank you, Major. While I am most appreciative of your flattering offer, I regret I must decline. We would not suit, I fear.' And that was the answer she always gave.

The textbook response to her refusal would be a manly statement of regret and the hope that further consideration might change her mind. This she would counter by a kind, but firm, negative. The gentleman would bow and leave with further well-bred statements along the lines of his desire to always be a friend and of service to her.

It appeared that Adam had tossed the textbook aside after the first two pages. 'I fear that is not an acceptable reply, Miss Tatton. Your father and I are in full agreement that you must marry me.'

'And I, Major Flint, being of age, cannot be bound by whatever cosy agreements you and my father have come to about the disposition of my person.'

At which point the textbook was not so much tossed aside as hurled through the window. 'So that is what this is about?' Adam demanded. 'You have taken against being told what to do? You'll ignore what is right, what is honourable, simply because you've some damned romantic notion in your head about true love.' He took a deep breath. 'I apologise for my language.'

'You sneer at my *damned romantic notions*, but you do want my damned person?' Rose enquired and tasted blood as her teeth closed over her lower lip.

Chapter Fourteen

'Oh, yes, I want your body and you have shown every indication of wanting mine,' Adam said drily. His gaze caressed her mouth, then hardened. 'What have you done? There is blood on your lip.'

The square of white linen he offered her was pristine. *Maggie's laundry*, Rose thought with a stab of homesickness for the simple uncomplicated warmth of that house. She took it from his outstretched hand, expecting him to move in closely and dab at the sore lip himself. But he was angry, she guessed. Angry and keeping his distance from her, the cause of the thoroughly unpleasant day he must be experiencing.

They stared at each other while she pressed the handkerchief to her mouth, smelling the clean tang of starch and soap. 'One of us is going to have to say something,' Adam remarked after the silence had hung heavy between them for a while.

'I have said it. No.'

'It is not an acceptable response. Not for your parents, not for my honour. Certainly not for your welfare or for that of the child you may be carrying.' His accent was indistinguishable from the well-born gentlemen he had learned to imitate, without a trace of the faint country burr she had grown to love. That was the voice he used to speak to his men, his horse, his dog and, when he had believed her to be his social equal, the voice he had used to her.

Whatever the choices Adam would willingly have made about his future, now it seemed he had accepted there was only one. He was going to mould himself into an English gentleman for her whether she wanted that or not.

'Your father tells me you have always held out for a love match. I am sorry for that, sorry for sneering at the notion just now. But if you do not marry me, I doubt you will be able to hide from another man that you are no longer a virgin.'

Rose sat down blindly on the nearest chair, jarring her spine when it proved to be an upright one and not the armchair she was expecting.

A love match? I could love you, Adam Flint. Perhaps I already do. But I have entrapped you when your only fault was to save a woman from an awful fate and then to fail to recognise that she was not what all the evidence proclaimed her to be. And now, even if I ever do find the right man for me, I have to hope he will be uncommonly forgiving.

'Rose, don't cry. It is not going to help.'

'I am not.' Then she realised she had pressed the handkerchief to her eyes to shut the world out, not to absorb any tears from her dry eyes. He must think she was trying to gain his sympathy, to soften him, as if that was possible. 'Yes, I want a love match.' She clasped her hands around the handkerchief in her lap. She did not want Adam to believe she would try to manipulate him by weeping.

He sat down on the matching chair facing hers, his forearms on his knees, head bent as if in thought. Or perhaps just to avoid looking at her and letting her see exasperation with her stubbornness on his face. 'You had held out through several Seasons against proposals of marriage. Why, then, did you elope with Haslam only to decide within hours that you did not love him?'

'Why indeed? You think I haven't asked myself

that, over and over again? There are still things I cannot recall, things that do not make sense, but I know I have always felt like that about marriage and I have always felt repelled by the Marriage Mart.'

Rose swallowed, wondering how much she could safely admit. What if he told her parents that there were still gaps in her memory and they sent for a doctor, someone as cold and unfeeling as Lieutenant Foster? But she could tell Adam. 'When I try to think about Gerald, really force myself to think about what happened, I hear that scream in my head again.'

'Then you must not force it.' He sounded as clinical as Lieutenant Foster. She could feel his eyes on her, almost hear him thinking. 'You do not want to tell your parents that things are not right with your memory yet, do you?'

'No. And how can I make a decision about this?' She swept her hand out in a gesture that encompassed him, the room, her every fear and frustration. 'How do I know who I am, what I believe, while I still cannot remember everything?'

'I believe you will recover all your memories,' Adam said slowly. 'Just that not all of them are accessible at the moment.'

'Is that all it is?' She wanted so much to believe him. 'But I have changed, haven't I? I am not the woman you rescued, Adam.'

'She was there the whole time. I have seen what battle can do to the strongest, bravest man. I have seen soldiers stunned by the noise, the horror, the exhaustion until there was nothing but an empty shell. Not all of them came back, but you did. It would be a miracle if you were whole again in days, even weeks. Wounds take time to heal, Rose, whether they are of the body or the mind.'

'Thank you.' He might have spoken as he would to any traumatised fellow officer, but at least he was showing he understood. She wanted to climb into his embrace, be held by those strong arms, be looked after and comforted. She wanted, weakly, to let him carry all the burden of what she had done. She was stronger than that, surely? 'You are very kind to me, you always have been. But I cannot marry you, trap you that way.' She bit her lip. 'Unless there is a child.'

'When will you know whether or not you are with child?'

That she knew with certainty now that her memory was coming back to her. 'Four days.'

'Whether you are with child or not, I am going

to marry you, Rose. I am going to court you, very publically. If you are with child then we will marry as soon as may be. If you are not, we can afford a little more time. You agree?'

'Yes…' She would not do to a child of hers what had been done to Adam, saddling the poor babe with a lifetime of being thought second best because of his parentage. Adam would stop at nothing to prevent that, she was certain, and he was right. 'I agree to that, but if I am not pregnant, then I do not expect you to abide by this. I wish you would listen to what my sense of honour dictates, as well as your own.'

He smiled then. It was a trifle wry, but it was a smile. 'You mean your sense of honour allows you to trifle with me, Miss Tatton? You seduced me and now you want to cast me aside?'

'Oh, you—' Reluctantly she laughed. And perhaps he was right, perhaps she had taken something from him at the same time as she surrendered her virginity that night.

'How do you propose to go about courting me?' There was no point in labouring this now, somehow she must try to discover what the right thing was for both of them.

'I must be guided by you. I am out of practice—'

He checked himself. 'I am not in the habit of wooing respectable young ladies.'

But you have once? And it did not end well, quite obviously. 'You could call tomorrow and take me walking in the Parc at the fashionable hour; that would be a good start. After that I will see if we receive any invitations. Mama will be doing her best as soon as she recovers a little, I have no doubt.'

'Invitations?' Adam sounded as though she expected him to attend a witches' coven.

'Of course. I doubt there will be balls or any large events. Too many people will be in mourning. But there will be dinner parties, suppers, small musical evenings, I am certain. Adam, do you realise you have gone positively pale?' Perversely this sign of weakness in him strengthened her. She needed to stand on her own two feet again and the temptation to simply lean on Adam was strong. It would be easier if he needed to lean on her, just a little.

'I can dance,' he said. 'During the Peninsula campaign, Wellington would have probably shot as unfit for duty any officer who couldn't cut a figure. But dinner parties? Suppers? And what the devil would I be expected to do at a musicale? No.'

His alarm would have been amusing if there was

not a quicksand waiting for just one wrong step and it would be Adam's pride that would sink if she got this wrong. His expression forced the first laugh from her all day. 'Adam, you go into battle on a regular basis. People try to kill you, brutally. You handle explosives and command men who need ferocious discipline, yet you are alarmed at the thought of a dinner party?'

'Yes,' he said bluntly. 'Look, I know perfectly well which knives and forks to use and I won't drink the water out of the finger bowls or remark that the blackberry jam tastes of fish if caviar is served, but I have no experience whatsoever of parties where respectable young ladies are present, or ferocious chaperones or men who want to talk about anything other than war, tactics, hunting, hounds or sex.'

'Adam!' Rose clapped her hand over her mouth to stifle her laughter. It was so good to laugh with him again.

'You wanted the truth,' he said darkly. 'I have no small talk. I don't know what is permissible to say or do with young ladies, let alone their mamas. As far as society women are concerned I am used to army wives and dashing matrons.'

'Respectable young ladies are easy. The game

they are expected to play is that they are ignorant and innocent. They have no opinions, at least none on serious matters and certainly none that might contradict what a gentleman says. Their role is to look pretty and make you feel rich, handsome, clever and dashing. Your role is to make them feel beautiful, charming, fragile and, in the most chaste way possible, desirable.'

'How the devil do I desire a woman chastely?'

'Desirable as a wife, the perfect mother of your children and an uplifting moral influence on your life.'

'May I go and start a small war somewhere instead?' Adam enquired. 'It would be easier.'

'No. Now concentrate. You do not touch them, except to take their hand. You do not stare down the front of their gowns and you never, for a moment, allow yourself to be alone with one of them. With me, as you will be courting me and I am going to encourage you, you may flirt. You do know how to flirt, don't you?'

'With a respectable woman?' When she rolled her eyes at him his mouth twitched into his rare half-smile. 'Very well, I shall pretend I am on a spying mission behind enemy lines. At least no one will shoot me if I let my language slip.'

'No, you will be withered by some terrifying dowager instead. It is Sunday tomorrow. Come with us to the Protestant service at the Chapel Royal. You may find the hymns in my hymnal for me and look solemn.' Rose stood and went to put her arms around his shoulders, rested her cheek on the top of his head. In her embrace Adam went very still. 'I need a hug.'

'I may not touch young ladies except on the hand,' he said as he turned his face into the swell of her bosom. 'If we are to succeed in this without arousing suspicions, Miss Tatton, we cannot afford to slip.'

'That is not my hand you are touching, Major.' She slid down on to his knee and rested her head on his shoulder. 'I need a hug and a kiss, Adam. Just one for courage.'

'So do I,' he said and closed his arms tight around her. 'In this position I can hug or I can kiss.'

'Kiss.' She twisted round, wondering when, if ever, she would have his mouth on hers again, his hands on her body, her hands in the springing texture of his hair.

His lips were bold and sensual, the taste of him on her tongue was achingly familiar and yet she sensed a restraint, as though he was shielding his power from her. He knew they should not be doing this and he was holding back. But it was difficult, she could sense that in every taut line of his body, and she felt a guilty pleasure in that sensual knowledge.

Rose told herself that she was pleased to see Adam the next morning because the evening with her parents had been so difficult, but she could not deceive herself it was not more than that.

'Good morning, Miss Tatton.' He turned from handing his shako and gloves to Heale.

'Good morning.' She moderated her headlong rush down the hall to a ladylike glide. 'Do come into the drawing room. Mama and Papa will be down directly.' Heale opened the door for them and then, very properly, left it wide open.

'What is wrong, Miss Tatton?' Adam was as correctly turned out as the day before.

'Adam, please call me Rose. I cannot get used to being Catherine or Miss Tatton.' *Especially not from you.* 'I keep finding someone has been speaking to me for a good minute without me realising.' She frowned at him. 'You have had your hair cut again.'

'Is that all that is wrong?' He rested one booted

foot on the low fender rail and seemed intent on checking the highly polished leather for scuffs.

'Your hair? No, although I prefer it longer.' It had curled strong and soft between her fingers as she ran them into it when he kissed her. Now she closed her hands tight to stop herself reaching for him. 'No, it is nothing really. Just my name and the fact that I miss Maggie and Moss and that cosy kitchen.' And feeling so guilty about her parents and frightened because being in familiar surroundings had not yet brought all of her memory back.

Adam glanced towards the door and stood up straight. 'Good morning, Lady Thetford, my lord.'

Rose noticed that her mother barely inclined her head in acknowledgment although her father returned the greeting.

'Catherine, do you have your prayer book?' Her mother fussed around her, rather too obviously not looking at Adam. At breakfast Lord Thetford had had to remark sharply that this was the Sabbath before she had stopped declaring that she would be seen in church with *that man* over her dead body.

'Yes, Mama. And money for the collection plate.' *And a clean handkerchief and a large and brooding artillery officer.*

Her father had ordered the landau with the roof

down and the pair of match bays in harness. He and Adam settled opposite the ladies and embarked on a stilted discussion of horses while Lady Thetford sat, fidgeted with her parasol and glanced around as if expecting crowds of hissing ladies, all pointing at Rose and crying scandal.

It was hardly worth taking the carriage—the chapel was at no great distance for a summer's day stroll—but Mama liked to be seen in such a smart equipage and, as she had pointed out the evening before, appearances were even more important now that her daughter was teetering on the brink of disgrace.

In Rose's opinion the large English community in Brussels attended the weekly Protestant service at the Chapel Royal as much for the social event as for devotional purposes. Certainly the latest hats and smartest outfits were being flaunted in the morning sunshine as ladies gathered in small gossiping knots in the square. Rose swallowed hard. This would be worse than her first appearance at Almack's under the critical eye of all the patronesses.

But her father had timed their arrival well. The bell was ringing and the congregation began to enter the building as their carriage drew up. By the time Lady Thetford had fussed her skirts into perfect order, dropped her prayer book, twitched Rose's bonnet ribbons and taken her husband's arm, they were able to join the stragglers without attracting attention.

Adam crooked his elbow and Rose placed her fingertips carefully on his forearm, resisting the temptation to cling on tightly. 'Do you have your own pew?' he asked as they stepped into the shadowy interior with its ornate white marble and grey-veined pillars.

'No, not an allocated one. Mama likes to be about halfway down the aisle on the right though. Have you not attended services here before? They alternate between German and French. It is French today.'

'Not services, no.' He glanced around. 'I brought some of our officers back here the other night.'

It took Rose a moment to realise that he meant he had brought their bodies back, not that a group of them had come here to pray. 'Your younger brother, too?'

'Yes.' He stood aside for Rose to follow her mother into the pew. 'My brother Gideon, too.'

Rose knelt, unable to find anything to say. After a moment she opened her eyes, conscious of her mother on one side and of Adam kneeling on the other, one hand covering his face. Was he thinking about his comrades lying so close? The half-brother he hardly knew? Or his own situation, trapped into play-acting the suitor?

Slightly in front of their pew, on the other side of the aisle, was a familiar blue bonnet. As if Rose's gaze was a touch on the shoulder the woman wearing it turned. Lady Sarah Latymor stared back at them, her eyes red-rimmed, her face pale. Her coat and gloves were black as if in a distracted attempt at mourning. She looked from Rose to Adam's bowed head and back to meet Rose's gaze. Her lips moved soundlessly as she gripped the back of the pew in front and began to rise.

'Adam,' Rose whispered frantically. *'Lady Sarah. She is going to denounce us.'*

Chapter Fifteen

The organ thundered, Lady Sarah turned to face the front and the congregation rose to its feet.

Rose let out a shuddering breath. 'She looks dreadful,' she whispered under cover of Adam helping her find the first hymn in her book. 'But yesterday she was angry, not upset. Do you think Lord Randall, or Major Bartlett, are worse?'

'We will find out after the service,' he murmured. 'No one here looks entirely normal.'

All around were women in mourning of one shade or another, men with bandages or slings, drawn faces. Very few of the English residents would have escaped without the loss or wounding of someone they knew.

Somehow Rose got through the service without standing during prayers or singing the wrong hymn. Finally the organ thundered out the processional again, the clergy and choir filed away to the vestry and the congregation began to get to its feet.

'May I escort Miss Tatton back through the Parc?' Adam asked before they left the pew. 'I can see my half-sister, Lady Sarah Latymor, over there. She appears to be alone.'

'Please, Mama?'

'After yesterday, I thought you two girls were not on friendly terms.'

'I wish to make up,' Rose said earnestly.

'Very well. It is Sunday, after all. I suppose we must all do our Christian duty.' With a look that spoke volumes about her expectations of his behaviour, Lady Thetford nodded in Adam's direction and swept off down the aisle on her husband's arm.

'Miss Tatton.' It was Sarah, right by her elbow.

'Lady Sarah.' Rose took one look at her face and swallowed her apprehension and anger, with the other woman. She was in distress, not plotting more mischief.

'I must speak to you. Both of you.'

'Outside, then.' Adam offered an arm to each and they made their way out of the church. 'Well? Are you satisfied now, Sarah?' he demanded as soon as they were around the corner and into a side street. 'Miss Tatton had lost her memory. If you had stopped, just for a moment, to talk to her, you would have been able to help. Now you have distressed her parents and thrown her into turmoil while she is still recovering.'

'I'm sorry.' All the fight seemed to have gone out of Lady Sarah. 'I was sorry the moment I spoke to your parents, Catherine. But I was so angry with…' She looked at Adam. 'With Adam, my brother. And Gideon was dead and Justin is wounded and they wouldn't let me near him. And Tom—I thought for a while I'd lost him, too.'

She drew a deep breath and visibly got control of herself. 'I saw Justin this morning. He is going to be all right. And we talked about Gideon and how he died so bravely and that you were both with him. And Justin told me you brought him back here, to this church, and didn't leave him out there in that awful place. I won't make any more trouble for you.'

'You had better come with us.' Adam turned and walked back to the church entrance. 'You can't go wandering about Brussels by yourself.'

'I'll be all right, it isn't far and I must get back to Tom.' She stood on tiptoe and kissed Adam's cheek, a sudden glimmer of her old smile back on her face. 'I don't want to be a gooseberry and you seem to have courting to do.' She took half a dozen steps away and then turned. 'I promise I won't make a scandal, tell anyone about you,' she said earnestly, waved her hand and hurried off.

She had forgotten to keep her voice down. Her clear words seemed to echo off the stones, cut through the clear summer air. Heads turned.

'Do you think anyone heard what she said?' Rose made a business of putting up her parasol.

'Probably not.' Adam looked round at the slowly dispersing crowd. 'Or if they did, it wouldn't make any sense and they'll think they misheard. I can only hope she'll not try to be any more help, or I may end up strangling the chit.' He shook his head. 'You know, I can't help liking my little half-sister and I never thought I'd hear myself admit that. At least the news about Randall is good.'

Flint took Rose's arm and made for the steep side street leading up to the Parc. He sensed she was unsettled after that encounter with Sarah and that she was nervous of the attention they were attracting. Enough people knew him, knew who he was, for gossip to start about his courtship of a viscount's daughter. He was ready for it, but he doubted Rose was. Had she ever been the object of gossip in her life? He doubted it. He had, and he knew what they would be saying now.

What is Lord Thetford's daughter doing with Earl Randall's bastard brother? Surely she was flirting with that nice young Haslam who was killed? I don't recall seeing her after the supper dance at the Duchess's ball. Did you see them with his half-sister Lady Sarah just now? What has happened that Thetford would countenance such an escort?

And they would put two and two together and make three or eight and some—and it would only need a few of them—might arrive at something like four.

He had to hope that she was not pregnant, that their courtship could be prolonged to the point where all gossip would die away. And yet... And yet the thought of Rose carrying his child filled him with a sort of wonderful terror. A child to be loved, one with both parents, a child with Rose's eyes.

'Mind that loose paving slab.' He guided Rose with the upper level of his consciousness on the footpath, on watching for pickpockets or loose horses or any of the other myriad hazards of city life, and the deeper level wrestling with unfamiliar hopes.

'I feel much better now,' she confided. Her hand was tucked firmly into the crook of his elbow and she looked up at him with a smile from under the brim of her bonnet. 'Lady Sarah will be no danger to us, your brother is recovering and attending church is behind me now. It will be easier from now on, I am certain.'

I am not. Easier, when she is still so unsettled, when we are about to stir up the whisperers? 'That is a most provoking bonnet, Miss Tatton.' *Flirt, don't worry her with your doubts.*

'In what way, Major?' She was being circumspect now they were nearing the Parc with its promenading crowds. 'Bonnets may be frivolous or expensive or dowdy, but *provoking*?'

'I can see very little of your face.' He leaned down and murmured, 'And I certainly cannot kiss you.'

As he hoped, Rose laughed. 'Wretch, putting me to the blush here of all places.' He felt her stiffen. 'Mrs Harrison and her daughters are going to stop.'

Flint saluted and allowed Rose to introduce him to the Harrisons, Mama and three very pretty daughters rather younger than Rose.

'Major Flint.' Mrs Harrison smiled and nodded. She obviously had no idea who he was. 'You escaped the battle without serious injury, I trust? Our own dear Charles is still laid up with a nasty bullet wound in the leg, but regaining his strength daily. He is in the Rifles, you know.' She did not pause for him to answer, but turned to Rose. 'And you, my dear, I declare we haven't seen you since the Duchess's ball. It was so affecting, seeing all those brave officers leave like that. Mind you, I thought it did the Duchess no credit, the way she ran around trying to make people stay.'

'I...I left before that, Mrs Harrison. I found it difficult to witness.' Flint watched with some concern as Rose bit her lip and seemed to falter, then breathed out as she smiled and confessed, 'I have been such a coward. It was all so awful I have been at home ever since. I was not well and then Mama would not allow me to go out with all the men on the streets—such dreadful sights.'

'But now you are quite recovered again, I can tell. Excellent, my dear.'

The Harrisons moved on and Flint squeezed Rose's arm against his side. 'Well done.' He wanted to hug her, kiss her, take her mind off all the nosy biddies. He wanted to take her to bed, and that had nothing to do with her welfare, as he knew perfectly well.

The truth was, he had grown accustomed to her, attuned to her, in a way he had never experienced with another woman. She had become a necessary drug to him, both stimulating him and soothing him. Was it because he was her first lover? He was going to be her last as well, he was determined on that and he recognised the possessive instinct that swept over him as something new.

Never before had he fought against that moment when it seemed time for a parting of the ways, but now he knew he would do whatever it took to keep Rose, regardless of whether she was carrying his child or not.

This business of walking in the Parc was simple enough, Flint concluded after twenty minutes of uneventful socialising. Smile, salute, keep half an ear on the small talk, make certain he showed Rose nothing but the most respectful, and slightly distant, attention. He obviously had a highly inflated opinion of his own notoriety for no one had so much as raised an eyebrow at being introduced to him and several ladies had given him their card and pointed out the days they were At Home.

They had almost reached the far end. 'Would you like to walk back along another path and look at the palace? There's nothing much to be seen around headquarters, everything is packed up to follow Wellington towards Paris.'

'Then let us go back towards the palace by all means. It is too nice a morning to go inside before we have to. Do you wish you were with the army, Adam, not stuck in Brussels?'

'Yes. No. Hell, I don't know. Napoleon is in Paris, they say, Wellington's chasing, he's probably at Cambrai by now. They may need artillery there, but they've got enough without me or the Rogues.'

He never thought he would say that, never thought he would lose his taste for a fight. Was this attachment to Rose making him soft? Probably not. He had come to the end of that chapter of his life, the world was changing, he was changing and it had taken this situation to make him face the fact.

'I'm probably best doing what I can here. The soldiers need keeping an eye on.' As men began to recover they were more of a handful, although to be honest he was grateful for the work to take his mind off Rose and the fact that his bed was cold at night.

'Adam, I think those ladies over there know you.' Rose's elbow was sharp in his ribs. 'They seem to be trying to attract your attention.'

Ladies? Surely not. Pointing or muttering, perhaps. Or Rose was too innocent to recognise a high flier when she saw one. He followed her gaze and almost turned on his heel. An expensive bit of muslin would be preferable to the two bearing down on them.

'Lady Archer, Mrs Gardener.' *Just nod and carry on past...* But, no, they had to stop and exclaim in delight over his being safe and well. They begged an introduction to Rose, they said nothing whatsoever out of place and their smiles and their eyes and their fingertips on his arm all shouted as loudly as a scream that they had both been in his bed and would be pleased to repeat the experience.

He dared not snub them, certainly had no intention of responding to their overtures, but they seemed to understand why all too well and their expressions as they studied Rose said quite clearly that they admired his enterprise, and probably his presumption, too.

'Do look after our hero, Miss Tatton,' Mrs Gardener said, smiling at Rose in a way that had Flint itching to pitch her into the nearby fountain. 'He is such a dear friend from Peninsula days. Good day, Major. You must come to the little reception I am holding tomorrow. Don't stand on ceremony.' She lowered her lashes over wide blue eyes. 'But then, you never did.'

Rose must have been holding her breath until they were out of earshot, he heard her expel it in one furious *whoosh*. 'Two of your mistresses at once, Major? They were your mistresses, I take it? Are we likely to encounter any more?'

She tugged her hand out from his arm and stalked off to the nearest bench, her skirt flicking in time with her angry gait. Flint took one moment to admire the sway of her hips and the hint of deliciously rounded bottom the swinging skirt outlined, then joined her. Rose sat and crossed her arms in as clear a display of rejection as he'd ever seen. 'Well?' She was furious and he found it curiously arousing. *She is jealous.*

'They were never my mistresses. Lovers, yes, occasionally.' He set one booted foot on the bench halfway along and leaned his elbow on his knee, his body as he turned towards her effectively screening her from passers-by.

'Both together?' she asked in an outraged squeak.

'Certainly not.' Although they'd have been game for it, he was quite certain.

'And they are widows?'

'No.'

'Then that, Major, was adultery.' She turned and stared at the fountain as though it was of riveting interest. 'And their husbands were your fellow officers, I presume?'

Flint swore silently in Spanish, French and gutter English. Put like that it sounded both dishonourable and immoral. 'They are both in marriages that were in name only.' He hated justifying himself, let alone to Rose, but the cat was out of the bag now, she would never trust him if he could not make her understand. 'Archer is considerably older than his wife and no longer able to get it...I mean, no longer able to perform his marital duties.' Now he sounded like the parson. 'Gardener is not sexually interested in women. And you will not repeat that.'

'I have no intention of discussing your amorous encounters,' Rose snapped. 'What do you mean, not sexually interested in women? You mean he has taken a vow of celibacy?'

'No,' Flint retorted. 'He prefers men for sex.'

'What?' She stared at him. 'I had no idea, I have never heard of such a thing.'

'Because it is against the law and a hanging offence.' Flint grounded his foot and sat down beside her, disconcerted by the hazel eyes fixed on his face. 'It isn't all that uncommon, actually. One just ignores it.'

'You…I mean…um…' Rose looked away so he could just see the curve of her cheek. It was flushed pink.

'No. You may have noticed I find women desirable,' he said drily. 'Anyway, lonely, frustrated women will look for a lover, more often than not. In this case their husbands looked the other way.'

'How convenient for all concerned.' Her voice was bleak. 'I am obviously very unsophisticated about marriage.'

'Rose, when I marry you I will not go with other women. I will not take a sudden interest in pretty lads and should my wedding tackle ever fail to function I can assure you that you will not be left unsatisfied. Is that plain enough for you?'

'Exceedingly plain.' Rose's cheeks were a hectic red now. 'As I said, I am apparently very naive. I was not so foolish as to believe that you'd had no women in your life before, you told me as much.

But somehow I did not expect to meet them. Is that likely to happen very often?'

There had been a few years after the humiliation of the fiasco with Patricia Harte when he had been glad to salve his wounded pride with willing, neglected ladies. Gradually he had become conscious of a growing distaste. He was using them, they were using him and it felt underhand. He began to have liaisons with camp followers, women who had a warmth and a practical loyalty about them that encompassed the uncertain life expectancy of their partners. He knew he was not easy to live with and he never attempted to hold them in the relationship. It had seemed a better way to carry on than—

'I see.' Rose stood up and he realised that his few seconds of thought had appeared to her to be a tacit admission that Brussels was probably swarming with his past lovers.

'Rose, I honestly do not know. Not many. I am hardly Don Juan. I am sorry, it never occurred to me that you would be embarrassed by this. '

'Or that I would ever find out, I imagine. I would like to go home now.' She set off down the path and unfurled her parasol, almost putting his eye out with it as she did so.

'Rose, I cannot help my past, all I can do is to promise you that I will be utterly faithful to you.'

'Forgive me, Major Flint, but somehow I do not find that very reassuring.'

'Damn it!' She kept on going. Flint strode past and stood in her path. 'Are you doubting my word?'

That confounded parasol stopped him seeing her face, she wielded it with the skill of a fencer. '*I do not know!* Adam, I thought I was in love with you. Now…now I have no idea what I think.'

Love? It knocked the breath out of him for a moment, long enough for her to sweep past him. Rose was in love with him? Flint struggled to breathe as though someone had punched him in the solar plexus. What the devil did that *mean*? If she was in love, then why fight against marriage?

'Rose, calm down. This is getting out of hand.' Even as he said it he knew the words were a mistake. You did not tell a woman who had just declared that your past behaviour had probably killed her love for you to *calm down.*

She kept going. 'Did I say I didn't know what to think? Silly me. I know precisely what I think. And I am as calm as I wish to be. Good day, Major Flint.'

Short of throwing her over his shoulder he did

not see how he could stop her. French cavalry was easier to deal with by a long mile. Flint fell into step behind her imperious, furious figure across the Parc and the few hundred yards to the house.

It was just a tiff, he told himself. Her nose had been put out of joint, that was all. They had been in perfect harmony before, she thought she might be in love with him. It would soon blow over.

He stood at the foot of the steps as she hammered on the front door, waited while Heale opened it.

'Miss Tatton,' the butler said on a gasp.

'That man—' Rose turned and pointed at Flint. 'I am not At Home to that man. Ever.'

The door banged closed in his face as he took the steps, three in one stride. 'Rose.' *Rose.*

Chapter Sixteen

'Miss Tatton.' Heale's voice stopped her as she reached the foot of the stairs. 'Lady Thetford is not yet home. Shall I send your maid to you?'

'No, thank you.' It took a moment to collect herself sufficiently to fix a smile on her lips when she turned back to the butler. 'A lovers' tiff, Heale, that is all. Please do not say anything to my parents.'

The smile seemed to reassure him. Heale was, she recalled, a terrible romantic behind the stiff butler's facade. 'My lips are sealed, Miss Tatton.'

Rose ran upstairs to her room and locked the door. The nagging memories had crystallised into a certainty, the knowledge that she had been avoiding marriage because men let her down. Or perhaps, she thought as she took off her bonnet and pelisse and curled up on the window seat, perhaps she had been very naive in her expectations.

She looked down at the empty street. Of course Adam was not pacing up and down outside, distracted with despair because she'd run from him. *He's got more sense*, she thought with a little laugh that threatened to turn into a sob. There was an ache in her midriff over that encounter with his past lovers. It had hurt and shocked her far more than it should have done, given that Adam was a soldier, not a monk. Of course he'd had lovers, she told herself. And why should he tell her about them? No gentleman would reveal such things to his betrothed.

I can forgive him those women, even the society ladies, yet I was never so forgiving in the past. Perhaps I never loved anyone enough to forgive.

Would her diaries tell her more? She had never thought to read them once the therapy of writing was done. Rose went to the chest at the foot of the bed and lifted the stack of blankets out to reveal the piece of paper concealing the base. That lifted away and she could hook her little finger into the knothole in the middle and lift the board out. The space created by the ornate carving around the bottom was packed with slim leather-bound books.

Rose lifted out the most worn, then sat back on her heels and stared at it.

Catherine Tatton. Her Diary. 1809.

That was her name and for the first time it felt real, as though it belonged to her. This was the diary she had been given by her godmother for the Christmas before she made her come-out and the others had arrived every year since.

Rose piled the volumes on her writing desk, set the room to rights and rang for her maid.

Jane came in and began to gather up her discarded bonnet, gloves and parasol. 'Was there anything else, Miss Catherine?'

'Should my mother enquire, please tell her I am reading quietly in my room.' With any luck, given that it was Sunday, her mother would assume she was perusing the book of sermons she had left rather obviously on top of the dresser the day before. 'I will take a light luncheon on a tray, here.'

'Yes, miss.' Jane draped the pelisse over her arm. 'I'll tell the kitchen.'

As soon as she was alone Rose took the first volume and curled up in the armchair. There were the details of six years of her life to restore. Perhaps when she had reached the end she would know what had made her the woman who had so recklessly run away with Gerald, the woman who found it so difficult to trust even the man she was almost certain she loved.

'Ah, there you are.' Lady Thetford looked up from her embroidery as Rose entered the drawing room. 'That is a pretty gown, I knew I was right about the floss trim at the hem.' She regarded the evening dress with approval. 'Your papa will be down shortly. And how was your walk with Major Flint this morning?'

'It was very pleasant, Mama. We met a number of ladies of our acquaintance.' *And two of his.* She found her own sewing box and took out the hand-kerchief she had been decorating with a mono-gram. She had gone to the box without having to think about it, another sign that her memory was returning, and bending over the intricate white work was as good a way to shield her face and her emotions as any.

'And so did we.' Lady Thetford held up several strands of pink silk to the light and regarded them dubiously. 'The salmon or the blush pink? The blush, I think. What was I saying? Ah, yes. I had several useful encounters and have three invita-tions to show for it.

'Lady Hemmingford is holding a small soirée

tomorrow night and invites all of us, including the major. She says it is quite impromptu as she was seeing who was in town first. Then Mrs Grace tells me that the dinner party she had invited us to several weeks ago is still to go ahead. She has had to revise the table somewhat as her nephew was injured, but that means she can fit in the major. And Lady Anderson is having an afternoon tea party in her garden on Thursday, provided the weather holds. And of course I secured an invitation for Major Flint.'

'Thank you, Mama.' A pinprick of blood welled up on her finger. How had that happened? 'Everyone we met was friendly. It seems no one suspects anything even though I have not been seen for several days.'

'Such a relief. Are you still feeling very low about all of this, Catherine, dear? I think I may become resigned to your major, you know. His behaviour and appearance this morning were beyond reproach and your papa has told me he is impressed with his straightforward manner.' She threaded her needle with bright green and began to attack a pattern of trailing vines.

'His birth is highly regrettable, naturally, but then, if you will go refusing a succession of perfectly eligible gentlemen, Season after Season, and crown it all by running off with a penniless lieutenant, we must be grateful for a good-looking man with manners and money in the funds.'

'Funds?' Adam had no money, surely? He seemed to have his uniform, half a dozen shirts, a horse and dog to his name.

'Of course he has, dearest. And letters from his bankers to prove it. I must admit that was when I began to think more positively of him, for I can acquit him of fortune hunting. Your papa says he seems to have simply saved everything he has earned for years and invested it very wisely. Which is particularly gratifying because it does demonstrate that he is not given to expensive vices like gaming or…er…'

'Loose women?' Rose enquired. Adam didn't need to pay for them, it seemed—they lined up for admission to his bed.

'Really, dear! A lady does not acknowledge such creatures. We have discussed that before.'

'How is one to know whether a prospective husband indulges in vice in that case?' Other than overhearing him bragging to his friends. That was what had saved her from her first mistake when, halfway through her debut Season, she had found herself outside the library door at a ball and heard Lord Philip Weston informing his brother that not only had he found himself a well-bred heiress, but the silly little peahen believed herself in love with him.

The peahen in question had cried herself to sleep for a week and then cut Lord Philip dead when she next encountered him. The diary had charted the heartache of a wiser and more cautious Miss Tatton. Handsome young lords were obviously not to be trusted, but older, more sober gentlemen could not be so two-faced, surely? The Earl of Harwich had seemed perfect. His respectful courtship, his manly declaration of love, his respectable way of life all convinced her that she was safe to give him her heart. It was his—until her best friend Miss Winstanley whispered that there had been the most terrible scene outside White's the night before when the discarded, pregnant mistress of the earl had waylaid him on the steps and demanded he provide for the babe.

And so it continued for Season after Season. Miss Tatton learned to investigate her suitors with great care and all of them proved to have feet of clay in one way or another. They harassed female servants at house parties, they gambled excessively, they were cruel to their horses or they lied about their wealth. Her judgement of men was obviously completely awry, she had confided to her diary on the third of March last year. Either she could not bring herself to trust or she could not fall in love with the right man.

Love was important, Rose thought now. Mutual love, or how could men resist the lures of other women? Even honourable men seemed to find it acceptable to keep mistresses. It was an impossible situation, she pondered, sucking her sore fingertip. If she allowed herself to love and was betrayed, then her heart would be broken and she would be tied to the man who broke it. If she made a marriage without love then she might as well resign herself to betrayal from the start. Adam would never deliberately hurt her, she was certain, but it would be a cold thing to marry a husband you loved but who did not love you.

When she had cautiously probed the subject with Mama months ago she had been told merely that a lady did not even think about husbands straying. Such things were below her notice and one ignored them as loftily as one did when one's carriage horse passed water in the middle of Rotten Row.

That had chilled her. *What if Papa...?* she had begun in her diary that night and then hastily crossed it through. Every man who courted her had some flaw in his character which meant she could not give him her respect, let alone her heart. In March she had begun to worry that the fault lay with her. Was she attractive only to fortune hunters or cynical rakes? Or was she, in turn, only attracted to that sort of man?

Which was why, she now realised, she had talked herself into love with Gerald. He was good-looking, he was kind and, as an officer, he was surely courageous. He was not, she confided in her diary, exactly intellectual. But then a kind heart was far better than a cutting wit. Even her most exacting enquiries had revealed nothing to his discredit and perilously eavesdropping outside the billiards room at a party had caught him confessing to nothing more wicked than attending a prize fight.

It had been a shock when Papa had refused his suit on her behalf, but to Gerald's credit he had not suggested the elopement. That had been her idea.

'Why are you moping?' Mama demanded, jerking her back to the present.

'Am I?' She supposed she was. Reading six years of romantic disillusionment in one sitting was enough to make one positively blue deviled. But at least she now knew what her instincts had been trying to tell her. She was a dreadful judge of men. 'I was thinking about poor Gerald.' The anxiety that she had used him for her own purposes was weighing on her conscience. Was she no better than the men she despised for deceiving her?

'It is very sad, but you can console yourself with the thought that his fate had nothing to do with the elopement.' Lady Thetford was robust. 'And he was doing his duty in a noble cause.'

'Yes, Mama.' And she had been some comfort to him all through that dreadful night, she thought now. But her motives had been selfish. What a mess. At least she could make amends for heaping the sins of those other men on Adam's head. But they must still talk, she still wanted, *needed*, reassurance about how he looked at marriage. 'I must write to Major Flint,' she said. 'Is there time before dinner?'

'I think so.' Her mother glanced at the mantel clock. 'You will want to tell him about the invitations, I imagine.'

Those, of course, and to apologise for slamming the door in his face and denying him the house. She owed him that, at least. If she had not eloped in the first place, none of this would have happened; it was up to her to put things right. If she was not with child, then perhaps she could persuade him, and her parents, that he need not tie himself to her. She wished she knew what was the right thing to do.

When the note was written she handed it to Heale. 'Please see this is delivered to Major Flint's lodgings as soon as you can spare a footman from dinner service. And, Heale, I did not mean what I said about denying me to the major. He will be received whenever he calls.'

Flint flattened the single sheet of notepaper under his hand and read it yet again. It had arrived last night while he had been out at a meeting with the other officers and NCOs who had been left in charge in the city, and he had tossed it, unread, on to the litter of reports on his desk.

To the devil with all women, he had thought as he pulled off his clothes and fell into bed. He could do without pages of reproaches on top of a heap of medical reports, statistics, charge sheets and the court martial of a corporal accused of rape.

This morning, fortified by one of Maggie's breakfasts, he had opened it and found, not a lecture on his sins, but one side of neatly written apology for Rose's 'overreaction' and a list of social engagements. He had to confess himself surprised. Rose had been distressed and embarrassed and he could appreciate why. She had been in tears and that felt…uncomfortable.

In his experience distressed, embarrassed ladies expressed themselves with flying china and raised voices. Rose, it seemed, was out of the ordinary. Unless, of course, reflection had shown her that far from thinking herself in love with him, she really did not care enough to be angry.

Flint stared at the list of hospitals he was to visit that day until the words blurred out of focus. Which was better? A wife who loved him and who he was bound to hurt because he had no idea how to love a wife in return, or one who could barely tolerate him and who had been forced into the marriage to escape ruin? What did love even feel like, anyway? He certainly was not in the besotted state he had occasionally observed in his friends, although half the time he suspected they were being led by their wedding tackle and not their hearts.

That he could understand. Sex was straightforward. A memory of one lady and her tricks with a pair of silk stockings and a hairbrush gave him pause. *Mostly* straightforward. Making love with Rose was better than with anyone else in his experience. Perhaps that was because she was so fresh, so unjaded. He dipped his quill into the inkpot and then sat while it dripped on to the desk as he thought about pale, silky skin, the perfect weight of her breasts in his hands, the taste of her on his lips.

Yes, sex was straightforward. But the way he felt after he had made her so upset, no, that was not straightforward at all. 'Damnation!' He blotted at the ink with his pen wiper. Now he had to spend the next two evenings trussed up in his dress uniform doing the pretty. Just what did one do at a soirée anyway?

It appeared that at soirées one stood around and talked whilst being deafened by shrill female voices and at the same time tried not to spill one's drink down the gown of the lady nearest you or be caught rolling your eyes at other male sufferers. It was also necessary to keep one's temper with simpering chits who wanted to coo over him because he must be a hero, male civilians who thought they could have fought the battle better than Wellington and anguished ladies who wanted to talk about the poor dear young men who had been killed or wounded.

It was all made considerably worse by the need to drag Rose off to some secluded corner and kiss her until that cool, bleak look vanished from her eyes.

Finally, under the pretext of presenting her with a glass of lemonade, he managed to say, 'I want to talk to you.'

'We are talking.' She was wearing a moss-coloured gown that made her eyes more green than hazel, striking amber jewellery and her hair was swept up into a complex of swirls and plaits that made him want to remove every single pin in it.

'Alone. And not at the top of our voices.'

'What do you want to talk about?' She sipped her lemonade and smiled at a passing captain of dragoons in a way that had Flint's hand tightening on the hilt of his dress sword.

'Us. Yesterday.'

Her lips pursed in a little pout that did nothing for his internal turmoil. 'It is rather warm and there is a terrace at the side, I think.' Without waiting for his reply she turned and led the way through the crowd, nodding and smiling and exchanging the odd word here and there. Finally they arrived at a curtained alcove. 'Through here.'

Flint followed her, across a lobby, through glazed doors and on to a deserted terrace. 'Excellent. How did you know this was here? Is this where you would flirt with Haslam?'

Rose turned away abruptly. 'Beast!'

'I am sorry.' He was, he discovered, jealous that she could be so touchy on behalf of the unfortunate lieutenant. 'Look, Rose, about yesterday. If I could have kept you from meeting those two, I would have done, not because I am ashamed of my past but because it *is* the past.'

'But you condone adultery. Obviously you do or you would not have slept with two married women. And those are just the ones I know about.'

'I did not break those marriages, they were already broken. I cannot imagine being unfaithful to you.'

She turned a shoulder, almost as though she was shrugging him off.

Flint moved closer, lowered his voice. 'If you are carrying my child, Rose, then you will marry me, trust me or not.' She would wed him anyway, he had ruined her, but at least if she was not pregnant he had longer to make her happy about it first. 'You said you thought you loved me.'

'Love?' She turned then, so close he could gather her into his arms, so he did, expecting a slapped cheek. But she came easily, slid her hands up to his shoulders, tilted her face to look into his.

It took him time to get his impulses under control and give her the kiss that was prudent for a couple only feet away from a society gathering. He did not feel prudent. What he wanted was to ravage her mouth, tear off that lovely gown, plunge into her body and take her over the edge again and again, gasping his name. He wanted...Rose. *Just Rose.*

'Love,' she murmured again. 'What has that got to do with it, I keep asking myself? I don't know, Adam. I wish I understood marriage, what it would mean for me. For us.'

Flint did not understand marriage either, he was quite certain about that. All he knew was that he wanted Rose, that he did not need to explain the fact with nonsense about love and that he was weary of balancing on the edge of his career, on the edge of a new beginning, on the edge of honour. So he kissed her because it was easier than talking, easier than trying to make sense of this. He kissed her and gave up on prudence.

He took her mouth as though it were a cup of water and he was dying of thirst. He lashed her to him with one arm as she gasped and he pushed the fragile sleeve of her gown from her shoulder with fingers that shook as they closed over the curve of her breast and found her nipple. Rose gasped again, shuddered and raked her fingers into his hair, dragging his mouth to hers.

The silk and gauze slipped and her whole breast was cupped in his palm and he had no idea if the moans came from her throat or his. It was only when he found his other hand was on the falls of his trousers that reality hit him like the butt of a rifle. 'Rose.'

She opened her eyes, wide and dark as though she had used belladonna drops. 'Adam. We can't, not here…' She fumbled with the bodice of her gown, pushed up the sleeve, turned and walked swiftly back to the doors. 'I'm sorry. I wish…' she murmured and was gone.

Chapter Seventeen

Adam came back into the reception room ten minutes later. Rose told herself that it was her imagination that he reminded her of the Devil who had come out of the smoke and the mud to kill the demons who threatened her, that the bleak darkness in his eyes and the unsmiling set of his face was simply the expression of a man irritated by inane chatter, an overheated room and sexual frustration. Should she have found some secluded corner with him? No, he was uncomfortable about compromising her here, he had stopped first, after all.

'My dear Miss Tatton, your major is a rather intimidating beast, is he not?' Lady Grantly fluttered her fan in the direction of Adam, who had propped one shoulder against a pillar and was eyeing the room over the rim of a champagne flute. 'He looks like a great cat wondering which poor little mouse to pounce upon next. Quite…thrilling.'

'I suspect Major Flint merely has a headache, Lady Grantly. And he is hardly *my* major. We have only recently become acquainted.'

'Oh? I mustn't leap to conclusions, must I?' The older woman's gaze sharpened on Rose's face. Rose did her best to look calmly amused and not like a wanton who had been locked in an indecent embrace only minutes before.

'No doubt I misunderstood what I overheard that sad romp Lady Sarah Latymor say outside the Chapel Royal on Sunday. She is the major's half-sister, I believe.'

'Yes. As you say, she is rather too lively on occasion and she delights in teasing the major. Do excuse me, I see the Misses Hughes bearing down on the poor man. I must go and rescue him.'

'Adam?' She had no need to touch him. He seemed to have eyes in the back of his head and she was quite certain he knew she had been working her way through the guests to his side.

'If you say you are sorry again,' he remarked softly, 'I am going to announce our betrothal here and now.'

'Then I will say that I regret not keeping my

feelings to myself until we had the opportunity to…talk in private.' She bowed to some passing acquaintances and tried to ignore the way his lips curved into a sensual, mocking smile at her euphemism. 'I have been doing a lot of thinking. I found my diaries, you see.'

'And you will take up your pen and start to add entries again? I would be interested to read them.'

'You think it would flatter your self-esteem?' She showed her teeth in a smile, used her fan, did her best to give the impression of flirtation. How could she write about making love with Adam? The paper would scorch if she ever found the words.

'I would like to think so. But perhaps not. You said you might love me.'

What had prompted her to such an admission, one that laid her open to such pain? She shrugged and lied. 'I was upset. Women prefer to gloss their physical desires with a coat of love, I fear. It makes us feel more…ladylike.'

That surprised a snort of laughter from him. 'Admitting to hypocrisy, Rose?'

'Aren't we all hypocrites? Or, at the least, very good actors? Look around you. Look at us. How can any of us ever know what is really going on in the mind of other people?'

'You know it when people are pushed to their extremity,' Adam said, all the laughter gone. 'When they are afraid, that is when you see cowardice and courage, fears and resolve. And again, when they make love, everything, all pretence, is stripped away.'

'Truly?' That had never occurred to her. What had she seen of Adam when she lay in his arms, when they had been stripped of everything but the most primal pleasure? She had seen a strong man without his defences or pretence, she realised. 'But women who are…professional, don't they have to pretend all the time?'

'Yes.' Adam drained his glass and set it down on a nearby table. 'And they are very skilled at it. But you can tell if they are holding back, reserving themselves behind a mental wall.'

Is that where they might see the truth in each other and learn to trust? In bed, making love? But now that intimacy was denied them, closed off until they were married, by which time it would be too late. *Or is it?*

'Look, Mama is signalling that they are about to leave.'

'Will they allow me to walk you home, do you think?' Adam rested his hand in the small of her back, guiding her as they made their way over to their hostess to take their leave. She wanted to lean back against that broad palm and those long fingers, that focus of heat and that possessive touch. 'I would like to talk with you alone.'

'It is not so very far.' Perhaps it was for the best, too much had been said tonight to leave unexplored. And perhaps they would kiss again. 'Ask them.'

He already was, his rare, and very charming, smile deployed to tactical advantage. *Mama is already more than resigned to him as a son-in-law. So is Papa.*

'There is a full moon,' Adam said. 'And such a beautiful view from the ramparts walk in moonlight. I would like to show Miss Tatton.'

'Do not let her get chilled,' Lord Thetford said, the sternness countered by a nod of approval.

'You have won them over,' Rose said as Adam swirled her evening cloak around her shoulders and her parents went down the steps to their waiting carriage.

'I have simply been straightforward with them.' He tucked her hand under his elbow and flipped one side of his own cloak back so his sword hand was free. Rose did not think he expected footpads in the well-lit elegant streets, it was simply an automatic gesture of readiness that made her heart beat a little faster. She was being protected by a warrior.

'Your father appreciates that I did not attempt to wriggle out of responsibility and the fact that I have money enough for comfort, if not luxury. Your mother finds me alarming and more than a little shocking, but she is also comforted by the thought that I would put a bullet in anyone who threatened you.'

'Mama is not so bloodthirsty!'

'Believe me, she is in the defence of her only daughter. I would not have given a fig for my life if she had been holding a loaded gun when I walked into your drawing room the day you returned home. Wait until you have a child and see if you are not prepared to kill or be killed for her. Giving you a large, fierce mongrel guard dog makes perfect sense to Lady Thetford.'

'Was your mother so protective of you?' Was this dangerous ground to stray on to?

'Lord, yes.' She could feel him relax beside her. 'She was a miniature dragon. All this—' he waved his free hand down the length of his body '—is purely my dearest papa. My mother was about five foot three, a pocket Venus with the heart of a tiger. I suspect the only thing that stopped her putting a bullet in the earl was the thought that she'd be abandoning me.'

'But you joined the army so young,' Rose protested. How could any woman let a fourteen-year-old boy go off to war?

'I went when she was at market.' The tension was back in the long body so close to hers. 'My grasp of tactics was good even then.'

'But you saw her again?' *Oh, that poor woman.*

'No.' There was a long, aching pause. 'She died the following year giving birth to her husband's child.' Another pause. 'I had thought she was safe once she was married.'

Rose wanted to stop right there and weep. Instead she made her voice as steady as his. 'When did you hear about it?'

'A month or so after the funeral. A lad from our village joined up.'

They walked in silence for a few minutes while she fought for some composure.

'Rose? You are very quiet.'

'I am trying not to cry.'

'Over me?' Adam sounded bemused.

'Of course over you, you great clothhead.'

'Other than my mother I do not think anyone has ever wanted to weep over me,' he said eventually.

'No heartbroken women?'

'I do not break hearts,' he said firmly.

Only mine. I do love him and yet I cannot see behind that facade, she thought as she swallowed the tears he would reject. He would have her believe he was not affected by his upbringing, but she was certain the scars still hurt. Under that tough exterior was the rebellious boy who feared he had abandoned his mother. He called himself her *fierce mongrel guard dog*. This pretence of a courtship was forcing him to confront the fact of his birth every minute they were in company. If they married, would the whispers ever stop? *Mrs Flint? She's the daughter of a viscount, but he's base-born, of course...*

It mattered not one whit to her. Adam had made himself a gentleman in every way that mattered, but she feared she would never convince him that was what she believed. And what basis was that for a marriage, where one partner knew he had been trapped and the other had no confidence he could remain faithful to her when all the time he was being punished for gallantry and kindness?

'Explain love to me,' Adam said abruptly. 'Not mother and child, or friendship love. Love between men and women.'

'I'm not sure I can.' Rose stopped under a street lamp and tried to see his face.

His shako shadowed his expression, but his voice was faintly mocking when he said, 'You thought you were in love with Haslam.'

'And I was not. I believe now that I had become afraid that there was something wrong with me, that I could never trust enough to love. Gerald was very sweet, very open. It was all on the surface with him, no dark, hidden corners.' *Not like you.*

'Hmm.' Adam's mouth twisted as if he had bitten a lemon. 'No dark corners, but he was prepared to elope with a young lady, marriage to whom would be advantageous. He took you even after your father had turned him down, even when his duty should have told him he would be needed to fight at any moment.'

'Are you saying Gerald wanted me for my money? Because I was a good match?'

Flint shrugged. 'Yes. Obviously.'

It took a moment for the full insult to sink in.

When it did her face stung with the heat of the blood in her cheeks. 'I do not know, Major Flint, which is more breathtaking, your complete lack of tact or your opinion that no man would want me for anything other than mercenary gain!' The fact that she had confided those fears to her diary did not excuse him coming right out and saying it, damn him.

'Did he know you well? Was he a friend, a lover?'

'No, of course not. You know he was not my lover.' There was a nasty acid knot in her stomach. Gerald hadn't wanted her for herself either. *Obviously.* She had been deceived yet again and everyone else could see it but her.

'And nor was he your friend. Rose, listen to me. I know you. I *am* your lover, I have seen you in circumstances that strip a person's soul bare. I know I want you because of who you are, what you are, not who your father is or how large your dowry.'

She tried to make sense of his words, unwilling to focus on them too hard in case she misunderstood. But she had to ask him. 'Adam, are you saying you're in love with me?'

He shifted abruptly and now she could see his face. It was not that of a lover, it was the face of a tough, unsentimental fighter backed into a corner. 'How the blazes do I know?' he demanded. 'I've just said I don't understand love. Why is that women are so fixated on it anyway? I'm in lust with you, I like you, I want to look after you and it is my duty to marry you. Isn't that enough?'

'No. No, it isn't.' Rose backed away. One step, two. 'I cannot trust without love, I cannot see beyond the surface without love.' Adam reached out and caught her by the wrist before she could retreat any further. 'You say you have never broken hearts, but you would break mine even more easily than you could break my wrist.'

His fingers closed over the narrow bones, the stammering beat of her pulse, encircling them completely, a hold as careful and as unbreakable as Dog's jaws closing on a newborn lamb that needed carrying. 'Rose, take what we already have, stop thinking so much.'

'I cannot stop thinking,' she protested.

'We've got this.' He tugged gently until they were toe to toe, then traced the curve of her lips with his forefinger, the calloused, slightly rough tip fretting at the delicate skin. She shivered, wanting more. Wanting him. 'You came to my bed, Rose. There must have been something you desired, even then.'

'I still do,' she admitted, unable to look away from his mouth. The corner kicked up into the secret smile he seemed to save for her alone. 'I had never thought about men like that before, not... carnally.'

'Carnally. Fancy word for something simple. All your barriers were down, Rose, that's all. You weren't thinking then, just feeling. You went with your instincts to trust me.'

'That makes sense.' Her voice seemed to come from a long way away and she still could not tear her gaze away from his mouth. His evening beard was just beginning to grow back, despite a close shave, and the dark shadow threw the sensual curve into sharper relief. There was a tiny scar at the right-hand corner. His own finger rested lightly under the swell of her own lower lip, quite still. She opened her mouth and touched it with the tip of her tongue and Adam's tongue moved over his own lips in response.

'I miss you in my bed.'

'I miss being there.'

'This close to your courses there is little risk and besides, I would be careful.'

'Adam, this is not sensible, not when we are both

in such a muddle over what to do.' Her protests sounded thin to her own ears.

'Whatever else I am in, it is not a muddle.'

'Well, it is academic anyway. We most certainly cannot go back to your rooms and I can hardly lower a knotted sheet from my window.' It was as though she had drunk too much champagne. One minute confused and on the edge of angry, now yearning to be tangled in Adam's arms, their bare skin—

'It is a warm night. The grass is dry.' He was eyeing the railings around the Parc with a speculative eye.

'Outside? In a public park? Adam, that is wicked!' A laugh escaped her, an excited, scandalised laugh. 'Besides, I could not climb that fence.'

'No, I suppose not, in that gown.' His mouth curved into a wicked smile. 'On the other hand, there are no railings to keep us off the ramparts walk.'

'Outside?' Rose repeated. 'What if anyone were to see us?' She was already halfway to agreeing, she realised. Adam started walking again, taking the side turning that led to the ramparts, now a grassy promenade lined with trees.

'It is deserted. See?' They stepped out on to

the walk, the view of the forest beyond bathed in moonlight, tranquil and mysterious as though a battle had never been fought beyond its borders. 'Besides,' he whispered in her ear, 'that little *frisson* of fear adds to the excitement.'

'Adam, you are outrageous!'

'I intend to be.' He took her hand and led the way down a winding path down the outer bank, a thin dark line in the moonlight. It vanished into a patch of small trees and bushes.

'How did you know this was here?'

'Dog chased a rabbit into here the other day when I took him for an early walk on the way to headquarters. I thought then that I would like to make love to you on this soft grass.' He swirled off his cloak. 'Does that gown crease easily?'

'I don't know!' She was excited, flustered and, Rose realised with a touch of alarm, aroused by the wicked risk. 'I've never made love in it before.'

She saw the flash of white as he grinned. 'Let's try this.' Adam unbuttoned his falls, let his sword belt drop and knelt down, sinking back on his heels. 'Just lift your skirts and straddle my thighs.'

It was like an unbearably erotic exercise in deportment, Rose thought wildly as she gathered up her skirts and sank down, trying to concentrate on keeping her balance, not crushing her skirts. Then she forgot all about deportment as their naked flesh met.

'Slowly,' Adam murmured as he supported her with his hands at her waist and lowered her down until they were joined. The fabric of his uniform trousers rubbed against the bare skin of her inner thighs above her garters; the faint, musky perfume of their arousal mingled with the honeysuckle scent from the bush behind Adam's broad shoulders; distantly, from the city, came the sound of music and laughter.

'Don't lean forward, you will crush your skirts,' Adam cautioned. 'I cannot move more than half an inch.'

'Then how—?'

'Squeeze,' he said. 'Just…squeeze. Like that—' He broke off on a gasp.

It was slow, exquisite, frustrating and wildly arousing. Rose caressed him with all the inner muscles she was just learning to control, dug her fingers into the epaulettes on his shoulders, panted with the effort to channel the rising excitement. Adam closed his eyes, rocked her gently, inexorably, pressed and withdrew until he was gasping with the effort of control.

'Adam, I can't...'

'Now,' he urged. 'Let go, Rose.'

So she did and felt him let go with her, hold her as they shattered together. When she opened her eyes they were forehead to forehead. 'I may never move again,' she whispered.

'I think we must. Can you reach your reticule and find a handkerchief?'

'It is still on my wrist,' Rose said, surprised. 'I never noticed.' She found the linen square and stood cautiously, shaking out her skirts.

Adam got to his feet, picked up his cloak, then kissed her, long and slow and tender. 'I promised to show you the view from the ramparts,' he said as he raised his head. 'I hope you were paying attention.'

'Idiot.'

'At least I made you laugh.' He turned and offered his arm. 'We had best get you home before your father starts loading his shotgun.'

The thought of Papa with a shotgun jerked her back to the realities of their situation. *I should not have made love with Adam just now.* She was not pregnant, she was almost certain. The shifts in her mood tonight, the slight dizziness, were all familiar symptoms.

He doesn't even need my money, so I cannot pretend I am making a fair exchange for his freedom. If she could only come up with a reasonable plan for her own future that did not involve marriage, then she was certain she could win her parents round. That might work if she was thirty-three, but not at twenty-three… And persuading Adam that his honour did not require it was another matter altogether. The inevitability of this marriage was beginning to loom larger and, heaven help her, she could not resist it as she ought.

'That was a big sigh. Are you tired?'

'No, not really.' Rose rested her head against his shoulder as they strolled round the corner. 'More…'

'Feeling cornered?'

'Yes, exactly. How do you know?' He didn't answer. 'Of course, so are you.'

'Is that what you think?'

'Naturally. You had a whole world of choices before you and only yourself to please. Now you will have a wife to consider. You cannot deny that marriage changes a lot of things.'

'Perhaps that is good. I find I rather like the idea of children and I most certainly do not intend to father any out of wedlock.'

Oh, unfair! Now she had the image of sturdy little boys with a belligerent attitude and bright blue eyes clambering all over their large, patient father. She was not so sure what the girls would look like. Brown hair certainly. They would adore Adam and he would probably be putty in their hands.

'I like the idea, too,' she admitted. Her resolution was crumbling, she could feel it, just as she felt the sincerity of his words.

'We are agreed, then? You are going to stop resisting me?'

'I never was able to resist you, you infuriating man. But that is not what you meant, is it? I will agree to the marriage, I will stop arguing, on one condition.'

'What condition?' They had reached the house, but Adam stopped at the foot of the steps. 'This is marriage, Rose, not a ceasefire negotiation.'

'On the condition that you are honest with me. Promise that and I will marry you.'

'Is this about mistresses, Rose? I keep my promises. I might be a scoundrel, but vows are vows.'

'It is about everything. Secrets and feelings. Decisions. Involving me. Telling me when things go wrong. Telling me when you aren't happy and why.'

The drawing-room window was unshuttered and the light chequered the pavement, illuminated one side of his face and left the other in shadow. For a moment she thought he would agree, give her a simple *yes*, to what seemed to her to be the essentials for a true marriage. But it was taking him a long time to say that single syllable.

'I will be faithful to you,' he said when the apprehension about his reply began to knot her stomach. 'I will involve you in decisions. I will protect you, and our children, with my life. I will not lie to you. Is that enough, Rose? Because you are asking me to become a different person from the man I am if you think I can open up my mind and my feelings like that. I've been alone too long.'

Was she being unreasonable? Rose found she did not know. Then she realised what it was that she was really asking. *Do you love me? Can you ever love me?*

'That will have to be enough,' she agreed, then heard the disappointment in her own voice. 'I'm sorry, I sounded grudging and I did not mean to. It was honest of you to say what you did and I respect that.'

'Thank you. You are a romantic, Rose. I am not,

that is all it is. Now, may I have a kiss goodnight?'
He took off his shako, bent to touch his lips to hers.

It was polite, sweet and quite unlike Adam. But
at least it was the kiss of a man she could trust.

Chapter Eighteen

'Whatever is the matter, Catherine?'

'It's *The Times* for last Thursday. Papa left it on the table, I suppose he picked it up at the Reading Rooms yesterday evening.' Rose mopped her eyes, blew her nose and folded the paper down beside her breakfast plate. 'It is the Duke of Wellington's dispatch and reading it… Oh, dear, I can't seem to stop crying.'

'You know why, do you not?' Her mother directed a swift glance at the closed breakfast room door. 'The time of the month. Things will happen just as they should tomorrow. That *is* good news. I must confess that the thought of facing down all the gossip and arranging a hasty wedding was weighing on my mind.' She reached for the coffee pot. 'I think I will begin to drop hints about the major and then when anyone raises an eyebrow I will make it quite clear it is a love match and we are still discussing whether to hold the wedding here in a month or two, or perhaps in Paris if the major is ordered there, or England. Nice and vague and not at all concerned about haste.'

A love match. Rose eyed her damp handkerchief and sniffed resolutely. *Stop it. Stop wishing for the moon and be grateful for what you have. Be thankful you are marrying a man who will not lie to you for an easy life.* 'You seem quite reconciled to Adam, Mama.'

'I must confess that I am, much against my better judgement. He is so reassuringly large and fierce. Not that I mean I have *seen* him being fierce, but he very obviously can be and I like that he is protective of you. And I had such a comfortable coze with him yesterday. I meant to tell you, but what with one thing and another it slipped my mind.'

The thought of Adam having a *comfortable coze* with anyone, let alone her mama, was so improbable that Rose dropped her slice of toast, marmalade side down.

'How? I mean, where?'

'I met him just after I had left you at Madame Fanshaw's for your dress fitting. He took me for tea at that darling little café off the Grand Place.'

'And you had a comfortable *coze*? With *Adam*?'

'I had to carry the conversation, of course. No man is at his most articulate in a bijou café full of society ladies while he is trying to eat dainty *macarons* without getting pistachio cream on his uniform. But I gave him great credit for not running away and for having very gentlemanlike manners and for not trying to do the pretty and persuade me he is not what he is.'

'He did not mention meeting you,' Rose said faintly, trying to imagine Adam perched on a tiny chair, faced with overly sweet pastries and fragile cups while a room full of ladies either ogled him or shot disapproving looks and his mother-in-law-to-be made lethally innocent conversation.

'I am not surprised, poor boy,' Lady Thetford said.

Poor boy? Adam? 'I am glad you like him, Mama.'

'Now, Mrs Grace's dinner party tonight. Will you feel up to attending or should I make your excuses?'

'I will be quite all right, I am certain, Mama.' Rose found a smile was curling her lips. 'And I cannot wait to tease Adam about the *macarons*.' They drank their coffee in companionable silence for a while before Rose recalled something she had been meaning to do. 'I would like to call on Mrs Moss, Adam's landlady, and return the clothing that she loaned me, now it is laundered. Might I take the carriage?'

'Of course, dear. And one of the maids. Just send the carriage back straight away, I will be paying some calls this morning, dropping hints about the major.'

'There's no need for a maid, Mama. If Adam returns for luncheon he can walk me back or, if not, I am sure Mrs Moss will lend me her servant for half an hour.' Lovely as it was to be on such good terms with her mother again, the phrase *comfortable coze* conjured up thoughts of letting her hair down with Maggie about things she could never discuss with Mama.

The clocks were striking ten when Maggie opened the door. Pierre, the coachman, carried the basket of clothes through to the kitchen then went whistling on his way to return the coach to Lady Thetford.

'You look so fine, lovie!' Maggie enveloped her in a hug, then stepped back to admire her. 'Miss Tatton, I should say.'

'Rose, please, Maggie. I'm still not answering to anything else without having to think about it. How are you? And Moss and Lucille? And all the men?'

'Everyone's fine, Rose.' The older woman cast a glance upwards at the ceiling. 'Excepting for the major.'

'What's wrong with Adam?' Had she depressed him so much last night with her talk of love and trust that he was cast into gloom? 'It isn't that wound in his side, is it? It isn't festering?'

'No, nothing like that. He had to hold a court martial yesterday and the man was executed afterwards. Raped a nun in the hospital where he had been nursed, can you imagine? Anyway, the major's fierce on that, especially since Badajoz, but he's not the sort to go hanging and flogging with a light heart either. And then he sat up half the night drafting new guard rosters for the nunneries. None of that makes a man light-hearted, not when he'd rather be chasing the Frenchies back to Paris along with the Rogues.'

'And he had to spend yesterday evening attending a vapid soirée with me and then listening to me agonising on the subject of marriage.' *And making love to me.* 'Why didn't he say?' Maggie opened her mouth, but Rose swept on. 'Because he was doing his duty to me as well as obeying orders, I know. And now I've promised him for a dinner party this evening. Could you give him a message, Maggie? Say I will make his excuses.'

'Tell him yourself,' Maggie said as she reached for her bonnet. 'I'm off to give Mrs Herring a hand with her new baby. It isn't sleeping so the poor soul isn't either, as you might imagine. You take the major a nice cup of tea and stay as long as you like. It's Lucille's day off,' she added as she scooped up a basket and made for the door. 'Kettle's just off the boil.'

'Maggie—' But the other woman was gone. Rose took off her bonnet and spencer and began the familiar ritual of making tea in the homely kitchen. Adam liked his strong, black and sweet. She poured hers first and waited while the brew darkened. She was in no hurry now, content to know he was upstairs and they had the house to themselves.

When she climbed the stairs the door stood ajar so she pushed it open without knocking and looked in. Adam was bent over the desk with his back to her. His boots were set neatly to one side and he had hooked his bare feet around the legs of the chair like a schoolboy, she thought with a pang of tender amusement. Dog lay beside him and as she entered he wagged his tail, two heavy thumps on the floorboards.

'Quiet, Dog. Thanks, Maggie, can you just put it down here?' He didn't look up from the page he was covering in writing that looked as though he was constraining a naturally bold hand to fit the page.

Rose put the mug on the table and rested her hands on his shoulders. 'I could have been a French agent armed with a knife.' It was a measure of his control that the quill did not blot. She laid her cheek against the crown of his head. 'Have you got a headache?'

Adam laid the quill across the standish and lifted his hands to cover hers. 'Just the usual report-writing headache. What are you doing here, Rose?' His big hands enveloped hers, his thumbs closed over the pulse points in her wrists and began to stroke gently back and forth.

'I came to bring the borrowed clothes back to Maggie, but she's gone out to help a neighbour so she left me to make your tea. I'll go away again now, Maggie said you'd been up all hours working. I wish I had known last night.' She slid her cheek lower so she could kiss the upper rim of his right ear. It was not a body part she had ever imagined might be arousing, but the strong curve and the intricate whorls were sculptural and sensual. What would he do if she followed them with the tip of her tongue? 'There's no need to come to the dinner party tonight, I can give your apologies, say you are on duty.'

'But I won't be. And this is finished.' He released her hands, picked up the quill to scrawl his initials at the foot of the page and added it to the stack.

'Are all your nuns safe now?'

'They had better be.' He swivelled round in the chair and pulled her down on to his lap. 'They are doing impressive work. Very valuable work. Our medical facilities in England could learn a lot from them. Men will be walking out of their wards who would otherwise have left as cripples or in a coffin.'

He broke off to remove Dog's head from his knee where the hound had thrust it, slobbering gently, in an attempt to lick their linked hands. 'Bed!'

Dog slunk off to the door looking beaten.

'Bed sounds a good idea,' Rose said. 'Come and

lie down and rest, you've a ferocious dinner party to fight tonight.'

'*Bed, you* and *rest* in one sentence?' Adam's gaze seemed to smoulder when it rested on her.

'Rest to start with. Mama knows I have come to see Maggie and expects either you or Lucille to walk me home after luncheon. Maggie is working her magic on a fractious baby and its exhausted mother. We have the whole morning.'

Adam stood up with her in his arms, which made her gasp. He set her on the bed, closed the door, turned the key in the lock and studied her as she began to unlace her half-boots and roll down her stockings. 'Your mother knows you are here?'

'Not in your bedroom. But she had her coachman drop me off just now. She thinks I am visiting with Maggie. You have quite seduced her, you know.' She reached up her hands to unpin her hair.

'Leave it.' Adam's voice had thickened. '*Seduced* her?'

'I believe the sight of a big fierce warrior sitting in a dainty teashop wrestling with tiny sweetmeats quite won her heart.' Her gown joined her stockings on the chair.

'It seemed only courteous.' He narrowed his eyes at her. 'You are teasing me.'

'It is irresistible. I only have to think of *macarons* and I start to giggle.' Her stays joined the pile of clothes leaving her in her shift. 'Does no one ever tease you?'

Adam stopped in the act of hauling his shirt over his head and just looked at her.

'No, I suppose not.' She sat with her chin in her hands, admiring him as he stripped. 'The wound in your side is better.'

'I heal fast.'

Not used to being teased, will not admit to being hurt or tired... Co-existing with this man as a husband was going to be a challenge. And he was tired now.

'May we nap?' Rose asked, stretching out on the bed. *Tactics, my girl.*

'I am perfectly—'

'Only, tomorrow my courses will begin and that makes me tired and my back aches rather.'

'Ah.' He lay down on the bed next to her, over six feet of naked, muscled masculinity.

Rose took a firm grip on her desires and snuggled against his side, her head on his chest. 'Just half an hour.' She curled her arm round until she could stroke the angle of his shoulder and neck and he put a big, warm palm against the small of her back and rubbed gently.

The tension went out of him so suddenly that for a moment she was frightened. Then she realised he was still breathing, long, slow deep breaths. His body was limp, more relaxed than she could recall it had ever been during the night she had slept in his arms. He was asleep, thank goodness. Rose smiled and let herself slip into a light doze.

Adam woke swiftly. One moment he was relaxed beside her, his breathing deep and rhythmic under her ear, soft snores stirring her hair. The next his body had come alive, small muscles flexed, his breathing was lighter, the fingers of the lax hand lying on her hip curved into a caress.

Rose pressed her lips to his chest and kissed the smooth skin under the ruffle of hair.

'How long have I been asleep?' He wrapped his arms around her and shifted so they were nose to nose. His whole body was awake now, she realised, conscious of his erection against her stomach.

'An hour, I think, not much more.' She let her hand stray downwards and smiled at his hiss when her fingers closed on the length of him. 'You are very awake now.'

'Stop it.' He made no move to still her hand.

'Why?'

'Because you will be sensitive at this time of month and you are making it very difficult for me to resist you.'

'How do you know these things?' Rose demanded, planting both hands on his chest to push up and look into his face.

'I've lived with the kind of women who make their feelings about ill-timed male attentions very clear. And I don't want to hurt you.'

'Perhaps if I was in control,' Rose mused as she came up on her knees and then straddled him, her thighs closing on the narrow hips. 'Last night was…illuminating.'

Flint growled and reached up to cup her breasts.

'Oh, those *are* tender!' She caught his wrists, one in each hand, and pushed them back above his head. 'Keep your arms there.'

His eyes narrowed, but he clasped his hands together and lay with his arms stretched above his head. Rose wriggled, provoking another growl, then found the right angle and let him slide inside an inch. 'Keep quite still,' she ordered, seized by a heady feeling of power. Between her thighs she felt his hips flex, as though she was riding a horse bareback, but he did not thrust.

Cautiously Rose began to rise and fall. She was exquisitely sensitive and knew Adam was right to be wary of hurting her. But like this the sensation was bliss and to watch the effect it was having on Adam was almost as arousing as the feeling of him within her, the leashed power at her command.

His eyes were closed now, his hands gripped the bedhead rails as though to stop himself falling, he was shaking with the effort not to surge into her. She bent down, her nipples grazing the coarse hair on his chest, and kissed the hard line of his mouth.

Adam gasped, opened to her, his tongue thrusting into hers with a desperation she had never experienced before. He broke the kiss, his head turning on the pillow in a kind of desperation. '*Rose*, for pity's sake.' His hair was dark with sweat, the muscles in his arms corded with effort. Inside her she could feel him becoming larger as the muscles gripping him began to tighten and she felt sensation build, focus.

She closed hard with her thighs and began to move fast, shallowly, finding the exact angle that tightened the notch of her pleasure higher and higher. Then it broke, she shuddered, clung to him. 'Adam, yes, *now*.'

His hands came down, gripped her hips, lifted her so his desperate thrusts were shallow. *One, two, three* and he shouted, arched his back and came apart beneath her.

Flint swam up from fathoms down to find Rose curled up beside him, her cheek on his chest, her arms lashed around his waist. When he moved she gave a little hum of satisfaction.

'Are you all right?' There was a thread of uncertainty in her voice that cut through the haze of utter satisfaction. He had never been with a woman who asked him that, sounded so much as though she cared for his feelings. For a moment his focus blurred, almost as if his eyes had filled with tears.

'All right? No. I'm a wreck.' Flint gave his voice a sardonic edge, armouring himself against the disgrace of letting that moisture flow. 'I've gone into hundreds of fights expecting to get killed, but I never expected to be tortured to death by pleasure.'

She chuckled, and sat up, curled round so she could look at him. 'You have the most incredible self-control.'

'You are mine,' he said gruffly and swung his

legs over the side of the bed so his back was towards her and he did not have to meet those candid hazel eyes, so full of trust. If she told him again that she loved him, what could he say? 'I do not hurt what is mine.'

Something hot and wet swiped at his foot. 'The devil!' Dog wriggled out from under the bed and sat, tail thumping, with what Flint could have sworn was a grin of fellow feeling on his whiskery face.

It broke the mood. Rose laughed and scrambled out of bed to scratch Dog's ears as she passed on her way to the washbasin. 'Getting under the bed was very tactful, Dog.'

Flint dropped his gaze from Rose's body as she soaped the sponge and began to wash, relaxed and unselfconscious in his presence. What was he promising her? He would give his life not to hurt her physically, but mentally? What did he know about keeping a woman happy for months? Years. A lifetime. When a lover had become too close before he had always ended the affair. Now this was marriage he was facing.

He was going to fail her. He was a highly trained killer, an expert with explosives and in commanding dangerous scum. He was so damned insensitive that he'd tipped his half-brother into a critical condition, so tactless that he couldn't extract his half-sister from the bedside of a semi-conscious gazetted rake and so unimaginative that he still had no plan for their future together. Was it really the honourable thing to do to tie this woman to a man like him?

Chapter Nineteen

'Adam! Your hands.' Rose had come back as he sat there, his hands loose and open on his knees. Now he looked down at the red-and-white grooves and ridges that had been pressed into the flesh as he clung so desperately to the bedhead. 'Does it hurt?' she demanded, lifting them in hers.

'No worse than gripping a sword hilt for hours in battle.' He rubbed them together. 'You'll have to tie me up next time.'

He had been joking to wipe the worry from her face, but Rose looked at him, head cocked to one side and unmistakable erotic speculation in her eyes. 'Would you like that?' Before he could answer, she murmured, 'I might quite like it if you tied me up sometimes, too.'

She began to dress, apparently unaware that she had rendered him incapable of rational thought.

When she shook out her skirts and slipped her feet into her shoes she looked across at him, still sitting naked on the bed. Naked and now achingly erect again. 'Adam? Was that a dreadful thing to suggest?'

'It is probably the most arousing thing anyone has ever said to me,' he admitted as he grappled for some self-control.

'Oh, good.' She began to fiddle with her hair, suddenly blushing as she twisted loose locks and stuck in pins. 'Only…I know you are used to women with a lot of experience and it must be rather boring for you that I am so ignorant.'

'No.' Flint strode over to the washbasin and poured cold water, wishing he could go and stick his head under the pump. 'No, I am not bored.'

Was this love, this chaotic, unsettling feeling that was stopping him sleeping, ruining his concentration, replacing all his old certainties with doubts? It didn't seem to get any better when he was with her, it simply intensified into the need to hold her, be inside her, make her laugh, protect her. Could he say it? *I love you, Rose.* But he would only hurt her, do the wrong thing, say the wrong thing. All that he could promise her was that he would die before he let harm come to her and he suspected that she wanted rather more from a husband than that.

'Good,' she said from the doorway. 'I will go and see what there is for luncheon. Come on, Dog.'

Adam was almost silent all through the meal. Rose told herself it was not anything to do with her. He was quite patently not given to inconsequential chatter so if she spent their marriage cast into apprehension every time he fell silent then she would be in despair most of the time. And heaven forbid that she should expect an exchange about topics as unmanly as feelings and emotions, she thought with a wry smile as she washed dishes and tidied the kitchen.

'What is amusing you?' Adam might be taciturn, but he was also observant.

'Nothing is amusing me.' She shook out the dish-cloth and untied Maggie's apron. 'But I am happy.'

His lids were hooded over his eyes, the only feature she ever felt betrayed his emotions, which meant he was hiding something. Most men would counter her words with a declaration that they, too, were happy. But not, it seemed, Adam, who was not going to lie to her even to spare her feelings.

The warm feeling inside vanished as she felt her smile falter.

'I'll find a hackney.' He stood up and reached for his shako.

'No, let's walk. It is a lovely day. Adam, don't frown at me. I might have been a helpless waif when you plucked me from the battlefield, but I am not usually such a poor creature. Some exercise would be very welcome.'

'A *poor creature* was not how I thought of you.' He clicked his fingers at Dog. 'Come on, you need the exercise, too. Just remember you are escorting a lady and leave the cats alone.'

Rose stood by the front door as he locked it, juggling key, Dog's leash and his portfolio of papers. Inevitably they became entangled and by the time Rose had ducked under Adam's arm and freed the leash from his sword hanger they were both laughing. She reached up and straightened his neckcloth with a final proprietorial pat on the chest. 'You look very handsome, Major Flint.'

'Thank you, Miss Tatton.'

A carriage rolled slowly past, setting Dog to barking. 'That is smart for this street,' Rose observed. 'I wonder where they are going.'

'Shortcut to the Botanical Gardens, perhaps. Although considering that was a wagon park while we were mustering, it is probably still more of a ploughed field than a garden.' Adam got Dog to heel and offered Rose his arm. 'Tell me who I am likely to meet this evening.'

'I warned Adam that Mrs Grace numbers the worst gossips in Brussels amongst her friends,' Rose remarked as she sat on the *chaise* in her mother's bedroom and watched her maid fasten a dashing little spray of plumes in her hair. 'I told him he must flirt and charm them all, even the worst dragon, and he gave me that look that Papa gives you when he doesn't want to make after-noon calls.'

'A trifle to the left, Annette. Yes, it cannot be anything but an ordeal for a man under the eye of that collection of harpies, I am certain. But the two of you have behaved perfectly at church and at last night's soirée and I have been dropping hints about how charmed I am by the major. He only has to hold his nerve and he'll brush through in style.'

'I expect he would prefer to be facing a French cavalry charge, Mama. There's the knocker. I'll go down and see if I can soothe both our menfolk.'

Adam had the look of a wolf that had been forced

to wear a jewelled collar and pretend to be a lap-dog. *The French cavalry would be shaking in their boots if he looked at them like that*, Rose thought as she joined the men in the drawing room.

'You both look very handsome,' she said as Adam snapped to attention and bowed. 'Don't worry, it will all be over by midnight.'

'They said that about Quatre Bras,' he rejoined gloomily.

'Have a brandy, Flint.' The earl produced the decanter. 'You'll need it.'

It was every bit as bad as Rose expected. Since the soirée the gossip mills had been turning, grinding out their speculation and half-truths. Their hostess inspected Adam with blatant curiosity. 'You're related to Colonel Lord Randall?'

'My half-brother, ma'am.'

'He recognises you, does he?'

'We recognise each other, ma'am. Fortunately we resemble each other closely, so we rarely get confused and recognise someone else by mistake.' Adam said it so earnestly that for a moment Rose was persuaded he really had misunderstood Mrs Grace's question.

'They are a devoted family,' she interjected, administering a sharp kick to his ankle. 'And there is Lady Sarah Latymor as well. Major Flint is so very fond of his sister. We were all together in church on Sunday.'

'That flighty little miss,' Mrs Grace began.

'Ma'am?' Adam, without moving a muscle, had that wolf look on his face again.

Mrs Grace took a step back. 'Mr Grace, won't you take our guests through to the drawing room?'

Her husband, an anxious host at the best of times, ushered them through while making disjointed small talk. 'Such lovely weather... Our gallant troops... News from the Duke at Peronne... My wife is most put out at not being able to procure a good turtle for soup, but of course, with the late trouble...'

There were already about half of the party of twenty assembled. Rose was conscious of sharp, assessing looks behind the smiles of welcome. One palely elegant lady, a few years Rose's senior, drifted across. 'My dear Miss Tatton, such a surprise to see you!'

'Indeed, Lady Fitzhugh? Why is that?'

'After you vanished at the Duchess's ball, one did wonder...' Her voice trailed off suggestively.

'If I was indisposed?' Rose smiled back with

great warmth. 'Yes, a touch of the influenza. How kind of you to be concerned.' Out of the corner of her eyes she could see Adam looking vaguely bored.

'Oh, was that all it was? I thought you must have run off with a gallant solider,' Lady Fitzhugh rejoined with a trill of laughter. 'You were so close to the unfortunate Lieutenant Haslam, were you not?'

'Would have been very bad tactics on his part,' Adam remarked so unexpectedly that both women started. 'Eloping into a battle, that is. No soldier is going to do that. You need a clear field before taking off, no pursuing fathers and certainly no charging cavalry. Ladies expect a certain romance about the thing, wouldn't you say?' He raised an eyebrow at Lady Fitzhugh, smiled his wicked, slow smile. 'A certain…finesse.' The drawl and the innuendo brought the hairs up on the back of Rose's neck and, from the other woman's widened eyes and fluttering fan, they had their effect on her also.

'My goodness, Major. Do you have much experience…of that sort of thing?'

'Elopements? None at all, ma'am. But my strategy is excellent.'

'I should have introduced you at once, do forgive me,' Rose said in haste before Lady Fitzhugh's smouldering gaze ignited Adam's hair. 'Lady Fitzhugh, may I present Major Flint of the artillery?'

'Major.' It was a purr. 'Are you in charge of a *very* big, very long, gun?'

'I am, my lady.'

Rose trod firmly on Adam's toe. 'We mustn't monopolise Lady Fitzhugh, Major.' He bowed and they moved off. 'For goodness' sake! She was going to start quizzing you about the size of your shot next, the hussy—and you were encouraging her.'

'Stopped her poking at you though, didn't it? Who is this glaring at me?'

'General Anstruthers. He's about ninety-nine and thinks Wellington is a young upstart. Good evening, General. May I introduce Major Flint?'

'Hah! Artillery, eh? What do you think of the direction of the battle? Eh? Not how I'd have done it.'

'I was rather in the thick of it, General. Difficult to assess the overall strategy as yet. What is your view, sir?'

That was tactful, Rose thought, and tried to feign interest as the General launched into a critique of the deployment of troops at Quatre Bras. The problem was, they were probably trapped until dinner was served.

Across the room she could see Mrs Grace talking to Lady Fitzhugh and the last arrival, Lady Glenwilling. From the direction of their gaze it was obvious that she and Adam were the subject of their conversation.

'Lady Fitzhugh is taking an interest in your magnificent major,' murmured a soft voice behind Rose.

'Lady Grantly, good evening. Hardly *my* major.'

The other woman's expression was far less friendly than it had been last night at the soirée. Rose suspected she had taken the trouble to find out who Adam was. 'No? He came with you tonight, did he not? A risky acquaintance for a young lady.'

'Why? Because his parents were not married?' Rose murmured outrageously as she turned her back on the General and Adam.

'Well, that of course. And his naughty reputation. I have heard that they called him the Grass Widow's Comforter in the Peninsula.'

I can well believe it. Rose kept her smile in place with an effort. 'We are not in the Peninsula now,

Lady Grantly. He is a friend and my parents approve him as an escort.'

'I suppose young women who turn down a succession of eligible offers must take what they can before they are at their last prayers,' Lady Grantly observed. Rose recalled, rather too late, that one of the offers she had turned down out of hand was from her ladyship's nephew.

She had not taken one of the glasses of champagne that footmen were bringing around, which was a good thing. Rose itched to tip one over Lady Grantly's carefully tinted coiffure. As it was she could only fix an insincere smile on her lips and turn back to the two men. The General was apparently ten minutes into Quatre Bras.

'Dinner is served, madam,' the butler announced as Mr and Mrs Grace swept through the room, organising gentlemen and their partners. Adam, with no rank at all, was left with Mrs Grace's companion, a depressed spinster cousin, while Rose found herself on the arm of the General's grandson, Lord Philpott.

When they were seated she was diagonally across from Adam who was several places further down the table. He flashed her a wicked look and bent to listen to the companion's nervous chatter.

'I am certain I saw you this afternoon, Miss Tatton,' Lady Glenwilling remarked across the board with a lofty disregard for convention. 'We were on our way to see what damage had been done to the Jardin Botanique and you seemed to have just come out of a house.'

'Yes, I believe I saw you, too,' Rose rejoined brightly. Her stomach gave an uncomfortable lurch. That carriage…and it had passed as she was standing on the doorstep adjusting Adam's neckcloth or something equally possessive. There was nothing for it but to attack. 'I have to confess that I have quite fallen in love with two of the gentlemen in that household. Shocking, is it not?'

The whole company stared at her, then, when it became obvious from her smile and the very outrageousness of the remark that this must be a joke, relaxed.

'They are both black haired and both very handsome foreigners,' Rose continued in a confiding tone. 'One is Spanish and one Belgian.'

'My horse and my dog,' Adam explained, his voice rueful. 'Miss Tatton has developed a passion for the pair of them and I fear I am quite cut out and reduced to the office of mere escort.'

There was general laughter around the table,

but Rose was not deceived. Her name was now firmly linked with Adam's but not, as Mama had hoped, as a couple at the beginning of a courtship. Adam had been escorting her unchaperoned, she had been to his lodgings, she was familiar with his animals. If she had acquired those pieces of gossip about another unmarried lady she would have put them together and reached a perfectly accurate, and perfectly scandalous, conclusion by now.

'That did not go well,' Flint said as they got into the carriage. He felt faintly queasy and it was not as a result of eating too much *confit* duck.

Lady Thetford was visibly upset now she was away from prying eyes and the viscount's face was stony.

'They know you left the ball early, at the same time as the officers,' Lady Thetford said with a sigh. 'There was some gossip about you and Lieutenant Haslam, but now they obviously believe you left with Major Flint and that you were with him from then until your reappearance. They will come up with a version of what was the truth, that an elopement was planned and foiled by the sudden order to march to Quatre Bras.'

'It was bad luck that we came out of the house

just when the only English lady obsessed with gardening took it into her head to inspect the Jardin Botanique,' Rose said flatly. 'And worse luck that she is a spiteful gossip.'

'We will announce our betrothal immediately. That will silence the worst of the talk,' Flint said flatly. Enough of this play-acting. Rose was his and he was weary of discussing it.

'And return to London for the wedding,' Lady Thetford declared, with a flutter of her fan.

'Retreat, ma'am?' It felt like running away to Flint. 'What is wrong with the Chapel Royal? We can find an English cleric or one of the army chaplains. What do you want to do, Rose?'

She was so silent that for a moment he thought she would not answer, then she said, 'I do not mind. I do not want to drag you away from your duty. We know there is no hurry.'

Surely women liked nothing more than plotting every detail of weddings? Rose spoke as though it was a visit to a rather dull house party that they were discussing.

'I will tell Lady Anderson in strictest confidence when we attend her garden tea party tomorrow,' her mother continued, looking more cheerful now she was planning. 'That way it will be all over the city in no time at all. Major Flint can finish his duties here and then make arrangements to resign and then you can be married.'

'Yes, Mama.' Rose was looking out of the carriage window, her face expressionless.

'And we will have ample time for your trousseau. How fortunate that lace is so very affordable here.'

She chattered on, making plans, organising guest lists. Flint let the words flow over him as he watched Rose, his sense of unease growing. She was too passive, too uninvolved. He had expected anger, resistance—or acceptance and some sense of relief that a decision had been made. She was thinking, turned in on herself as though the decision had not been made at all. He hated seeing her like this with the spark and the laughter drained out of her. This was not his Rose, this was Miss Tatton, a woman he did not know, chilled into propriety by the cold winds of social disapproval. He was going to have to act, take control of this courtship, get his Rose back.

My Rose. The concept startled him. Possessiveness, protectiveness, desire…and something else. 'A word with you, my lord, if you please,' he said as the carriage pulled up outside the Tattons' house.

'Of course.' The viscount ushered his womenfolk into the house, kissed Rose's proffered cheek, muttered something to his wife about not waiting up for him and waved a hand towards the study door. 'The decanters will be out.'

Flint took the proffered brandy, sat and let the fumes tease his nostrils while Lord Thetford fussed about and finally sank down in the chair opposite him. 'I am concerned about Ro…about Catherine,' he said abruptly.

'So am I,' Lord Thetford agreed. 'I'm afraid she'll baulk at this now there's no…'

'No child on the way? Quite. She isn't happy.'

'Tricky.' Lord Thetford stared gloomily into the depths of his glass.

'I'll speak with her alone, tomorrow.'

'Very well.' The older man got to his feet. 'I'll wish you goodnight then. You can let yourself out.'

Left alone, Flint stared into his glass. *I'll tell her the truth, because I believe I do love her. I do not think I can live without her, not and ever be happy again. I would die for her and I will give up the army gladly for her. That, surely, is love?*

He raised the glass to his lips and found his hand was shaking. His hand *never* shook, not since that first day's baptism of fire when he had walked out of the screaming cauldron of battle and found he was still alive.

Unless she had changed her mind, she loved him, too. He was not given to prayer, he had heard too many fervent petitions on the battlefield cut off in a scream, but now he sent an incoherent plea to whatever deity looked after poor bloody soldiers. *Just give me this and I'll never trouble you again.*

Chapter Twenty

Rose woke to the confirmation that she was definitely not with child and with a perfect excuse for pale cheeks and a lack of energy. Dosed with willow-bark tea for her aches she settled to a morning of list-making with Mama who was throwing herself into the wedding planning with enthusiasm, undeterred by Rose's lacklustre responses.

'You'll be yourself again tomorrow,' Lady Thetford said, cutting into her thoughts. 'A pity we have that garden tea party this afternoon, but it won't do to vanish from sight, not after last night. Still, you can sit in the shade and rest. Yes, Annette?'

'Major Flint has called to speak to Miss Tatton, my lady.'

'He is very attentive, is he not, my dear? Annette, take your mending down and sit in the small salon with the door open to the drawing room.'

Rose found Adam in the drawing room looking exceedingly formal and serious and Annette tucked herself away discreetly in sight, but out of earshot.

'Miss Tatton.' He bowed.

'Major Flint.' She dropped the hint of a curtsy. 'Won't you sit down?'

'In a moment. There was something missing from my earlier proposal.' Adam opened his hand to reveal a small blue Morocco-leather jeweller's box, then went down on one knee beside her chair and opened it. 'I hope you will do me the honour of wearing my ring.'

It was a yellow diamond, an oval set around with small brilliant diamonds. Adam took her left hand and slid it on to her ring finger. The fit was perfect. The sight of her fierce, tough warrior forcing himself through this charade of gentility was heartbreaking.

'It is very lovely.' Rose tried to inject warmth into her voice. 'But why now, Adam?'

'Because we are about to make this official.' He hesitated, his head bent over her hand. Adam never hesitated. After three heartbeats he looked up and met her questioning gaze, his blue eyes shadowed. 'And because I have come to realise that I love you and it would mean much to me for you to wear my ring.'

It sounded stilted, rehearsed. *Untrue.* Adam had always told her the truth before, always been clear, never hesitant. He had dropped her gaze and was looking at their linked hands again. *This is a lie.*

This was worse than she had feared. Now Adam Flint, the man who said he did not understand love, the man who had resisted using the words to her because he was so honest, had produced them as the ultimate argument.

'I had hoped you would not say it, that you would not feel you had to, that we could do this with honesty between us,' she said before she could lose her nerve.

His face hardened. Anger that she doubted his word, she supposed. 'It is the truth.' *He really is not a very good liar*, Rose thought drearily. But there was nothing to be said or this would simply descend into a circular argument about lost virtue, honour, duty… But at least he felt strongly enough to compromise that honour by telling her the falsehood he thought she wanted to hear.

'Of course, I am sorry. And I love you,' she murmured, truthfully, and leaned forward into

Adam's kiss before he could see the tears that blurred her sight.

It was the truth from her, at least. She loved him, she knew that as a certainty now. She would give him all that love, in bed and out of it. She would bring him land and connections and support in whatever path he wanted to take in the future. She would, she prayed, give him children to love. But now she could no longer give him her trust, just as she had feared. He would lie to her when he thought it was for her own good, he would probably lie to her when he thought it would protect her feelings when he tired of their lovemaking and sought other women.

On the battlefield, when Adam had found her tangled in those briars, she had believed he was the Devil come to take her down to hell for her sins. It was her own fault that she was in this situation, but the hell she faced was one of unrequited love and the knowledge that she had forced the man she loved to change his life utterly for her sake.

All she could hope was that she could at least make him happy, give him children to be proud of. Adam would have wealth beyond his own prudent savings and with that came choice, Rose told herself in an effort at reassurance. And he would be safe from death or hideous maiming. Surely no man really *wanted* to fight wars, not once his country's enemy had been defeated. Adam had had no choices before, she told herself as her eyelids drifted closed, now he had.

Lady Anderson's tea party was blessed with sunny weather and her extensive garden was set about with rugs and cushions, little tables and chairs. Footmen lurked behind every bush ready to proffer platters of sandwiches and dainty savouries whenever a plate became empty.

Rose shook hands with her hostess, nodded to numerous acquaintances, all of whom were staring at Adam, settled into a nest of cushions, accepted a cup of tea and waited for her ring to be noticed.

It did not take long. She was soon surrounded on her rug by half a dozen young ladies, lavish with good wishes and greedy for secrets.

'How lovely,' Miss Watts cooed after the ring had been admired and meaningful glances exchanged. 'Such a rapid romance, was it not? Are you quite well, Miss Tatton? You look so pale.'

'Yes, I am not quite myself today,' Rose admitted and leaned forward, dropping her voice to a whisper. 'I wouldn't mention it to anyone but you, dear friends, but…' She lowered her voice still further as they crowded closer, agog for a scandalous revelation. *'It is that time of the month.'*

'Oh.' Lady Althea Tate gaped at her. 'Then you are not…I mean, what a nuisance not to feel well at such a lovely party when you must want to celebrate your happy news.'

'Isn't it?' Rose sipped her tea. 'But there is plenty of time to enjoy being betrothed. After all, we are in no hurry to set a date.'

'You aren't?' Miss Watts said, then bit her lip.

Attack, Rose thought. 'Oh! You surely did not think that the major and I…that I *have* to get married? Oh, my goodness, what a suggestion!' She glared at the young woman, who turned an unbecoming shade of blotchy pink.

'No, no, you quite misunderstand me,' Miss Watts gabbled. 'I mean, so many people are getting married quickly because of the end of the war, officers selling out, that sort of thing.'

'Oh, I see.' Rose smiled as innocently as she could manage. 'Well, Major Flint and I have still to decide where we are getting married, let alone when. And I have my trousseau to plan.'

As she hoped, that sent the young women into a frenzy of clothes talk. Rose sank back against her pile of cushions and let it all wash over her. They would tell their mothers, their mothers would talk amongst themselves and the news that Miss Tatton might have made a somewhat unconventional choice of husband, but that there was no scandal attached to the marriage, would percolate along the gossip channels of Brussels society. Everyone's reputations would be saved, Adam would become a wealthy man with choices about how he lived his life and she…she would learn to live with heartache.

Where was Adam? She had told him to stay away so she could deal with the unmarried ladies, now she wanted to look at him and draw some strength from the set of his shoulders, the blue of his eyes, the exchange of a smile.

Rose saw him at last standing alone in the shade of a cherry tree. He looked relaxed, successfully hiding any boredom he was feeling. Perhaps the knowledge that he had done the honourable thing, even if it had meant lying to her to achieve it, gave him some satisfaction. His head came up as a late-comer caused a flurry by the entrance. A tall, slender man in the same blue uniform jacket as Adam, his head swathed in a bandage, appeared to be flirting with Lady Anderson whose laughter could be heard clear across the lawn as she rapped him playfully on the sleeve with her fan.

The artillery officer caught up her hand, pressed an outrageous lingering kiss on the back of it and sauntered over to where Adam stood. Neither man was so relaxed now. Rose caught a subtle alertness in Adam's stance and a wariness in the other man. Surely they were not going to fight? Then Adam smiled, shook his head and the other man gave him a friendly buffet on the shoulder before they moved off, deeper into the shade to where a pair of chairs had been set apart.

Curious now, Rose got to her feet and wandered around the edge of the lawn towards the shrubbery. It wasn't that she wanted to eavesdrop, exactly, but she did wonder who the stranger with the head wound was. Could it be Major Bartlett, the rake that Lady Sarah had taken up with? If so, Adam was being exceedingly friendly, given the threats he had uttered.

As she loitered, wondering if she could get closer, the man strode out from behind a large rosebush right in front of her and caught at her hand to steady her when she stopped dead and almost tripped over her feet.

'Ma'am! I do apologise, inexcusably clumsy of

me.' He did not release her hand, simply drew her a little closer.

Rose blinked back at green eyes, a charming smile and a look that would make any woman's toes curl in their satin slippers. If this man was not Major 'Tom Cat' Bartlett, the Rogues' notorious rakehell, then the army had more wicked artillery men on the strength than seemed probable.

'Are you Major Bartlett?'

'I am. I do not believe I have had the pleasure of an introduction.' He did not appear surprised to be recognised, but then he was probably used to women discussing him.

'How is Lady Sarah? I do hope she is…well.' Her voice trailed away as the smile chilled on his lips, leaving a grim-faced man of undoubted intelligence regarding her as though she had just crawled out from under a small boulder.

'You are Miss Tatton, aren't you?' Bartlett said.

'Yes, but—'

'Congratulations.' The soft voice was a drawl. 'I never thought I'd meet the woman who could ruin a man like Flint. It seems I was wrong.'

'Ruin? What can you mean?'

He stepped back amongst the bushes, pulling

her inexorably after him, his grip on her hand no longer caressingly flirtatious. 'I came to talk to him because Randall is leaving the army, which means there is a vacancy for the command of the Rogues. There are only two possible candidates— me or Flint. But he tells me he's resigning, marrying you, becoming a *damn farmer.*' He said the two words as though they were an insult.

'He is not! He will be a landowner, a wealthy man. He—'

'Adam Flint is the best hands-on artillery officer I know. The men will follow him into hell and out of it. He can sight a gun by eye while I'm doing sums in the back of a notebook. I'm the better diplomat, the better at the big strategic picture, but that man is artillery to the soles of his boots. I expected to have to fight him for the Rogues, now I've been handed it on a plate.'

'But you must be pleased about that,' Rose began.

'Pleased to know I got it by default? Pleased to see a friend emasculated and turned into a lapdog for some empty-headed chit?'

'Stop right there!' Rose jerked her hand free of his grip. 'Adam Flint is most certainly not emasculated and he is not a lapdog, he's a wolf and I am not empty-headed, you rude man. You don't know me. You don't know anything about this.'

'No? I know Flint as well as a brother. Better than a brother. We've fought together, been wounded together, half-frozen and starved together. I've been drunk with him, I've chased women with him, I've told him things in the small hours of the morning when I expected to die the next day that I daren't even think about now. So do not tell me I don't know him.'

'The war is over.'

'This one is, but there is always a place for soldiers. Do you think Flint wants to spend the rest of his life pretending he is something he is not, just for the sake of your reputation?'

'Reputation? I know *you* do not care about reputations. After all, you are the rake who seduced Adam's half-sister.'

'We are getting married and she is following the drum.' There was a look in those hard green eyes that made Rose's breath catch in her throat. Pride and love. 'Sarah's a woman with the courage to become a soldier's wife.'

'And I am not?'

'Quite obviously not. Good day to you, Miss Tatton. I wish you well of your marriage, I am sure it will be everything you hope for, because you are marrying a man of honour who will never break his word. He will never let you see that you have scooped out his soul like an oyster and left an empty shell in its place.' He gave her a bow that was an insult in itself and strode away.

Rose heard his voice, light and amused and charmingly apologetic. When she looked at the entrance he was bidding Lady Anderson farewell.

She rubbed her hands up and down her arms in an effort to stop the shivering, then realised she was standing in a patch of full sun. She could not be cold. She wondered vaguely if she was going to faint and whether she should move off the gravel path to do so on the grass. Everything had gone very quiet although she could see people were laughing and talking. An edge of darkness rimmed her field of vision.

'Rose?' A warm hand caught both her cold ones and an arm went around her shoulders. Heat, shelter, protection.

'Adam.'

'You aren't well, you're as white as a sheet. Here, sit down before you faint.'

The iron garden seat was hard and chill, but she clutched at the arms and let the back with its moulded ferns stiffen her spine. 'Adam,' she said again.

'I'll get your mother.'

'No.'

'Then I am taking you home, now.'

'Home?' Home for Adam was a tent, or a bivouac in the ruins of a shelled building or lodgings, warm and honest and simple, like Maggie's house. Family were his soldiers, his fellow officers, the whole army.

'Yes, home. Can you stand?' He took her arm as she came to her feet. 'Best not to make a fuss about it, we'll just slip out and I'll send a footman with a message for your mother.'

'I am all right.' Sound had come back fully now and she was warm, almost too hot.

What have I done? I almost let him make his whole future a lie. Major Bartlett was right, I am trying to turn a wolf into my lapdog. I even forced him to mouth lies about love.

'Take me back to Rue de Louvain, please.' That was not home, not without Adam, but then, nowhere ever would be now.

He took her out of the garden through a conservatory, down a corridor, without meeting anyone until they reached the front door. Adam sent the footman off with the message then guided her out on to the street and hailed a hackney coach. 'Faster than waiting for the carriage to be sent round,' he said as he bundled her in, sat down and pulled her on to his lap. 'There now. Tell me what the matter is. Just women's troubles?'

'Yes. No.' To lie back against his chest was blissful indulgence. 'That was…difficult.'

'You are overtired.' Adam settled back and closed his arms around her. 'You'll be better for a night's sleep. It went very well. I was hearing the whispers all around the garden. The hard-to-please Miss Tatton has confounded everyone by choosing to take on the Latymor mongrel, with the subtext that I scrubbed up reasonably well and that as it isn't a wedding at the point of a shotgun, then I must have hidden depths.' He paused. 'Or heights.'

'I wish you wouldn't put yourself down,' she murmured into the knobbly front of his uniform jacket.

'Calling myself a mongrel? But I am. Not my fault any more than it is my sister Sarah's fault that she's inherited the Latymor nose.' Again that hesitation. 'You want me to pretend I am something I am not?'

She hated that anything she said or did made Adam hesitant. 'No. *Never.*'

'Good, because we might fight if you did.' He sounded more thoughtful than annoyed.

Tell me you love me, make me believe it. 'Adam, you do love me, don't you?'

He stared at her, eyes narrowed, as though he had scented danger. 'Of course I do.' The carriage juddered to a halt. 'We're here.'

Suddenly the way was quite clear. 'Kiss me. Now.'

'In a public hackney, on the street in broad daylight?' When she twisted in his arms she saw he was smiling. Relief that she was not pursuing that awkward question of love, no doubt.

'Yes, please.'

For a kiss that had to last her for the rest of her life it was not perfect. The carriage smelled of mould and tobacco. Adam was being careful, too careful, not to be anything but respectful. Rose breathed in deeply, filling her senses, her memory, with the scent of his skin, the smell of warm wool and clean linen, metal polish and leather soap and the faint tang of black powder that he never seemed to be able to wash off.

When he opened his arms and lifted his head she

turned her face away, unable to meet his eyes, not wanting him to see the truth in hers, not able to cope with the well-meaning lie in his. 'Goodbye. Don't come in.'

'All right.' He climbed down, helped her descend, then took her arm as she climbed the steps to the front door that Heale was already opening. 'Rest, Rose,' he said and then she was inside and he was gone.

Chapter Twenty-One

'What the blazes do you mean, she's gone?'

Lady Thetford winced at the volume and sank back on to the sofa behind her handkerchief. Her husband thrust two letters and a small package at Flint. 'See for yourself. The opened letter was to me, but read that, too.'

The package was obviously his ring. Adam shoved it into his pocket and thrust a thumb under the sealing wax on the letter with his name.

I am sorry, Adam, but it will all be my fault, no one will blame you, they will all be too busy talking about my dreadful reputation for refusing men...

I know you don't love me, that it was a well-meant untruth. You have always been so honest with me, so I could tell this was different, that you were making yourself say those words.

Even so, I let myself believe you would have more choices, more freedom married to me. That you'd be safer.

That was foolish. Major Bartlett made me see that. He says you are the best artillery officer he knows. I should have realised that safety and comfort and choice don't matter if you are doing what you were born to do. It seems that loving you doesn't make me understand you. It only made me find excuses for selfishly keeping you. And it forced you to lie to me.

You saved my life, you saved my reason and you showed me another world. I won't marry anyone else, I wouldn't want to—not after you. But I am going to find something useful to do with my life...the life you gave back to me.

Go after the command of the Rogues, fight Major Bartlett for it, and one day, when you are a general, I will boast that I met you once, on the field of Waterloo.

Rose

Flint ran his fingers over the marks where tears had fallen, blotting her writing. *I won't marry anyone else...I will boast that I met you once...the life you gave back to me.*

He waited until his vision cleared and his hand

was steady before opening out the other sheet. She had left in the night, taking her maid with her. Papa was not to worry, she had plenty of money with her and she knew the way. She was going home to England to think.

'How will she be travelling?' He realised that Lord Thetford had a greatcoat slung around his shoulders, and his hat and gloves lay on the table.

'Canal passenger boat would be cheapest, but she has funds. I imagine she has hired a carriage to Ostend for speed.' He picked up his hat. 'Why has she done this? I don't understand it.'

'I thought she loved you,' Lady Thetford said, glaring at Flint over her handkerchief. 'What did you do to drive her away?'

'Failed to listen to her.' Failed to speak to her about what was in his heart with conviction because he was so shaken by it himself. Failed to make her trust him. *Failed her.* 'If she hired a chaise and four, she'll be almost in Ostend by now. If she can catch the tide she'll be at sea by the time I get there. Where will she go in England?'

'The London town house or the place in Kent she inherited from her godfather.' Lord Thetford turned to the door. 'Come on.'

'I'll ride, go alone, it will be faster. Give me the

addresses. You stay here with Lady Thetford, sir. She needs you and it will cause talk if both of us leave Brussels.'

'Moss!' The ex-sergeant was on his feet as Flint slammed into the kitchen. 'Find Major Bartlett. Tell him to go to headquarters, tell them I have had to leave the country on urgent family business. Give him my papers and tell him to take over my work.'

'You're going absent without leave?' Moss was already jamming his battered hat on his head.

'Rose has left, gone to England.' Flint grabbed pen and paper and scrawled two lines. 'Here. That's my resignation. Give that to Bartlett, too, tell him to deliver it. And tell him I'm going to jam his teeth down his throat and tie his balls in a knot next time I see him.'

Maggie, uncharacteristically grim-faced, handed him his wallet from the dresser. 'I'll pack a valise. You going to hire a carriage?'

'No. I'll ride. Just what you can fit in a saddle-bag while I fetch Old Nick, Maggie.'

He did not stop to hear her reply, but ran. The stallion, sworn at, behaved. Dog, ordered to his bed, cowered. But Maggie stood her ground when he brought Old Nick to a snorting stand in the yard and took the saddlebag from her.

'Do you love her?'

'Yes.' He tightened the straps and gathered up the reins.

'Tell her, then.'

'I did. She doesn't believe me.' He gave the stallion its head, hooves skidding on the cobbles.

Behind him he heard Maggie shout, 'Don't talk to a woman about honour and duty, you id—' The rest was lost in the noise of the street.

Four days after he had left Brussels, Flint watched the harbour at Margate come closer as the Channel's choppy waters finally calmed in the shelter of the breakwater. The easier motion was a relief: the aftermath of the gale that had kept every ship in port at Ostend had done nothing for guts already churning with anxiety for Rose.

The harbourmaster confirmed that a passenger hoy for Margate had left a few hours before the gale struck. It was a sturdy vessel with a reliable, experienced captain, the man had assured Flint, but his imagination, always so reliably under control, was running away with him. Rose drowned,

Rose clinging to wreckage, Rose driven ashore goodness knew where...

'There you are, Major, the *Channel Star*, last packet boat out of Ostend before the gale blew up.' The mate of the fishing vessel Flint had chartered leaned on the rail beside him and pointed. He scratched his chin and eyed the furled sails and bustle of activity around the vessel tied up on the Margate pier. 'She's been in a while by the look of her, they're reloading and taking up a powerful lot of room doing it. We need to find a clear stretch to get that animal of yours ashore.'

It had taken considerable persuasion backed up by a great deal of hard cash and some unsubtle hints about secret military business to get them to winch Old Nick on board. At least a trained warhorse knew all about boats and the men had been vocally surprised at how co-operative the stallion was at the indignities of winches and hobbles. The stallion's rolling eye promised retaliation to come, just as soon as his hooves met solid land.

'Come on, you bloody-minded animal.' An hour later Flint dodged snapping teeth and loosened the hobbles as the winchman pulled the canvas sling free from under the horse and scuttled to safety.

'Behave and you can have a rest and a feed in a minute.'

He led Old Nick across to the man who stood at the foot of the *Channel Star*'s gangplank, a list in one hand. 'Sorry, sir. Full complement of passengers and we don't take animals.'

'I don't want to sail with you. I'm interested in your last load of passengers. Was there a young lady, brown hair, hazel eyes, slightly above average height, slender, accompanied by a maid?'

'Aye.' The man sidled round behind a bollard out of range of Old Nick's teeth. 'Poor lass.'

'*What?* What's wrong with her?'

The man took another unwary step back, his heels on the edge of the dock. 'Dreadful seasick she was. It was a right rough passage and I don't think she was too good to start with. I'd have thought her a lady what'd lost her husband in the late battle if it weren't for the fact she wasn't in mourning and she didn't have a ring. White as a sheet, hardly a word to say for herself, then she took to the cabin.'

'Where is she?' *In mourning?* Perversely the thought raised his spirits despite his worry. If she was grieving over leaving him then there was hope. Just as long as Rose was not simply laid low by the fact she thought he had lied to her. 'Did she go to one of the inns?'

'No, sir. Sent a boy to the livery stables for a chaise and pair, had her bags loaded and off they went. Not what I'd want, one of those yellow bounders to travel in, not right after a rough voyage.'

Neither would Flint. He led Old Nick to the livery stable the seaman described, and fed and watered the stallion while he questioned the staff.

'Aye,' the head ostler confirmed. 'Right poorly she were, the young lady. Still, she'd not far to go, which would be a mercy.'

'Not London?' Flint eyed Old Nick, solidly demolishing a bucket of feed after inhaling a bucket of water. He wouldn't want to push the animal on to London, but if Rose had gone to the Kent house that was not such a stretch.

'No, sir. Whitstable way.'

She had gone to her own house and that, he reckoned, was twenty miles or so. He could do it by evening without killing the stallion. Flint pushed aside the urge to gallop the entire way. Years of army manoeuvres had taught him the importance of rest, of food, of getting where you were going in a fit state to fight.

It was just seasickness. No one died of seasick-ness, he told himself. But they did die of broken hearts, he thought as he led Old Nick out an hour later. *I love you*, she had said when he had given her the ring and told her that he loved her, too. But there had been sadness in her kiss, he recognised it now. She had believed he was lying to her and he hadn't explained, hadn't let her see how he felt, explained his inner confusion, his feelings.

That honesty had been what she had asked him for and he had been too much of a coward to let Rose see just how vulnerable he was to her, so he had sounded awkward, clumsy, like a man lying when he had never wanted to be so honest in his life before.

That thought kept him company on the easy ride to Whitstable, a black crow of conscience on his shoulder. *Coward*, it croaked in his ear as he reined the stallion into a walk down the hill into the port. *Half-breed excuse for a gentleman*, it muttered as he rode out of town again with directions to Knap Hill House, rehearsing all the reasons why Rose would be better off without him.

'Can't miss it, Major,' said an innkeeper with the unmistakable look of an old soldier about him. 'Up the hill, bear to the west, fork right at the gibbet. Two miles on you'll see the gatehouse.'

The middle-aged woman who opened the gate for him curtsied politely. 'Yes, Miss Tatton arrived yesterday, sir. We weren't expecting her, but there's always a skeleton staff up at the house.'

He touched his hat to her, tossed a coin to the small boy hiding behind her skirts and let Old Nick walk slowly up the curving driveway towards the house. It was old, he could tell that, and of no style he recognised. One wing looked ancient, built of brown stone. A more modern redbrick central mass was flanked by what once might have been a barn, now much altered. It looked like an overgrown farm that that collided with a small castle, he decided as he guided his horse towards the stableyard arch.

A groom on a sturdy cob clattered through the arch and reined in as he approached. 'Sir?'

'I have a message for Miss Tatton from her father.' That was true enough.

'Don't rightly know if she'll be able to see you, sir.' The man circled his mount impatiently. 'She's none too well, I'm off for Dr Fowler now. If you put your horse in the stable there, sir, I'll see to him when I get back. There's only me...' And he was gone, cantering down the drive.

Flint did not recall afterwards getting Old Nick into the stable or stripping off saddle and bridle. He pushed past the footman who opened the door and was halfway up the stairs before the man panted to his side.

'Sir! You can't go up there, sir!'

'Where's Miss Tatton's woman? Jane, isn't it?' Flint took the remaining steps in two strides and found himself confronted by three corridors, more steps, endless doors.

Naming the maid seemed to reassure the man that he at least knew the family. 'If you'll wait here, sir.' He hastened down one of the corridors and tapped on a door.

Jane emerged, pushing her hair back under her cap, her freckled face pale and drawn. 'Major!'

'How is Miss Tatton?' Flint demanded.

'Poorly, Major. She's exhausted. I've never seen anyone so seasick. Twenty-six hours at sea and she couldn't keep anything down, not even water. And she wasn't feeling too strong beforehand.' The look she sent him was cool. It seemed she knew who to blame for Rose's lowered spirits. 'I couldn't get her to rest at an inn in Margate, she said she wanted to come to her own place. She's worse today, so I sent for the doctor.'

'Where is she?' Flint went past her to the door she had emerged from.

'You can't go in there, Major, it isn't seemly.' Jane tried to push in front of him.

'Seemly be damned.' He shook off her hand. 'That's my betrothed in there. Go and get the cook to make chicken soup and soft white bread and bring up weak sweet tea at once.'

'Rose!'

She dragged open heavy lids. It was too much, she felt like death and now she was having hallucinations. 'Go 'way,' she managed to croak through lips that felt as though they were covered in rice paper.

The apparition of Adam neither vanished nor wavered. 'I'm not going anywhere and you are not going to die on me. You were too much trouble last time.'

'Adam?'

'Who else?' He raked one hand through already dishevelled hair and began to unbuckle his sword belt. 'Where's that girl with the tea?'

'Tea?' Vague thoughts of tea parties and dainty

cakes swam through Rose's mind. 'You're really here?'

'Give me that.' There was a clatter of china, then she was being hauled up into a sitting position and pillows stuffed down behind her back. 'Drink this.' A cup was pressed to her lips.

'Can't. It just comes back up.' She pushed the cup away with a hand that seemed as heavy as stone.

'This won't. Try for me.' The cup pressed against her lips again. 'Just sip.'

It was too much effort to fight. She sipped and swallowed and her stomach heaved.

'Don't you dare,' Adam said in the tone she'd last heard him use to Private Williams when he caught him trying to hobble out to find a gin shop.

Rose opened her mouth to protest and tea was poured in. This time her stomach accepted it. 'More,' she managed.

Adam tilted the cup again, then set it aside. 'That's enough for a minute.' He got to his feet, still snapping at her. 'Look at you, what the devil do you think you were doing? They must have told you it was going to be rough and you weren't feeling well to begin with. And then not to rest when you got to Margate is ridiculous.' He came back to the bed with a towel and a damp cloth in his hands and began to wash her face with a gentleness that was the opposite to his voice.

'I can be ridiculous if I want to,' Rose muttered. The cool cloth was bliss as he smoothed it over her crusted lips and sore eyes.

'Not under my command you don't. Have some more tea.'

She drank and the room stopped moving up and down and the pounding headache eased a fraction. 'I'm not under your command.' Oh, but it was so good to see him. So impossible. So wrong.

'All right. But I am responsible for you. We are betrothed,' Adam said.

Perhaps it was not so good, after all, if he was going to be dictatorial. 'I am responsible for myself.' Adam raised one eyebrow. He did not have to say it: she was not taking very good care of herself. 'Besides, I broke it off.'

'Your intelligence was faulty,' he said, his voice dry. 'You were taken in by enemy spies and you misunderstood what you heard with your own ears.'

None of that made any sense. Rose reached for the teacup and he filled it and put it in her hand. She drank it down slowly, thinking. 'How did you get here?'

'Your father sent for me the moment he found your note. I left at once and I was kicking my heels in Ostend for days, imagining you shipwrecked.'

The remembered anxiety in his voice caught at her heart and her eyes filled with tears before she registered what that headlong journey implied. 'You can't have just left like that!' She might not know much about military life, but she knew an officer did not simply leave on personal business. 'You deserted your post—they'll court-martial you and you'll never get command of the Rogues.'

'I resigned. Tom Bartlett has taken over my duties.'

'No. Oh, Adam, no!' He couldn't throw it away, couldn't be so impossibly honourable and gallant all because she had made one monumental mistake. 'Go back, tell them you have changed your mind. I don't want you, I have come to my senses.'

'You have?' He said it without a smile. 'So you did not mean what you wrote in that note?'

'I was emotional, and confused and grateful to you.' Rose made herself hold his hard blue gaze. *No man looks at a woman he loves like that, but a soldier faces an unpleasant duty with just that look in his eyes.* 'We had been lovers…I see now I was simply making up a romantic fairy tale to justify my wantonness when I thought I was in love with you. Of course I don't want to marry you.'

Adam sat silent, watching her, so she kept talking. 'And you are a dreadful liar. You do not want to marry me, so you can go back to Brussels and tell my parents that I am fine and they do not need to worry. Then you can get on with your own life.' She thought the smile she produced was really rather good, under the circumstances.

'I see. Very considerate of you.' Adam's mouth thinned to a hard line. He stood up and reached for his sword belt. 'I can hear the maid with your soup. Try to drink as much as possible and get some rest as soon as the doctor has seen you.' He walked to the door, held it open for Jane and then disappeared into the shadowy passageway.

Jane put the tray down and flapped a napkin over Rose's lap. 'I've told Mrs Weston to have a bedchamber made up for the major in the west wing, Miss Tatton.'

'Here?' She almost spilled the soup when Jane placed the tray in her lap.

'He's been travelling as long as we have, ma'am, and Mrs Weston says there isn't a decent inn until you get into Whitstable. I didn't think you'd want to turn him out. Besides, Jem in the stables says his horse needs to rest.'

'He brought Old Nick? On a *boat*?'

'Seems so, Miss Tatton. A powerfully determined man is the major.'

'Well, he can determine on going back to the Continent tomorrow.' Her hand shook with weakness as she lifted the spoon, but the soup slid down into her abused stomach, savoury and warm and comforting. 'But make sure he has a good dinner tonight, won't you?'

'Yes, Miss Tatton.' Jane gathered up the tea things. 'Shall I sleep in here tonight?'

'Why?'

'In case you feel uncomfortable with a gentleman in the house and no chaperone, miss.'

'Don't be ridiculous, Jane,' Rose snapped and wondered, rather desperately, where she had put her handkerchief.

Chapter Twenty-Two

'Is Major Flint about yet?'

'He's gone, Miss Tatton. He was up with the dawn.' Jane set the tray down on the window table in Rose's bedchamber and began to lay out cutlery. 'Cook's sent up a nice poached egg and a slice of mild-cure ham and some toast. That will all sit well inside, I'm sure.'

'Please thank Cook for her thoughtfulness.' Rose slipped on her robe and padded barefoot to the table. *Gone. Is it to be so easy, then?*

The day before, Adam had made no attempt to see her, but he had asked the doctor to call again and Jane reported that he was supervising the food sent up from the kitchen. She also said that Old Nick was rested. The doctor had been encouraging and had no doubt put Adam's mind at rest. His horse was fit to make the short journey to Margate. What was there to keep him, after all?

The window commanded a fine view over the small park at the back of the house where grassland edged with trees led down to the river in its shallow valley. She had slept in, for the mid-morning sun was bright on a swath of buttercups.

So Adam had given up and left. She had to be relieved, of course. It was good of him to go without saying goodbye, for that could only have led to more arguments or painful silences. Now all she had to do was work out what she was going to do with the rest of her life. It wouldn't involve a husband and children. Or Adam Flint.

Rose stabbed the quivering centre of the egg and watched the yolk run out. That had not been a good idea with her sensitive stomach. Or perhaps that unpleasant sinking feeling was despair, not squeamishness. Many women did not marry, she told herself, attacking the ham. She was luckier than most, for she had wealth and education behind her. She could, and would, find something fulfilling and worthwhile to do.

She forced her thoughts away from Adam and thought about the injured Rogues in Brussels. What was going to happen to all those wounded soldiers coming back from the war? How would the ones who had lost limbs, or their sight, fare?

And what about those whose wits had been turned by the ordeals they had been through? She had just touched on the edge of that horror and had lost her voice and her memory. What would happen to those who had gone through far worse and who never recovered?

She had heard of the horrors of Bedlam where the inmates were chained like animals and exhibited as a menagerie of horrors for the entertainment of gawping visitors and it was the stuff of nightmares, not the sanctuary it should be for those who had given so much for their country.

What those men needed was comfort and tranquillity, kindness and care and, if they were able, a suitable occupation. She could provide that, she was certain. Others would help her with such a good cause and she could begin here by converting the great east wing to house them.

Rose folded the remains of the ham into a roll and went to rummage in the bureau for paper and pen. With her sandwich in one hand she began to jot notes. She would need military help at a high level and lady patronesses. Medical advice… The list got longer as the ham cooled. Convert the east wing into separate rooms? Shared rooms? Dormitories? All three? She needed more advice.

* * *

When she reached the foot of the third sheet of paper she had to get up and stretch her stiff shoulders. Perhaps it would be best to look around the east wing now. Rose had her hand on the bell pull to ring for her bath when she saw the rider in the park. The horse she would have known anywhere, the rider...the rider was not in uniform. Adam might have left Old Nick here to rest up, but the stallion would kill anyone else who tried to ride him. It had to be Adam.

All the suppressed emotion surged up, filling her with energy that she thought she had lost for ever. Rose yanked on the bell pull and Jane came in minutes later, flushed and out of breath. 'Miss, are you all right?'

'Yes, perfectly.' Except for a racing pulse and a pain where her heart was. 'Who is that?' She pointed to where the rider had halted to survey the valley.

'Why, the major, miss.'

'You said he had gone.'

'Yes, but only into Whitstable to send a letter to your parents, Miss Tatton. And he said he had some shopping to do.'

Shopping for civilian clothes. Adam, what are

you doing? He had to get back to Brussels before they accepted his resignation as final.

'I need hot water immediately, then lay out a riding habit.' If a confrontation was inevitable she was not going to face it looking like a sickly waif trapped in her bed. 'Send to the stables and tell them I need a horse ready in half an hour.'

He knew less about farming and estate management than he did about French literature, but Adam thought he could recognise well-kept land when he saw it. The cattle were fat, the sheep satisfyingly woolly, the hedges had no gaps and the grass was green. The buildings all had sound roofs and the men who were working about the place were dressed in decent homespun and returned his greetings with cheerful grins.

He looked up at the beat of approaching hooves and doffed his hat when he saw the rider was female. The low-crowned beaver felt odd in his hand after a shako. He drew Old Nick on to the verge of the lane to allow the lady to pass. Strange that she had no groom to accompany her.

'What are you *doing*?' The rider reined in the neat bay cover hack he had seen in the stables that morning.

'And what are you doing out of bed?' he demanded. Rose, pale but healthy, rode as though she had been born in the saddle. An utterly inappropriate wave of arousal swept over him.

'Why are you still here—and dressed like that?' She did not appear very pleased at his civilian breeches and coat, his plain blue waistcoat and modest beaver hat. His boots were his old ones, his stock was decently tied and his linen clean. What was there to object to?

'I told you, I resigned. These clothes may not be very fashionable, but they are perfectly serviceable,' he said mildly.

'I do not care if you are wearing bright yellow Cossack trousers, a pink waistcoat and a cabbage in your buttonhole!' The bay was sidling uneasily, picking up on her agitation. 'You must go back to Brussels and withdraw your resignation immediately.'

'I do not want to.' And, he realised with relief, that was true. Now he was here he knew he was homesick for England again. He needed a challenge, something fresh in this new world the peace would bring. He wanted Rose. Above everything, he wanted Rose. 'Besides,' he said, trying to make her smile, 'I've written to Maggie asking her to send Dog over.'

'Good, he'll mope without you,' she said and, instead of smiling, turned pink. That, he thought was encouraging. Perhaps she was moping for him, too, just a little. 'What are you thinking about?' she asked and Flint realised he must have fallen silent, gazing not at her, but over the green hillside and the clear sparkle of the river.

'That I want you,' he said, meeting her eyes. She coloured up, a wash of warm colour. 'Not like *that*. Well, yes, like that as well. But I want to marry you, to be with you.' She shook her head, obviously exasperated with him, and something inside snapped. He urged Old Nick up close alongside her hack, reached across and simply dragged her into the saddle in front of him.

She gave a muffled shriek as she clung to him. 'Adam, what are you doing?' Old Nick curvetted sideways, then stood at a sharp command from Flint.

'Do you remember riding with me like this?' She nodded, her hat bumping his chin, and he pulled out the hatpin and sent the hat spinning into the nearest bush. 'That's better.' Now his chin rested on her hair. 'I smell a damn sight better than I did then, and you've got your voice, but it still feels as good to have you in my arms, against my heart.' She gave a murmur of agreement and tightened her hold.

'You said once that you knew me, that right from the start you knew you could trust me, even when you thought I was the Devil. What changed, Rose? When did you stop trusting me?'

She pushed against his chest and sat up so her mouth was no longer muffled against his coat. 'When I realised that honour was the most important thing for you. You said you were not the marrying kind, that you wouldn't stay faithful. But you were also insistent on marrying me, on leaving the army, on doing all those things that I knew you would hate. It did not add up, Adam.' Her fingers played with Old Nick's mane, twisting the coarse hair into knots. 'You would do your duty and marry me, because that was the honourable thing to do, but how could I expect you to be faithful?'

He let his breath out in a huff of relief. 'That is easy. To be unfaithful to my wife would be dishonourable. But there is a much stronger reason than that. I love you.'

'You had always been honest with me before, but

that morning when you gave me the ring, told me you loved me, you couldn't meet my eyes, you were hesitant. I knew you were making yourself speak of love because you thought it as the only thing that would make me accept marriage happily.'

'I've never had to speak of love before, I had no idea how to say it. You think I would lie to you?' That hurt, but not as much as she was hurting, he could tell.

'Yes, if you thought it was for my own good.' And that was bitter.

Flint sat with the sweet weight of Rose in his arms and tried to think. His mind was blank. How do you convince a woman that you love her when she has no reason to believe you and her own honour stops her taking the easy way of pretence and compromise? He knew what his instinct was telling him: let her go free, let her decide. Instinct had saved his life more times than he could count, had shown him the way when intellect was exhausted. He would risk his heart on an artilleryman's instinct, it was all he had left.

'I'll take you home,' he said and snapped his fingers at the cover hack who obediently trailed behind as he turned Old Nick's head towards the stables.

* * *

Rose sat in the drawing room and waited as Adam had requested, very formally. He was going to give up, say goodbye, she was certain. She raised her chin a notch. That was the right thing and she would not let herself down or shake his resolve by weeping all over him.

When he came in he carried the ring box in one hand and his sword in the other. 'You gave me this ring back and I will take it with me,' he said and pushed it into his pocket. 'And I will leave today, go back to Brussels, settle my affairs. I will not withdraw my resignation. But before I go, I want to show you, tell you, something.'

He picked up his sword, knelt in front of her and laid it in its scabbard across her lap. 'That is mine. When I was made an officer I had to have a sword, but I could not afford to buy one so I picked this up on the battlefield.' That explained its plain hilt and the battered scabbard, so unlike his dress sword that gleamed with fancy work and lived in an elegant, unmarked scabbard. 'This sword has been with me ever since. It has saved my life countless times, it is the symbol of my honour, of what I have made of my life. It is the only possession I would kill to keep.'

Adam laid his right hand on the hilt, took hers in his left hand and placed it on top. 'I swear, on this sword, that I love you, Rose. I swear that I want to marry you. I swear that I will always be faithful to you and that I want to make my life here in England with you.'

He lifted her hand away and stood up. 'Now I will leave unless you tell me to stay, tell me you believe me, trust me. That you still love me.'

Rose had learned to read the emotions behind that expression of stoical calm, the carefully controlled hands, the set shoulders. She could not do anything but believe that oath, but she would have followed him to the ends of the earth without it, just for the look in those blue eyes and the betraying twitch of the nerve in the corner of the rigid mouth.

'Stay, Adam. I believe you and I trust you. I love you, I never stopped loving you and I am so sorry I doubted you.' There was more, explanations, protestations, but, breathless, she never had a chance to say them. She was on her feet, in his arms and his mouth was on hers, hot and fierce and possessive. Somehow she pulled back. 'Adam, I swore I would not ask you for marriage.'

'I am the one doing the asking. I have proposed

before and you accepted. Are you going back on your word?'

'No. How can I, if you want me? I love you too much.'

He narrowed his eyes at her, calculating. 'Where and when do you want to get married?'

'Here?' Yes, that felt right. 'You do want to keep this estate?' She could not believe she was saying this, that this was happening.

He nodded slowly. 'I can see us here. And it is right to marry here, just as soon as your parents are able to come over. Shall we arrange everything for the end of next month?'

'Oh, yes. Perfect.'

'If you had pouted at me and demanded a big society wedding in London with months to organise it and arrange your trousseau then I wouldn't be able to do this.' He bent and scooped her up into his arms.

'Adam, it is one o'clock!'

'Had you invited anyone for luncheon?' He pushed open the door and strode towards the foot of the stairs. 'Jane. Your mistress is not at home to callers for the foreseeable future.'

'Yes, sir.' Rose caught a glimpse of the maid

bobbing a respectful curtsy, quite at odds with the grin on her face.

It seemed futile to protest and, in truth, she had no desire to, only the desire to lie naked in Adam's arms again and make love with her fierce Devil warrior who had sworn his love on his sword like a knight of ancient chivalry.

He undressed her slowly, letting the long skirts of her riding habit slide into an amber pool at her feet, untying the knot of her stock as though he had all the time in the world, brushing kisses against the tender skin at her nape as he freed her from the short corset she wore for riding.

'Look at you,' Adam murmured as he turned her in his arms and let his gaze caress down the naked length of her. He set her on the bed and began to strip, his gaze locked with hers until he was as bare as she.

'You lost weight, being so sick.' He stroked his fingertips down her ribs. 'I must feed you up.'

'While you never had any spare flesh on you to lose,' Rose murmured as he came down over her, his lips and tongue exploring the softness between neck and breast. 'How will you stay so hard and fit when you have no battles to fight?'

'You'll have to exercise me a lot,' he muttered

and took her nipple between his teeth, making her gasp and arch up against him.

'It makes a difference, knowing we are to be married.' Rose cradled his head between her palms as he shifted down her body, his tongue sliding over her ribs, working wicked magic.

'It does?' Adam lifted his head. 'More respectable, less exciting?'

'More serious. This is for ever. And more joyous—because it *is* for ever. I was always saying goodbye to you in my thoughts and now...*Adam.*'

He slid down between her parted legs and spread her wide for his scrutiny. 'You were talking about joy, my love?' His mouth, his lips, his tongue, took her and tormented her and worshipped the quivering, aching flesh of her until there was nothing but him and a single point of sensation and then an explosion of feeling that wrenched his name from her lips, over and over again.

When she came to herself Adam had come up her body and slid into her, filling her as he lay still and patient, waiting for her to rejoin him.

'I love you,' he said as he began to move and she shifted, curled her legs around his hips so he could plunge as deeply as possible into her heat, surging with the movement of his body as he drove them both into a tightening spiral of sensation. It broke in a shuddering fulfilment that seemed to reach the core of her and she felt Adam break, too, as she did, her name breaking from his throat in a cry of primal possession that somehow sent her over into another paroxysm of pleasure, her body pulsing around him.

'Adam, wake up.' A sharp finger prodded him in the ribs.

Flint opened one eye. 'Again?' he enquired. His body, against all reason, greeted the question with enthusiasm.

'No. Not until after dinner.' He opened both eyes. Rose was blushing adorably. She also, strangely, had her hands full of paper.

'What on earth?' He hauled himself up against the bedhead and began to pull scattered pillows together.

'It is my plan for what I was going to do when I thought I would never marry. I want to do something for soldiers coming back from the war who are disturbed in their mind. You saved me—my mind as well as my body. I cannot bear to think of those men condemned to wander, bemused figures of fun, or locked up in Bedlam with no one to fight for them. See what I have written already.' She thrust the papers at him. 'It is more questions than answers, but you will know what to do. We can do this together, can't we?' She frowned. 'I suspect we may be told we are mad ourselves to attempt it.'

Flint glanced at the papers. It was brilliant. And difficult, complex and, probably for some people, controversial. It would be a battle. 'I love it,' he said and pulled the woman who would be his wife into his arms. 'And I love you, Rose Catherine Tatton. I'm done with Randall's Rogues, let us plan for Flint's Folly.'

Epilogue

31st August 1815—Knap Hill House, Kent

Rose had told Adam that a wedding here, at the house that was now their home, would be perfect, and it was. The sun shone, the sweep of lawn down to the river was dotted with guests, with little pavilions and scatters of rugs and chairs. When it became obvious the good weather would hold they had simply moved the wedding breakfast outside and made a glorified picnic of it.

She stood for a moment, looking down from the terrace, searched for Adam and found him easily, standing beside Lord Randall. The two of them in civilian dress were surrounded by men in uniform, but it was obvious from their bearing that they were soldiers. And brothers. They looked right together and easy with each other at last. As she watched she saw Justin slap Adam on the back and the group's laughter drifted up to her.

Justin had been his best man in church that morning, finally bridging the divide between their father's sons.

She turned to take the sweeping steps down to the lawn and came face-to-face with two ladies, arm in arm. Mary, Justin's new countess, and Lady Sarah, Major—no, *Colonel* now—Bartlett's bride. *My sisters-in-law*, she thought, finding a smile. She knew neither of them, really, and now she felt wary. She'd had a fleeting encounter with Mary only as a desperate, brave woman fearing for her lover's life and Adam had described a tiny martinet, ordering him from Justin's sickroom. Sarah had been a furious, then penitent, avenging angel, a woman Tom Bartlett had described as full of courage and Adam as a foolish chit.

The polite words were forming in her mind, but she was enveloped in a double hug before she could say any of them.

'Our third sister,' Sarah said with satisfaction, stepping back to look at Rose while keeping a firm hold of her right hand.

She's grown up, Rose realised. There was a gloss of calm and style, an air of confidence that had replaced Sarah's wilful arrogance. *And she looks well loved*, Rose thought wickedly. She recognised that little smile of smug feminine satisfaction from her own mirror. Tom Cat Bartlett was obviously employing his famed amatory skills to good effect at home these days.

'I suppose we *are* sisters,' she agreed, returning the pressure of the two warm hands clasped around hers. 'I've never had sisters before.' The feeling was surprisingly good.

'Neither have I,' Mary said. 'It will be wonderful to have you both to confide in.' She looked softer, somehow. No less intelligent and alert, yet…

Rose let her gaze drop to the other woman's slender midriff and was answered by a blush and a laugh. 'Yes, but we aren't telling anyone yet,' Mary whispered. 'And Justin is driving me insane! You would think no woman has ever carried a child before.'

'He's a fusspot,' Sarah declared. 'And it is rather amusing to see my brother Lord Iceberg in a tizzy, you must admit. Tom will be perfectly calm when I am expecting.' She cast a glance over the balustrade to where her husband was bowing over the hand of a particularly pretty young matron. 'At least, I hope so. I refuse to be left at home, regardless.'

'Tom is a terrible flirt,' Mary observed. 'I would kill Justin if he carried on like that.'

'Tom will flirt until he's a hundred and ten and make every woman from sixteen to ninety feel wonderful. But he'll never stray,' Sarah said complacently. At that moment Bartlett looked up and the charming smile on his face changed to something so intense, so loving, that Mary and Rose caught their breath. Sarah kissed her hand to him and he grinned and strolled back into the crowd.

'Now we are sisters I want to know all about this hospital.' Sarah turned so they faced the scaffolding-clad wing of the house. 'If I wasn't going to follow the drum with Tom I would come and be a nurse for you. I was when Mary had the wounded men at her school in Brussels.'

'We can both be patrons,' Mary said. 'You need money, advice from the military and lots of support in society. Between the three of us, and our husbands, you'll have all that. And employment for the men who are able to work when they recover.'

'Thank you. It is such a relief to have female friends who understand,' Rose said, realising a lack she had never felt before. 'Adam is wonderful, but he looks at it from a male, army point of view, and I try not to worry him with the details while he's setting up the stud.'

'Oh, yes, that wonderful stallion of his. I've heard such stories about it from Justin,' Mary said as they linked arms and began to descend the steps. 'Has Adam bought any mares yet?'

'Just one. See, over there.' Rose pointed to a paddock where a black horse with a long, waving mane and tail was watching the activity in the gardens with interest. 'Her name is Belladonna and she's my wedding gift from Adam. And she's as sweet-tempered as Old Nick is evil, so we're hoping for a nicely balanced set of offspring.'

'Mrs Flint.' Tom Bartlett stepped out from behind one of the little marquees. 'My felicitations.'

'Colonel.' Rose found she was still a trifle annoyed with him.

'Am I forgiven?'

'What have you done, you wretch?' Sarah demanded, jabbing at her new husband with her parasol. 'I won't have you upsetting my new sisters, either of them.'

'I accused Miss Tatton of emasculating Flint and turning him into a lapdog.'

'Emasculating?' Mary gave a snort of completely unladylike laughter as the three women turned to scrutinise Adam's broad back, now only yards away. 'I rather doubt it!'

At the sound of his wife's voice Lord Randall

looked around, then walked over to them. 'My dear. Did you cry out? Are you all right? It is very hot.'

'I was laughing, that is all, Justin.' Mary tucked her hand into the crook of his elbow. 'We were just admiring your brother.'

'Were you indeed? In that case you are definitely overheated and I am going to take you off to a chair in the shade and feed you ice cream. Mrs Flint, Sarah, you'll excuse us.' He nodded to Bartlett and strolled off, taking Mary with him.

'Mrs Flint?' Bartlett was still looking at her with a rueful expression.

'Rose,' she said and smiled. 'Of course I forgive you for defending your friend. Now, if you will pardon me, I am going to take my husband away to tell him about my wedding gift to him.'

'Rose.' Adam turned at the touch of her hand on his arm. His eyes on her face were intense. 'I've been neglecting you.'

'You've been mingling with our guests, very properly,' she said with a smile. 'But come down to the paddock, I need to tell you about my wedding gift to you.'

'Have you bought me another horse?' He took

her hand and began to stroll towards the ha-ha that edged the lawn.

'No.'

'New boots?' He vaulted down into the ditch and held up his hands to swing her down.

'No. Nor a tiepin, nor a hound.' They walked to the paddock fence and Belladonna trotted across to nuzzle them in the hope of treats.

'What, then?' Adam lifted her on to the top rail of the fence and stood looking up at her, his big hands bracketing her waist.

'It is rather early to be certain, but I believe I am right to hope.' Rose took his right hand and pressed it, palm down, to her stomach. 'I'm late, you see, and I am never late. And I feel…different.'

'Rose?' Adam's face was a picture of shock, alarm and delight. 'You're pregnant? You are carrying a child? Our child? How?'

She laughed and bent forward to kiss him. 'How? The usual way, I imagine. And perhaps that very day you proposed over your sword. And it is most certainly ours, my love.'

'Oh, my God. Get down off that fence.' He swung her down. 'And I had you jumping off the ha-ha and you've been on your feet all day and it is hot and—'

'And you are most certainly Justin's brother.

Mary says he is driving her absolutely insane, fussing over her.' She clapped a hand over her mouth. 'You won't repeat that, they haven't told anyone else yet.'

'And I suppose, for the sake of your reputation, I had better not rush back up to the lawn, order more champagne and drink a toast to my pregnant bride, had I?'

'Indeed not. We must stroll back and continue to circulate and do our duty by our guests.'

'Until they all go and I can take you to our big bed and celebrate with champagne and strawberries and kisses.'

'That sounds like a perfect plan,' Rose agreed demurely. 'Provided I may have just one kiss on account.'

'Just one,' Adam agreed, taking her lips with a passion full of unspoken promises, then he swept her up in his arms and carried her back to the house and their guests and the rest of their life together.

* * * * *

This is the third and final story in the fabulous
BRIDES OF WATERLOO *trilogy*

Make sure you've also picked up
A LADY FOR LORD RANDALL
by Sarah Mallory
and
A MISTRESS FOR MAJOR BARTLETT
by Annie Burrows

Both already available

MILLS & BOON®

Why shop at millsandboon.co.uk?

Each year, thousands of romance readers find their perfect read at millsandboon.co.uk. That's because we're passionate about bringing you the very best romantic fiction. Here are some of the advantages of shopping at www.millsandboon.co.uk:

* **Get new books first**—you'll be able to buy your favourite books one month before they hit the shops

* **Get exclusive discounts**—you'll also be able to buy our specially created monthly collections, with up to 50% off the RRP

* **Find your favourite authors**—latest news, interviews and new releases for all your favourite authors and series on our website, plus ideas for what to try next

* **Join in**—once you've bought your favourite books, don't forget to register with us to rate, review and join in the discussions

Visit **www.millsandboon.co.uk**
for all this and more today!